Morris Craw Russell

Uncle Dudley's odd hours, being the vagaries of a country editor

Morris Craw Russell

Uncle Dudley's odd hours, being the vagaries of a country editor

ISBN/EAN: 9783743377264

Manufactured in Europe, USA, Canada, Australia, Japa

Cover: Foto ©Andreas Hilbeck / pixelio.de

Manufactured and distributed by brebook publishing software (www.brebook.com)

Morris Craw Russell

Uncle Dudley's odd hours, being the vagaries of a country editor

UNCLE DUDLEY'S

ODD HOURS

BEING THE

VAGARIES OF A COUNTRY EDITOR.

By M. C. RUSSELL.

ALSO, AS AN APPENDIX,

J. PROCTOR KNOTT'S FAMOUS SPEECH ON DULUTH.

DULUTH, MINN.:
Compiled and Published by Miss Susie M Russell.
1882

A Remark by the Author.

——‡——

This is the first book with which we have ever afflict-
ed a patient public. If any one doubts this statement,
we commend him to a careful perusal of its pages.
The author is not "stuffed up" with the idea that this
is the *first* book ever published,—excepting in the Zé-
nith City,—nor that it is destined to work a revolution
in the domestic affairs of the human family. Nor do
we anticipate that its sale, when placed on the market,
will exceed "Robinson Crusoe," the "Pilgrim's Progress," "Uncle Tom's Cabin," "Innocents Abroad"
and "Aesop's Fables," all combined. In fact, we have
no assurance that it will equal in general circulation any
one of these works. But, we dare to *hope* that enough
of them will be wanted by a charitable public to enable
us to pay the binder for his "lids" and the paper-mak-
er for his trouble in turning out the sheets. The bill
for type-setting and printing is already honestly adjusted, because we did it ourself,—that is, a member of the
"Dudley" tribe did it,—during "*odd hours.*" Whether
we shall ever publish another book, or whether we shall
ever produce a second edition of this one, remains, principally, with the present generation to say. If we find
that the people actually suffer for more, it might be just
like the author to comply with a clamor of that kind.
For the present, however, this book will have to stand
as our monument, and in all probability it will mark the
literary *resting place* of an ambitious but mightily mistaken book-maker, in the person of

Your sympathetic friend,

UNCLE DUDLEY.

THIS LITTLE BOOK IS AFFECTIONATELY DEDICATED

TO MY FRIENDS.

—{M. C. RUSSELL.

CONTENTS.

CONTENTS.

APPENDIX:

Hon. J. Proctor Knott's Famous Speech on Duluth.

"Hoo-hoo-hoo!" is all he says—night-murder, all he knows;
His wise-like stare 'mongst men is found, but ignorance, only shows.

Uncle Dudley's

ODD HOURS.

(By a Country Editor.)

BEING FUNNY.

NEVER strive to be witty, young man, unless sure you can make a success of it; for, an attempt at wit, followed by failure, is a most humiliating defeat, indeed. Most young persons—particularly young men, have a strong desire to appear as "wits;" to shine above those around them, as possessing brighter intellects; in short, as being a little smarter than anybody else. To become a Mark Twain, an Artemus Ward, a Doesticks, or a Nasby, *is* an object praiseworthy enough; and, it is all right to try yourself a little, for the purpose of finding out whether you possess the elements of a wit, and a humorist; nevertheless, all the tests necessary in ascertaining whether you have "got it in you" should be conducted strictly in private, for a considerable length of time, and the tests should be made very severe. Up in a hay-loft, or down in the most secluded corner of a coal-cellar, or in some retired portion of a calf-pasture, can be reckoned on as safe localities in which to begin. When you imagine you have "struck the soul to a good thing," just retire at

once to your retreat, and commence developing it; say
it over a number of times, just as it first came into your
mind, and if you find that you have to laugh every time
you repeat it, you can note progress; and if, after saying it over four or five hundred times, you laugh more
heartily every time, then you may consider it a fair specimen of humor, out of which a two-line joke may some
time be " panned ;" and if, in addition to this, you dream
about it every night, for a month, so that you are compelled to get up out of bed and laugh until your sides
ache, ending in a spasmodic fit of hiccoughs, it will then
be safe to write it out privately, and put carefully away,
where no one will find it, for future reference.   But, too
much care cannot be taken to keep your jokes and future intentions a secret, lest you be ridiculed, and become discouraged from having your sensibilities hurt,
and your ambition drowned in ice-water, thrown by
ruthless hands.

After you have accumulated several thousand " good
things," to draw from in emergencies during your future
career as a humorist—for, once "funny" you will be
expected to always continue so until gathered in by old
Time,—you may venture to offer some of the best samples for publication in the village paper, provided it has
but a small circulation; for, you must be careful not to
gain too much publicity at first, so that if your effort is
badly received, there will not be so many to receive it.
After this trial, nature will take its course, and if you
are not too thin-skinned, and can stand a good deal of
solid grief, you will doubtless succeed in attracting some
public attention and favorable comment by the time you

reach an age when your head will resemble a soap-bubble, or your hair, a tow-wad—provided it transpires that you actually contain a mine of native humor.— Otherwise, of course, you will sink under a load of disappointment; recline under the shadow of a great sorrow, and probably end your days as conductor of a wheel barrow, on the grade, or the superintendent of a coal-cart. So, young man, whilst it may be an easy matter for any one to become a congressman, you must reckon well the chances, before you aspire to the exalted throne of a humorist. We *feel* all this, because we have been there. During our "infant manhood" we accumulated a vast store of wit, reduced to writing, and looked forward through rosy glasses to the time when we would publicly open the flood-gates of our humorous soul and inundate a sorrowing world with a burst of laughter. The choicest item was submitted to an editor of more than average erudition; he examined it critically; when through, he turned sharply and asked if the article was intended to be a humorous one; we nodded our guilt, when he replied: "Young man, you would not make a humorous writer, if you lived a thousand years, and worked ten hours a day at nothing else —if *this* is a fair sample of your talent in that direction." That settled our "humorous hash." By a heroic physical effort, we made out to reach the open air, where we could cool off, and feel of our head, when we found, sure enough, that the "bump of wit" was an inverted one, and was a yawning hollow, instead of an able-bodied protuberance. We have never since tried to write anything more laughable than a death-notice, or an epitaph for the tomb-stone **of** some departed delinquent, who never paid the printer. These we write well.

AS A HAY-MAKER.

THE grass **had** become intolerably high round about our **domicil, and the cow was** "out of meat;" hence, we purchased a scythe. A lawn-mower is too new a contrivance to be recognized by **any one** having old-fashioned tastes, and so we straight-**way went for** the good old tool of our daddies. **We never had** interviewed a scythe before, and had **our** foresight at **that time** been as acute **as our** present hindsight, we should not have interviewed it then. A scythe seems to be made up of crookedness and fiend-ishness, mixed in **about** equal parts; and, how a man is expected **to** go straight **at his work,** behind one of them, is a little in advance of any mathematical knowledge we happen to **have** on hand. We cannot imagine that any man living **can** manipulate one of them successfully ex-cept he be a cross-eyed person; a **really** cross-eyed man **might be** able to get in **his work where** it was wanted; but, **if all** scythe-handles **are as** crooked as the one we have—and which we now desire to give away—we have shekels that say that no straight-looking person can cut down the grass he wants **to** cut, unless he strikes at some object in the next lot, or else throws it around the corner of the house and then runs the other way. You might as well try to drive a tack with a ram's horn—it isn't in it.

What made our defeat too humiliating for anything was, we had been lecturing our young descendants during the breakfast hour, upon the nobility of labor, and also upon the wickedness of running after every new thing that came out to lessen the labors performed by our forefathers; that we used a scythe instead of a lawn mower, as a matter of principle, and after breakfast we would show them how their lamented grandfather mowed his hay, and how their Maker intended hay should be mown—and didn't want they should ever become so averse to labor, or so filled with pride, as to countenance the use of a horsepower machine, or a sacriligious lawn-mower, in the performance of this ancient and honorable branch of labor.

After the frugal breakfast, we adjusted our hat and, followed by the family procession, went out where the tool was suspended in a plum-tree, whistling our favorite opera, "The conquering hero comes." It took us some time to get it down, but finally it commenced coming, and we ran out from under and let it fall just where it had a mind to. The boys laughed a little, but pretty soon it quit flopping around, and we advanced cautiously and got it by the tail, and one of the handles, and lifted it off the ground; it sort of swung around and came near cutting our left limb, pretty high up; we told the boys they'd better climb up on the fence till we were under way and got the "hang" of it a little. We finally captured it by both the handles,

carried it up to the edge of the grass, swelled our muscle and gave it a tremendous swing; it went skylarking
through the trackless air above the tall grass, and cut
off a fine plum-tree around behind us; and, had we not
let go all holds and dodged out through one of the
crooks, and made the top of the fence just ahead of it,
no doubt we should now have been running about without a head. The boys laughed immoderately, and we
reproved them severely for making light of so serious a
toil. After the establishment had quieted down again,
we advanced on the crookedest side, and grasping it
simultaneously by both handles, held it out at arm's
length to find its chief center of gravity; soon, we seemed to have it, and made another pass at the luxuriant
pasture; this time, the point of the scythe went into the
ground half way to the handle, and the tail-end kicked
us on the left ear and one of the handles vibrated vigorously against our stomach and we sat down to hold it
where it ached the worst. The boys laughed so hyster-
ically that they fell off the fence, and our ear swelled
up like a blighted plum. We made just one more effort
to "conquer or die;" the scythe skipped around, cut
a little row of grass, flipped off to the left, cutting a favorite rose-bush off close, then took a circle around o'erhead and brought up with a fearful crash and buried
itself in a fence-board, whilst we sprang out through
the "twist," ran into the house and locked the door.—
NOTE—If anybody wants one of those grass-tools of
our daddies, we hope he will come around and get that
thing out of the lot, ere it wipes the tribe of Dudley
from the face of the earth. It will be found to be a cap-

ital thing to set in the front yard for tramps; if a tramp ever came into the yard, and the thing was properly set, all that would remain to do would be to take a basket and go out and gather up the pieces and give them a decent burial.

P. S.—*Wanted*—A lawn-mower.

To TURN the grindstone, saw wood, carry a hod, and work, are the greatest vexations of life—unless it may be a mop-stick with an infuriated woman at the bad end of it.

"WAS Peter ever in Rome?" is a question that has for a long time been agitating the minds of the Catholic and Protsetant clergy. We know of no way to settle the dispute, but suggest that they send a delegate to Rome, with instructions to interview the oldest inhabitant, and look over the old poll-lists and hotel registers.

THERE is a man from Pennsylvania, now out on the Northern Pacific hunting to find a moose, whole, and an elk, whole. If he fails, and passes east this way, we shall endeavor to furnish our naturalist friend an able-bodied gopher-hole, or two, or a rat-hole, so that his western trip may not prove altogether a failure. They already have oil-holes and gimlet-holes in Pennsylvania.

COTTON AS A CARGO.

OUR domestic circle concluded the other day to make up a lot of bed-comfortables, and so, sent their venerable " Uncle " to the store for twenty-five pounds of cotton-batting. We informed the storekeeper what was wanted, and he asked what we had brought to haul it home in. We told him that if twenty-five pounds of cotton-batting wasn't any heavier than twenty-five pounds of anything else, we thought ourself man enough to worry it along on our shoulder. To assure him that there was no need of his doubting as to our carrying capacity, we began telling him of a few things we had done, as he proceeded to take down the cotton and pile the rolls up on the floor. Among other things, we assured him we had carried a bed-tick full of No. 1 wheat up three flights of stairs and then stood around an hour or so with it on our shoulder; that, when in the army, we once carried a sick soldier and his baggage, together with the company's camp-kettles and a bushel and a half of rice, forty-five miles, on a forced march, without stopping to eat or drink, beside pulling upward of a dozen mules out of the mud as we went along; we also told him several other things we had done, among which was, that we had once lifted the corner of a two story log house and held it up until a man, who had lost his jack-knife through a crack in the floor, crawled under and got it. Of course, these stories were *somewhat* exaggerated, but that man needed to be convinced that we could tote twenty-five pounds of cotton-batting, and he needed it badly.

About this time we noticed that he had nearly a wagon-load of rolls piled up on the floor, and we told him he was forgetting himself—that we only wanted twenty-five pounds. He said no, he hadn't more than fifteen pounds yet, and went on taking it down from the top shelf. We walked around the pile, and made the observation that cotton-batting must be very light to the pound. He answered that it *was* tolerably light. We didn't say anything for a minute or two, but began to feel rather uneasy as the pile grew to a size that it would require a hay-rack to haul it away. Finally we told him we didn't think we wanted so much—that the weather seemed to be getting warmer, and our folks could make the comfortables a little thinner, and use them for comfortables in the summer and for sheets in the winter. But he insisted that we called for twenty-five pounds; that he had got it pretty nearly all taken down, and he wasn't in the habit of working for nothing. We saw we were beaten on that pile, and badly beaten, and finally effected a compromise by paying him a dollar for his trouble, and buying five pounds instead of the quantity originally ordered; even then, we had about as soon have tried to carry off a bed-tick full of Northern Pacific No. 1 hard wheat, as that cotton. As we took our blushing departure, that cotton-vendor sort of grinned out of the corner of his mouth, as he said: "Come down some time, 'Uncle,' and spend the evening, and tell us some more stories about how much you can carry, on an average." We said "yes," and then slid around the corner underneath our cotton, and upon arriving home, told our folks the next time they wanted twenty-five pounds of cotton-batting, not to take us for a caravan or a hippodrome, or there would be trouble among the animals.

WHEN we see a neatly-dressed, refined and intelligent-looking lady, traveling on the cars, and occupying her time in knitting—whilst a score of other females are passing away the hours in the most frivolous gossip and pastimes—we kind of chalk her down as one of God's noble-women who escaped at the time of the apparent general destruction of her class. We actually saw such a woman a few days ago, improbable as it may seem.

THE season of spring has bloomed again. The shout of "dubbs!" and "knuckle tight!" is again heard floating on the ambient air; the croquet mauls will soon be bumping the balls; the hens have begun their annual labors, and the "roosters" are all on edge for a fight. House-cleaning and raking up the yards are among the house-wife's specialties. The excitements of the chase are again being enjoyed—chasing bedbugs out of one crack into another. Yes, spring has arrived, and we perspire copiously when we reflect upon the vast deal of hard labor that is to be performed—by others.

BROTHERS AND SISTERS.

ERE they to be the last words of advice we could give, they could be of no more serious import than to implore brothers and sisters, whilst together under the parental roof, to be loving and indulgent to one another; to bear with one another's shortcomings, and instead of chiding and wrangling, embrace the dear forms of those whom, from every natural and divine tie, you should love and protect, as you would the tender flower in the months of winter. Think for a moment, dear little friends, that the association you will be permitted to enjoy together, with your little brothers and sisters at home, is but a brief period at the most; when you are tempted to feel aggrieved at them, just stop a moment and think: "Why should I allow my temper—my bad disposition—to convert what should be happy moments, into a time of vexatious contention, by which my own heart is hardened and seared, and by which my acts and words may make a dark and callous impression for the bad upon the tender heart of my dear little brother or sister, that may last all through his or her life—even changing the character and place of their saddened graves at the end of all." These lit-

tle darlings are soon to start upon the rugged, thorny
path of life's journey, all alone, save being accompanied
by the sweet or bitter recollections of their home life
and their trust or distrust in God's protecting care, and
in the love of their brothers and sisters who loved and
counseled, or who contended with, and hated them
during the tender years of childhood. Oh, my little
friends, remember that when parents sleep in the grave,
and are powerless to comfort you, the best and only
true earthly friends you have left are your brothers and
sisters, if they have lived true to their duty as such.
Remember that there is no sadder, no more serious
thought that can come to your minds than the one,
" What is to be the future of this tender little brother or
sister ? Let it be a sad or joyful journey, I am now
bound, by the grace of God, to do my whole duty by
them, in the brief space given me, to indellibly impress
upon their minds the fact that I love them perfectly."
Such a resolution faithfully and resolutely carried out,
will not only brighten your own soul and heart, but will
in the future dark, tempestuous hours of your brother's
or sister's life, appear like a sweet angel of peace, in
their memory to strengthen and buoy them up in a sea
that, with no such fond proof of love to cling to, might
overwhelm and drift them to a speedy and a hopeless
destruction. Oh, little friends, remember that the present is a golden time in life; let naught but love and encouragement exist among you ; so that when you come
to separate at the door of the parental home, each can
carry with him the assurance that, though distant lands
may intervene and divide you, the pure and life-tried

love is whole, ample and sincere, and such as will prove
an anchor of hope, and a buoy that will land you safely
at last in that haven beyond the sky where the pure love
of life shall be doubly purified, and go on through all
eternity.

HOW SMALL WE ARE.

IF A MAN wants to realize how insignificant
he is, and how insignificant are all things here
below, in fact, let him scale one of the high
hills in the vicinity, and look down—then look up.
Let him attain the very peak therof, and gaze down
upon the cleft and troublous world, and reflect upon
what he sees. A monster globe of land and water with
human ants running, craze-brained, hither and thither
over its surface; and, ant-like, rearing their castles up
ward only to be despoiled and ruined by the heel of
Time. Away down there, are millions of human pig-
mies who are wrapt about with what they esteem to be
the great all in all, and what they call "human affairs."
They see naught but the "mighty things" they create;
they hear naught save the praises they sing of themselves; they think of naught save that which pertains to
their own aggrandisement among their kind. Poor,
puny insects—animate specks of nothingness, moths of
rolling years. They never look up to catch a glimpse
of vastness, nor even cast a thought toward the infinite.

They seem not to know that their proudest piles, which have cost them years of toil, are as naught by the side of mountains that have been thrown to the clouds by a single quiver of Nature; they dream that their little earth is all of creation, their gain is their god, and they worship at the shrine of the evil spirit of Mammon. They grovel in self-esteem, and shout defiance among themselves. They never realize that their world—in whose tiny web of tangled affairs they are hopelessly bound—is but a speck of matter, tottering in its transient rounds through space which is filled with countless worlds of immeasurably more importance than theirs, and yet the space between is measureless by all the powers of human calculation. Could we all, or any of us, even catch the faintest glimpse of our own smallness, we would stand abashed in the presence of our own reckless, thoughtless, fruitless and sinful struggle for prizes never reached, though we clamber over the prostrate forms of our fellows and cast our souls into the pool, to bridge us over to the mythical goal.

AUNT BETSY wants us to tell her how to persuade her cow to let down her milk. We do not claim to be particularly posted on how to make a stubborn cow allow her milk to flow, but you might try having one of the boys draw a buck-saw gently across her back just when you get a good hold on the teats; we cannot exactly tell what the result would be, but are of the opinion that something would "come down," which would certainly be some satisfaction, you know.

EVENING.

A S WE sit in the door-yard this quiet August evening, a strange silence prevails; not a sound is heard, save the creaking crickets about our feet, or the occasional notes of the katy-did; the sun has sunk behind the hills, and as it fades out of sight —continually painting morning splendors and evening sunsets in its ceaseless rounds—its last rays tinge the western blue with a mellow light that gives an awe-inspiring aspect to the silent landscape. The scene is one where the over-strung mind can turn from the turmoils of life, and peacefully contemplate the visible universe in one of its most enchanting moments; all is peace; all is harmony; the troubled world seems to have lulled itself to repose under the soothing influence of a perfect serenity. Such an hour is balm to the soul, a rest to the weary, fretful mind; the calm that pervades the scene, the gentle beauty of the view, gives one a glimpse of the harmonious world of rest beyond the tinted sky, and sooths the weary heart that has long since become sick in the battle of life. It is the last evening of the week, and seems to be preparing the sympathies of Nature to accord with the character of the sacred day to

follow. The busy week has gathered its chapter of
events, Time has written his record, and the Past is rolling up an historic scroll as against the inspection of the
Judgment-day, when Time shall end.   The doors of the
mart are closed, the busy shops are shut, and the family members are approaching the hearthstone to receive
the parental blessing, and to lay their measure of love
on the altar of filial affection. Oh, that this peace could
be extended—with its beauty, its love, its forgiveness,
its holy thoughts, its reverence and calm good will—
over all the remaining pages of Time.   How sweet the
enjoyment of one's better nature and purer thoughts,
when permitted to surmount the bitterness of Life's
struggle, through the peaceful influence of such an hour
as this.   The heart-aches, the animosities, the hatreds,
the jealousies and sinful thoughts are all forgotten and
buried, and that inner feeling of love, forgiveness and
kind regard for all our fellow travelers, holds the fullest
sway within us; and our souls rest in perfect conson-
ance with the blissful scene about us.   The harmony of
the hour is finally intensified by the sweet vesper-lay of
the birds as they hide away among the boughs, and pay
their good-night homage to the Author of all this glorious scene.   As night draws her somber robe o'er the
landscape, thankful humanity withdraw to their bed-
sides and, as become the recipients of His mercy and
blessings, bend the knee in honor of the Creator of all
this mighty universe, and in supplication before Him
whom we ask, in repentance, to guard us through the
night.

ON THE ICE.

THE skating season, having fairly set in, and there being a splendid opening for a first lesson in the gliding art, we resolved not to let the opportunity "slip" for finishing an otherwise brilliant education. With this object in view, we provided ourself with a pair of what they called "club skates," and by moonlight quietly betook ourself to the lake shore where, already, scores of boys and girls, lads and lassies, and some of maturer years were enjoying the rare sport. Fortunately for our bashful nature, it was not so light but that we could keep ourself incog.; we resolved to go up above the rest of the human family there assembled, and cut a few circles, and things, by way of finding our center, and after warming up to our bottom gait we resolved to go down through that crowd and show them what life on skates meant. We had never been on skates, but, after seeing mere infants gliding around in the most graceful and daring manner, it was not for us to doubt our ability to cut a magnificent swath after five minutes practice. We sat down on a stone and adjusted the implements, as we had been told to, and, after drawing our cap well over our ears and muffling our chest and neck, and adjusting our patent lung protector so that the sharp air would not chill us as we flew through space, as we proposed to do, we got up on our feet—or rather on our skates. They were a fine pair of the "latest out," and we felt ever so much at home on them. We struck an attitude that betokened grace, and then pushed our left foot out vigorously a little north of west, and the other one didn't wait for orders—it flew around in four or five different directions and caught us just back of our left ear; of course, we saw in an instant, that we were "whitewashed" on that heat, and so we reclined on our nose and went skimming along for a rod or so, just as it happened; and it turned out to happen very unsatisfactorily. We finally got our nose and chin wiped off, got our legs hauled around into position and sat up. The accident was altogether inexplicable; there never was a bigger, nor a more complicated disaster enacted in that length of time—it was the quickest work on record, we felt sure, and that was *some* satisfaction.

We concluded there must have been some error in our adjustment of the skates, or else we shoved out the wrong leg first, or else there was something wrong somewhere. In fact, we *felt* as though there was something wrong. A young lady just then flew past and asked if we were tired. We took off our hat and told her we were not exactly tired, but a little weary. Then we commenced getting mad a little bit, and resolved to commence skating without any further delay. We felt of our skates to see if they were in proper position, and also our nose, and then we just hopped up on our pegs,

and, after getting our balance, pushed the right gently
to the south'ard and fetched the left gently up to the
wind'ard; then the right, off on a slight quarter, and
the left straight ahead. About this time we sat down;
we hadn't contemplated resting so soon, but somehow
we did, and a pyrotechnic display greeted our vision just
as we took our seat that was only equaled by the Aurora Borealis on a winter's night. We had sat down in
so reckless a manner that we had bitten our tongue half
off, and the top of our head seemed to have gone up in
a balloon. When we got so that we could think intelli-
gently on any subject, we thought, among other things,
that such confounded amusement as this skating, must
necessarily tend toward shortening the spinal column
until a man's body and legs must be in about the same
proportion as the body and handles of a pair of nut-
crackers. We had a notion to quit; but after thinking
over matters a little we got mad again, and when we get
mad, there isn't any one pair of skates that can neutralize our feelings by any such conduct. We got up on
all-fours and after flying up in the rear a few times,
made out to erect a perpendicular once more, and just
naturally clattered ahead regardless of consequences.
After making half a dozen frantic lunges in all directions—our arms flying around like the arms of a wind-
mill—we commenced going to grass again; the last
thing that we remember was that the world had changed
places with the moon, while we flew through space,
playing the role of a comet, and suddenly several worlds
came together, and things here below had gone to eternal slam bang.

When we came too, we found we had struck all over, and were bu'sted in all quarters worse than a Chicago savings bank. We concluded to cease that sort of fun right then and there—unless we could be thoroughly cushioned and upholstered for the business—and we did quit. We were taken home on a friendly dray. No cards.

TIME IS MONEY.

T IS pretty generally understood that printers are hard-working mortals, and we, ourself, are no exception to the rule—we have been the victim of honest toil all our life, and the bread that we have consumed has been the direct result of a perspiring brow. A day or two since, we thought to take a few hours' leisure; the weather was pleasant and to leave our work and stroll about for a time, seemed good to us—indulge in a little physical inactivity and mental "slouchiness" to a reckless degree. Things were very quiet on the street; even the wickedest man in town leaned lazily over a drygoods box, with only life enough left to use one eye on some object of interest away up town. It was warm. Even the barber next door was sweating as he clawed around among the bushy beard of a frontiersman in search of a likely place to commence operations. We met a dog; his tongue was out a good deal longer than his tail—he was a stumpy-

tail dog. We felt sure, from the evidences around us.
that it was too hot for mortal to labor, and our conscience pricked us not for the idle hours we were trying
to enjoy. A show-window on the shady side of the
street attracted our attention, and like an idle, curious
boy, we leaned up against the frame and commenced
looking at the "things." There were dolls, some with
heads and no bodies, and some with bodies and no
heads, and others complete; marbles of all sizes and
colors, their cost so arranged as to suit boys of all conditions in life; jack-knives with bone and horn handles,
"barlows," admirably arranged for cutting a boy's
finger to the bone in the neatest style; there were glass
beads, tinseled and plain, big strings for a quarter and
little ones for a cent; just the things to lead into cap-
tivity the eye of the little miss; a "jumping-jack," with
his limber legs all set for business, his arms akimbo, and
staring at us with a look which seemed to say, " If you
don't believe I can git up and dust, just pull my tail a
trifle;" a little goat looked up at us saucily, and we felt
sure he said, "You're another;" we quit looking at
the goat. Pretty soon we discovered a little "savings
bank" among the mass of toy goods, and right over the
little hole where the coppers were supposed to be in-
serted, were these words in gilt letters: "Time is Money." This, taken in connection with the language of
the goat, was the least bit too heavy for our conscience;
and, after pondering seriously for a moment, we took
another small look at those ominous words on the bank,
and at that miserable goat, and then we went straight
home again—just as straight as we could go. We firm-

ly resolved that after meeting with such a rebuke from
so unexpected a source, we should never again cease to
make good use of our time—for tired hands are far better than a guilty conscience.

THE CAT.

WE KNOW but little concerning the ancient
history of the cat.   It is supposed, however,
that the world has nearly always had its full
quota of assorted cats.   We once saw saw an Egyptian
mummy that had been taken from the universal tomb
of the Egyptians—the Catacombs.   It was the body of
a full-grown man, and though it had not decomposed,
like the dead of to-day, it was terribly withered up, and
was about the color of navy tobacco.   His body had,
of course, been embalmed, after the fashion of the
ancient time in which this gentleman had been laid on
the shelf.   He had been encased in what at that time
was called linen; in these days we call it "old gunny
sack."   After being wound about with strips of this
three-cent fabric, from head to foot—much as we do up
a sore thumb—he had apparently been soaked in tar,
or something.   This not only excluded the air, but preserved the body from decomposition, and let the old
chap dry down, and sort of "set."   This ancient Egyptian had probably been dead for two or three thousand
years, and was as fine a specimen of "well-preserved"

humanity as we ever beheld. For the purpose of allowing his posterity to look upon the face of one of the most illustrious of real "old seeds," the coffee-sacking had been removed from about his head and shoulders, and, aside from his dark complexion, and eccentric cast of countenance, he had the appearance of having been a prominent man in his time—possibly a government gauger or the president of a savings bank. But, you ask, what has this ancient mummy to do with the cat story?

Well, the authorities who had desecrated the tomb, and brought away this effectually dried up individual, had also brought all the tomb contained. Among the other items was a cat, that had evidently been placed therein at the same time with its master. The animal had been wrapped and soaked in the same manner as he; and was preserved in as perfect condition; even the hair, and the color of the hair was the same as when it cantered around the back alleys of ancient Cairo, or Thebes, in quest of a stray mouse, or purred around the feet of one of the Pharaohs. It was the remains of a yellow and white cat, with an occasional gray spot, for variety's sake—a sort of calico cat. It was probably a favorite, and the master doubtless ordered, immediately prior to his demise, that the cat be killed and buried with him; or, possibly, the cat died first, and the master finding no further object in life, when the cat was gone, finished his own life, and both he and his cat were toted to the Catacombs together.

At any rate, this two-thousand-year-old cat conclusively proves that cats are no new thing; but, that the

ancients knew, as well as we, the beauties of a duet
on the garden wall at the low hour of twelve.   And if
they embalmed all their cats in those days, it shows how
utterly reckless we have grown in these latter days on
the cat question.   But if there was any good reason for
paying such respect to the cat, then the Egyptians neglected to "hand it down" to us; and, never finding any
reason for giving a dead cat any more than an ordinary
burial, we have drowned scores of them, hung several,
and smashed a good many.

A cat is supposed to have nine lives.   Just how this
fact was first discovered we are not aware.   We once
undertook to kill a very old and tough Thomas-cat,
however, and discovered the truth of this assertion.   We
drowned him once, but we had not got half way home
when that cat came purring against our leg, as if to rub
the water off his glossy fur.   Next day we mauled him
half an hour across a fence rail, supposing we had
broken every bone in his body, and threw him over a
bank.   That night a cat was heard at the door, and
upon opening it, in galloped Thomas, as lively as a
cricket; the mauling had apparently only limbered up
his joints, though he looked a little gaunt.   We killed
that cat every day for two weeks, in all the horrid forms
known to a determined nature; but, upon leaving home
some years afterward, there wasn't a livelier cat of his
age in the neighborhood.

Cats are great thinkers; they will often sit and sleep-
ily gaze into the fire for an hour; then suddenly start
off into another room or out to the barn and bring back
a mouse in each corner of their mouth.   They evident-

ly figure out, by a mathematical calculation, which mouse-hole is entitled to furnish the next lunch.

There is one thing about cats that always made us respect them; and, in fact, when we stop to reflect about it we cannot help loving a cat: It is because they have music in them—we always did love anything that furnished this hum-drum life of ours with music. There is probably as much music in a cat as in any other creature. Their in'ards are tightly strung in all the orchestras, and in all the gay ball-rooms of the world; and without the soothing, soul-stirring strains that fill the world with joy, emanating from the internal arrangements of the cat we should certainly realize that we are "all poor creatures." In fact, it would prove a great catastrophe in the world, were all the cats to be stricken out of existence.

WE saw a man going down street the other day, with an irregular gait, trying to sing that old, old song entitled " Hic ! " and endeavoring, between the verses, to smoke a clothes-pin.

HOW TO BEGIN ON A NEW FARM.

AVING been raised in the West, and it having become "noised around" that we knew something of how to commence on a new farm, or "claim," a young man has applied to us to write an article on the subject, as he and others have proposed to "go west," where land is cheap and plenty, and adopt the life of a farmer—anciently called tiller, modernly styled "granger." The young man was anxious to gain all the information possible on the subject of opening up a "claim," and we admire his good judgement in applying to a reliable source to obtain knowledge in regard to the most noble and ennobling occupation of man.

The first move toward farming a new claim in the west is to take possession of it; the next, to enclose a small tract of the land and put a roof over it; floors may be introduced, if the proprietor is pretty forehanded, otherwise they are a luxury that may be dispensed with indefinitely. There should be two apertures left in the walls—one for daylight to climb in at, the other to admit ingress and egress on the part of the proprietor. The furniture necessary to a good square start on a new farm, should be rather plain, to be in good taste; **for,** the vanity of pomp and show should never be allowed to invade the natural simplicity of a new farm. **A stool** with three legs—one on the south and two on the north side—should suffice for that **kind** of "paraphernalia;" at first, a little inconvenience may be experienced in trying to sit on it without tipping over; but any one with sufficient talent to master the art of riding a veloc- ipede, will very soon prove equal to riding one of these kind of chairs. It is less difficult than a one-legged milking-stool by just two-thirds. The table, for a new farm, should be a barrel, for **several reasons:** a salt-bar- rel, the open end up, and a board across the top; **this** is what we term an extension table—the longer **the** board the greater the extension. The inner recesses of **this table can be used** as a wardrobe and cupboard, in **which the settler may keep his** other shirt and the extra provisions away from the mice. By hugging the knees around the barrel when eating, the chair can be man- aged **with greater** dexterity. A tin plate and cup, with **horn-handle** knife and fork, a tin dish and spoon with **which to handle the pork and gravy,** should complete the table-ware for **a new farm, unless,** as we said before, the proprietor is forehanded, in which case a tin sugar- bowl might be added consistently—one painted brown, so that too great a contrast will not exist between the instrument and its contents—for if sugar is used at all, its hue should be somber; ten or twelve pounds for a **dollar.** All the supplies necessary to start a new farm are a hundred-weight of pork, a barrel of flour, **a barrel of salt,** the same of vinegar—to **eat with** "greens"—

and a peck of **beans**; if the proprietor is forehanded, however, he might **increase the** quantity of salt and vinegar, and add half **a** pound of pepper and a nutmeg.

The **next** duty of the proprietor of a new farm in a new **country** should be to kill a coon; this will wake **him up to** a sense of defensive and **offensive** operations; **but the chief** object to be gained by this is to get the **skin of** the animal to **nail on the** door; for if **there is** anything that seems **good to us, and that** ornaments the door of a house **on a new farm to an** appropriate perfection, it is a coon-skin artistically stretched and nailed up with the flesh side out; and then, **it's so** "lucky."

The proprietor should next tear up the bosom of the virgin soil with a twenty-two inch plow hitched to a **yoke of at least** moderately stout oxen; at first he may **grow impatient** to do too much plowing in **too short a time**; we warn him that unless patience is cultivated on a new farm, he will fail. If he breaks up fifteen or sixteen acres per day at first—with one yoke of oxen and a twenty-two inch plow—he is doing a good, reasonable business, and may safely estimate that he is succeeding as well as could **be** expected. He should "plow deep whilst sluggards sleep"—say about twelve or fifteen inches in depth. When plowing, or breaking, is done, let him be particular as to the quality and variety of his seeds, for planting an "old seed" on a new farm is of no earthly account. The variety of corn known as "sod-corn" is the best for the first year's planting. If a great variety of crops is desired on a limited area of ground, it would be best to mix the seed before sowing —wheat, rye, barley, buckwheat, flax, turnip and oats in equal parts, **and** put on about ten bushels to **the** acre. The winters being somewhat long in this country, the young farmer can employ himself during **the** snowy months, in sorting out his crops and getting them ready for the spring market. We advise the production **of poultry and pigs, and the cultivation of butter and beeswax; they are all saleable products, and besides, the turkeys and chickens are death on** grasshoppers and **bugs—a hundred turkeys** will alone **sweep** dozens and dozens of grasshoppers out of existence in a single summer, while chickens are a tangible terror to striped bugs that infest cucumber-vines. We trust these few practical suggestions, by one who has **been there and knows** as to these things, may prove more or less valuable to every reader who desires to start on a new farm.

WE recently attended church service in a frontier district, where the pioneers and their families were gathered in a log church and listened to the gospel as expounded by the good pastor, who performed his rounds in the wide field of his labors on foot, and often by moonlight, along the Indian trails of **the wilderness.** To be sure, in his earnest sermons, he did not bore with as large an auger as many of his co-laborers in city pulpits, but he came as near slaughtering Satan as almost any of them.

TOO MANY SUBJECTS.

WE HAVE received an invitation to deliver a lecture in one of the interior districts of the region which we inhabit at the present time. It grieves us to say that we shall have to decline the invitation, because we cannot lecture anyway—we're not that kind of a man. What our friends will lose, by our declination, we should feel sorry for, only their loss will be so very trifling that it will not warrant any extended season of grief on our part. But, when we refuse to lecture, in this instance, we know just what we're doing —when we declare that we cannot lecture we speak advisedly in the matter. We know better than any one else our capacity as a Demosthenese or Cicero, because we've tried it. A few years ago—just previous to the time when we found out we couldn't—the committee of a four-horse literary society invited us to deliver a set lecture. We smiled upon that committee, and told them they could feel assured their wish should be complied with—that it would give us great pleasure to furnish the grand occasion with one of the best efforts they would probably enjoy during the lecture season. Then they smiled upon us, and departed. We had about ten days

in which to prepare it. After spending a day and a
night in thinking up a subject we determined to write
all we knew upon several topics, so that if we failed on
one we could switch off on another—our bump of caution is remarkably well developed. The evening finally
came, and the hall was jammed full—this was very flat-
tering, though our knees perceptibly weakened upon
staring so many countenances in the face. In fact, we
wished there weren't so many countenances present.
Upon being introduced, as the renowned Ole Dudley-
son, from Scratchmyback Mountain, our heart commenced threshing around and playing pull-away in such
an outlandish manner that we came near tumbling off
the platform. We felt just as though we looked like a
man who wasn't much of a lecturer—a fellow who had
escaped the notice of the fool-killer, when he took the
last census. We had notes of all we knew upon four
different subjects, and had the four sheets of paper, one
on top of the other, with the heads to each written out
in a bold hand, excepting one set of notes, which had
no top head. This sheet lay on top of the others, as
we afterwards learned, and the next one to it was on
" Modern Feudalism." This one had the caption plainly written, and it projected just above the top sheet that
had no heading. Ordinarily, of course, we should have
noticed it; but our feelings were so intensified that we
never discovered our mistake, until after we had discovered that lecturing wasn't our *forte*. The *top* sheet was
on the subject of, " The Domestic Animals of America."
After stiffening our pedal extremities sufficiently, we advanced to the stand and remarked, "Ahem!" Then

we took a drink of water, glanced at the sea of faces in
front of us, and said, "Ahem," again. Then in order
to give our heart and gizzard time to play their game
out, we reached around to our coat-tail pocket for our
handkerchief, and wiped the water off our mouth.
Then we brushed our hair back, noticed if our neck tie
was in position, said "ahem," and felt for our manu-
script. We said: "Mr. President—ahem! The subject I have chosen for the edification and instruction of
the audience this evening, is "Modern Feudalism."—
About this time we were about blind with embarras-
ment, and could hardly see the writing that followed
the bold heading, and too much excited to notice
whether the body fitted the heading, or the heading al-
luded to the body. We continued: "Mr. President,
I repeat, that this lecture is a treatise upon Modern
Feudalism. There is no subject more interesting for
contemplation, for discussion, and kindly consideration
than our domestic animals. The ox, the cow, the
heifer, the steer, the calf; the horse, the mare, the colt,
the gelding, and—and so forth; the hen, the rooster,
the turkey and the turkey-gobbler; the cat and the dog,
and the—and the—the mouse and—and other domestic
creatures, etc., etc." About this time some unruly boys
began to whistle "down breaks," and the audience generally began to laugh and stamp their feet. At first we
we thought the growing tumult was that of approval—
though we hadn't thought the laugh came in so soon.
After some time, we tried to say that "of all the animals people had around the house, the bed-bug was
furthest from being valuable or desirable;" but it was

no use. The audience had gotten entirely away with the gentleman from Scratchmyback Mountain, and it was not until the President had adjourned the meeting, that we discovered we had announced *one* subject, and begun speaking on *another;* and after we finally became possessed of our usual composure and senses, we thought the matter over and concluded that lecturing wasn't the calling best suited to our natural bent—we didn't seem to be bent in that way. So we have "sworn off," as the old toper would remark on New Year's Day. Our ambition to grace the rostrum has become permanently crushed and battered down.

A YOUNG man of our acquaintance who grew up from the cradle with an unconquerable desire to become a brakeman on a railroad train, finally got a "sit" on a freight train. He worked at his favorite calling for six months, gross time; up to that time he had lost the thumb of one hand, three fingers off the other, had an ear scraped nearly off by a "bumper," had three ribs broken, the toes of his left foot smashed, and his back wrenched so as to partially disable him for life. When we last heard from him he had determined to retire from the railroad business, and what was left of him was negotiating with a gardener for a summer's job of breaking on a vegetable cart.

AN EXPLANATION.

EARNING early during our tender years that even an Arab who had never written a book, was set down as an article of Arab too worthless to even be accounted for in a census report, we secretly resolved to come up to at least an average specimen of that nationality, if we had to hire it done. We have never entered into any special line of training for the book-making business, because we desired to have an *original* work; and feared, that if we should ever read another book, ours might be too much like the one we read. We ventured once to read a portion of "Milton Lost in Paradise," (we believe that is where he lost his bearings), somebody's "Treatise on the Creation," a few snatches, by Homer, "Mother Goose's Melodies," and the "Early Voyages by the Northmen." Our regret at having done so, however, has always been a source of annoyance, as will be discovered by the careful reader of these pages, when bearing in mind that we *intended* to have it completely original. We have had the hardest kind of work to prevent our productions from being almost a copy of some of the best efforts of the above-mentioned writers. Some of our keenest articles are worded a little differently, but the *style* is almost precisely the same as theirs. We therefore desire to make this explanation, and thus remove any suspicion that we *intended* it to be so ; because, we solemnly aver that nothing was further from our desires. Although the original harmony of the enclosed productions is thus rendered inharmonious, we trust, under the circumstances, that our readers will not set us down as a literary pirate, altogether, but will give us credit for having made a fair onslaught upon originality. We forgive the authors named, for having been indirectly responsible for marring our book, as we are convinced that they did not write their books for that purpose, and the fault is mostly our own. We feel very much elated, however, as far as we have gone,; it having become widely "noised about" that we were soon to place a book "on tap" we have, up to this date, received orders for nearly half a dozen of them—from various sections of the country—and feel sure that if this kind of a rush continues right along, ten hours a day, we will be able to work off our whole edition of three thousand copies inside of two hundred years. After that, we shall be able to publish another book with more style about it, and then rest on our laurels, conscious that our literary calibre will then be equivalent to *two* separate and distinct Arabs, or *one* double-barreled Arab.

HOW IS IT?

YES, it is often asked, "How is it that homely girls can find chances to marry, and do marry?" We heard a girl ask that question just a day or two ago. It seemed to puzzle her mightily, in fact, as she puckered up her pretty lips and turned up her delicate little nose, more in contempt than in sympathy. We dare to suggest to her that, take 'em as they run, homely girls are best at heart, have sounder minds, are more amiable, are happier themselves—despite the consciousness of possessing a plain face—and strive more to make those about them happy. They come much nearer, as a class, being what God intended to honor by the noble name of *woman* than the pretty faced pets of the sex, who are too frequently marred in soul and character by their beautiful faces. When men desire to sow their wild oats, and appear at the festivities of the world, where show or outward beauty is the reigning master, then they choose the butterflies as companions, who can smile bewitchingly and glitter most brilliantly 'neath the gas jets. But men, as a class, are not so foolish as to select a brilliant exterior, alone, for a life companion; they ask the hand of a *woman*, when they seek

for a home-queen; a woman full of earnest purose, with
a loving disposition, a faithful trust and untiring patience
in her life-labor of making home happy, and one in
whose face, though it may be plain, shines forth the
radiance of a pure mind, a cheerful soul, and with a
faith both in the life of the present and the heaven of
the future.   These are a few of the reasons " why homely girls marry."

MAY BASKETS.

MAY-DAY morning, many of the young ladies
and gentlemen found, hung upon their door-
knobs, beautifully constructed May-baskets,
containing boquets of wild flowers.   Although neither a
young lady, nor an extremely young gentleman—judg-
ing from the number of youngsters who call us " Dad "
—we have to thank somebody for one of these pretty
little tokens of friendship.   It is a pleasant custom, indeed, and one that not only reminds us that the flowery
month is here, but makes one's heart palpitate with a
sort of secret joy in the consciousness that a mindful
friend has passed our way during the stilly hours of
night, and *not* a stealthy enemy.   We say again, blessings on all these beautiful little customs, which contribute so largely in binding human hearts together, and
bringing all nearer, and with greater thanks, toward
God, who so mercifully allows us to live and enjoy His
blessings.

COLTS.

A NEW colt —particularly a " blooded " colt—is anything but a picturesque spectacle, and is as awkward a looking contrivance as a wheelbarrow with one handle broken off.   Its legs stand around in rows with about the same regularity as the rafters in a bu'sted umbrella, and they have joints in them that look like the battered end of a pile-driver. Colts don't know much until they have learned something ; they give their dam a power of trouble, and when they go out in company the mother endures so much vexation that she sweats like a thunder-cloud.   When a colt gets where there are other horses, it is dead-sure to follow off the the wrong animal ; and, with an innocence that is per-fectly exasperating, will follow after a strange *horse* with a persistency sufficient to make its own mother turn grey ; when it gets a little foolish, by the presence of other company, it don't know its own mother from a two-year-old steer.   We have seen a colt run around a half-acre lot fourteen times, hunting its mother, when there wasn't another thing *in* the lot *but* its mother.   If they have their own way, they only take one meal a day, but that lasts all the time—probably they do this to keep from "piecing between meals." A new colt's tail looks like a cat's tail, when the cat is taking a survey of a dog, and its head seems so heavy that we always feel nervous for fear it will tip up and break its neck; their bodies are about as gracefully proportioned as a corn-cob, and about the same shape, and they look out of their eyes just as though they were looking at nothing. We don't like colts much when they're green, and when they get ripe they are more dangerous than a long spell of sickness, so we don't like colts in any shape—because they have no shape, anyway.

WE noticed a little pig on the street the other day, picking up stray kernels of corn under a wagon, to which a span of average mules were hitched. Pretty soon the little porker had taken in all the stray corn he could find, and so he thought he would just take a little smell of the off mule's north heel—that's just like a little fool pig would do, you know. Well, the mule stretched out his leg about that time, and the little innocent pig—little dreaming that he had placed his nose against the most artistic besom of destruction known to history—commenced to emigrate, and the last we saw of him he looked about as big as a bumble-bee, and was just passing out of sight over a neighboring hill-top.

THE BIRCH CANOE.

ITTING on the beach; the waters of the Lake are as still as the evening is peaceful; scarce a ripple is seen to mar the glassy bosom of the Bay, and the full round moon is duplicated in body and beauty, as it looks down into the deep blue waters from its azure field above. The evening star twinkles out from the bending vault, like a glittering gem—brilliant and new as the day it was placed there by the finger of the Almighty. All Nature seems hushed in repose, as if waiting with breathless respect for angels to peer out through Heaven's portals and smile upon a wicked world. Soon a plaintive sound is heard, and the mirror-like surface of the waters is seen to change to oval riplets as, from a neighboring nook, a canoe emerges, bearing two children of the forest; as they dip their paddles, the frail bark seems possessed of wings and glides gracefully o'er the water, and the dusky maiden, with wild, soft notes gives a musical melody to the otherwise silent scene. Viewing them in their primitive craft, we cannot but feel something akin to sadness, as we reflect that they are the final remnant of a rapidly fading race. The strain they sing seems to say, " Farewell! We leave these beautiful shores to the hands of the conquering pale-face!" For hundreds of years—yea, thousands—the blue waters before us knew no touch save that of the birch canoe, and the rocky cliffs echoed back no sound but the plaintive songs of the red man, and its own hoarse voice when torn by the ruthless tempest. Passing away!—Passing away! Instead of the birch-bark fleets of old, now are seen the monster ships, with great white sails and towering masts, raking the sky above and plowing the deep below; the giant monarchs, with smoke and steam, fly hither and thither like fiery monsters, and with their deafening yells start very Nature from its wonted slumber, and frighten the birch canoe away to a refuge in some rocky glen. Soon, the smooth Bay will no more reflect back the face of Nature's daughters, the cliffs echo with the war-whoop of the savage warrior, nor the laughing brooks gurgle an accompaniment to the lullaby of the Indian mother. The birch canoe will only be known to song; no longer will it kiss the mossy bank at its moorings, nor rock to slumber, on the bosom of the Bay, the infants of its passing race.

A REVERY.

OW solemn is the thought, as one sits by the hearth in the evening-hour, gazing vacantly at the wasting embers of the fire—thinking of many scenes of the past, and yet thinking of nothing in particular—when the toll of the faithful old clock reminds you that another hour has dripped into the receptacle of eternity. Again the never-resting wheels of your mind start back over the path of the past. The scenes of your life flit through the channel of thought like a panorama of lightning scenes, and carry you, in a twinkling, from the days of your swaddling-clothes to the very present. Then you retreat again, to pause for a moment and gaze over the threshold of some painful or pleasant event of your life and view it o'er again; then you leap to another and another, and see how you might have bettered it, or how narrow was the ecsape from a worse result. When all is past and gone, how many incidents you can recall that were keys to as many doors leading out from the path you traveled. Had you unlocked any one of them and passed through, whither would you have strayed and where would you have landed? Then you surmise and speculate. How thankful you feel to a protecting heaven that you did not stray out into many of the by-paths that tempted as you passed, and which, as the experience of maturer years has taught, would have led to speedy ruin of either soul, or body, or prospects—or all. Then you feel half inclined to murmur because you did not go into others that it now seems must have led to honor, wealth and happiness far beyond what you now possess. This latter is dangerous ground upon which to dwell, and is the sap-worm of contentment and the comforts you have already gained; this you must shun, lest you sin against yourself and the merciful Being whom you owe for all the innumerable blessings and favors of which you have been the ungrateful recipient. Again the clock strikes the hour, and you are startled from the deep reverie that absorbs your mind, and are partially brought back to the ever anxious present. Then you leap into the future, and out upon its broad area wander only through flowery paths and magnificent castles—no man sees monsters in coming time, who looks out through the window of hope. All views are pleasant, all pastures are green; the stream of future life is clear and its bosom unruffled by storms of adversity, The sunshine on the path of years to come is only shut out by the distant and ever receding horizon which, when finally reached, you have a confiding hope that you shall find a peaceful resting-place in the eternity of God and the home of your fathers. With feelings of resignation, yet a saddened mind, you retire to your couch resolving to hope for the best and prepare for the worst.

BUYING A COW.

NOT BEING a millionaire, we have never had
a single thought, or aspired to the dignity of
furnishing our barn-yard with a sure-enough Alderney cow.   They are the " rage," to be sure ;
but all of these fine-haired animals have been picked
up, and now adorn the rear landscapes of the bonanza-
kings' homes, who dwell here and there among us,
where they nip the delicate herbage and pan out thick
cream in the fore-milking with an after-piece, at each
sitting, of pure, gilt-edge butter, all ready for the table.
We are tolerably proud, though, if we haven't a bank
account or a mine, and to get a good cow—one that
would give right good common fluid, plenty of it, was
gentle, graceful in her motions, with an intelligent countenance,—was our ambition.   We thought we knew
most of the " points " of a good family cow, and so kept
our eye cocked for one that would please our fancy, for
a *good* cow, if she *wasn't* particularly picturesque in
some particulars.

The first cow we mistook for a "milker" proved to
be otherwise.   She was a long, loose-jointed affair, with
symetrical limbs, and had a real knowing look as she
would peak around at the lacteal artist from underneath

her lop-horn, on the near side. She was a little skittish, we noticed, but thought nothing about it, because she watched us very steadily. Pretty soon, however, we made a miss-Q, in some manner, and she handed us one, before we could apologize; and when we landed we **were in too much of** a pile to assume an apologetic position, **and so we went to the house and went to bed.** This creature kicked us into the middle of the next day, twice, and knocked daylight out, and starlight into us, once, and gave seven pints of very poor milk during the four days we owned her, and then the butcher gave us a little something for her, on account, and we began looking for another cow that wasn't quite so loose in the joints.

The next one was a monstrous ox-like animal, with a head on her like a pile-driver, and an udder as big as a bass-drum. She looked kind of foolish out of her eyes, and didn't know anything but "eat." It took a barnfull of hay and a wagon-load of shorts and corn to keep her from actually starving during the first week. She gave more milk than the first one,—say about five quarts a day—but it cost too much. We finally sold her to the butcher who said she would do to "corn," and he could sell her hide to good advantage for heavy belt-leather.

Number three was a gentle little creature—white, with **brindle** spots. She had only one teat that amounted to much, and that amounted to a good deal; when it was full it was about **the** only projection there was around there, and it was so huge that it took both hands to get around far enough to produce a pressure, and there wasn't strength enough in four average country editors to draw the milk from that cocoanut, without wearing themselves up to a stub in doing it. We had to put a porus-plaster on the back of the calf's neck to help it to draw enough sustenance to keep it alive—and it had a terrible suction, too, that calf had. We began to suspect that we didn't know so *very* much about selecting a cow, after all; and that people around here were working off their refuse stock on us. We paid big prices, (and sold them for what we could get) and got several of the most celebrated poor cows in the neighborhood. Folks got to whistling, and making mouths at one another, when they would see us coming along the road leading a new cow. The thing was growing pretty monotonous, and although we lost enough money, dealing in cows, to have bought a whole flock of Alderneys, we got mad, and were bound to strike butter and milk, outside of the Alderney strain, or bu'st. We kept on buying and selling cows,—losing five or ten dollars on each—averaging a new one every week, until we had ground through about all there were around, that any one wanted to sell. Our occupation seemed to be the *role* of a middle man between cow-owners and the butchers; both were making a good thing at our expense.

At last, however, after investing the last dollar we had, and giving several long notes, and after being kicked into every fence-corner on the place, we struck it—we struck it rich.

A poor man—and consequently honest—owed a debt, and in order to pay it he had to sell his last cow, and we gobbled her. Talk about your cows!—Your dark-eyed, brass-knobbed Alderneys! Our cow would not permit one of them to scratch against the same fence. The first evening, we filled everything in the house that would hold milk, including the wash boiler. In the morning, the cream had to be spaded off with the fire-shovel, and two churns were at once set to work. Upon going out to milk, we found the mess she gave the night before was only a priming. It was a regular Niagara of richness; there was no use in trying, we couldn't find store room for it on the premises, without using the cistern, and after filling all the tubs around the place, we had to turn the stream into the alley—it was awful. We had to go to feeding her saw-dust and mop-rags to dry up the current, and now we've got her choked down to about sixteen quarts of cream at a milking. Some people may think Alderneys are "old business," but the cow we have now can drown an Alderney in the milk she gives, twice a day, and roll out a pound of butter to the pint. We've gotten through supplying the butchers.

THE FARM FEVER.

EVERY so often we have a run of it. We get entirely discouraged with the narrow, contracted life of a newspaper man, and feel as though our Maker intened us to fill a bigger place—say about 300 acres or so. We itch all over to go right out and rip up the surface of the country, and raise wheat and oats, barley, hogs, and other vegetables. We want to get hold of the forked end of a plow, and play a long lash over a breaking team. This thing of shoving a five-cent lead pencil seems so utterly trifling—too light a business for a man who *knows* he could run half the farms in the State—into the ground, for instance. Our muscle is just humping up all over us, in great goose-pimples. We want to slash the seed into the ground, manage stock and be boss of wide acres. When one of these spells comes on we can hardly hold ourself; we have to go right out and jam something around and look about for somebody to buy us out—lead-pencil and all—just lumping the whole thing off for a dollar and a half and a yoke of oxen. Then again, we happen to think that, "He who by the plow would thrive, himself must either hold or drive," or words to that effect, and

that mostly cools us off, and lead pencils begin to rise.
If you want to buy a newspaper cheap, just take us
when the " farm fever " has a square hold of us.

A REAL TROUBLE.

NE of the old boss dogs, who assume the responsibility of keeping the common town dogs
and the green country dogs all straight, around
on the streets, got his dignified eye on an ill-
behaved canine, the other day, on the opposite side of
Superior street, who was doing something or other that
the old " boss," who ran that side of the block, conceived to be unconstitutional, according to the dog law,
and so he just made a fearfully impetuous break for him.
Having his goggles steadfastly fixed upon the special
object of his wrath, he didn't observe any intervening
obstructions. A husky old Scandinavian fellow citizen,
who had been ably discussing a cord of hard-maple
wood, and was located just between the two dogs, was,
at the time standing leaning on his saw, indulging in a
moment of rest; he was kind of lazily gazing upward
into the " mellow depths of immeasurable space," his
mind, no doubt far away among the hills and hollows
of his native land; mayhap, comparing the solidity of
American maple with that of Norway pine, with the
odds in favor of the maple, by a large majority; or, he
may have been engaged in trying to figure out why it
was that some men were beggars and some were bank-

8

ers, and others occupied that middle ground, wherein
they were permitted to manipulate a bucksaw at the
rate of seventy-five cents a cord—provided they carried
the wood up two flights of stairs after they got it sawed.
His face wore a serious expression at all events, and he
evidently didn't find a great deal in this land of milk
and honey, and things, worth laughing about; his face
was not that of an habitual laugher, by any means.
He was unquestionably a gentleman who always looked
the serious side of any object or proposition over first,
and after accomplishing this he found no time to lavish
upon the other side. But, we had almost lost sight of
the big law-loving dog, in question. He was a "heavy
dog," and he was certainly very much agitated by the
miserable cussedness of the dog on the other side of the
street—so much so that he went straight for him, that
he might direct the immediate attention of his erring
brother dog to some point of order, or some rule or
practice upon which he was seriously infringing under
the by laws then in force. He made a most impetuous
push for victory the first thing. In his forward movement upon the enemy's works he ran between the legs
of our reflecting Scandinavian friend, and was just high
enough to lift him from his feet and, with the head of
steam with which he started out he carried the wood-
sawyer nearly to the middle of the street, where the mud
was uncommonly deep and thin, ere he could set him
down. The Scandinavian said something about the
time he left his sawbuck, but he didn't say it in the
United States language, so we lost the probable force
of the remark. About the instant that he turned a

back somersault off the dog, and dove into the sea of mud, head and shoulders foremost, the big dog had the other dog by the ear, and he proceeded to give him what his conduct richly deserved, in less than a quarter of a minute. When he let him go, he went around the corner looking, for all the world, like a mud-pie with legs under it, and a handle sticking out behind. As our friend, the knight of the buck, arose to his feet, he looked like the tail-end of a brick-machine; he wiped the mud out of one eye, blew the superficial quantity out of his mouth, and then he made some further remarks, something like these: " Cone-futtle-tam-tog-er-rame-lukee-cutyhellee-bone-futchee-whoop-pe-hellee-time! " He got hold of a cord-wood stick and let it go in the direction of the dog, but it missed the mark a little and the old peace-maker trotted around the corner, while our friend adjourned the seventy-five cent struggle till he could go to his ivy-clad cot and shovel the mud off his clothes and dig out his ears, and the other eye.

PIC-NIC-ING.

WHEN our young folks want to have a real good time, they go on a picnic; and so do many of our old folks. We caught the picnic fever a few days ago, and went. Arriving at "the prettiest spot on the face of the earth," etc., we prepared to enjoy the immeasurable glory of a first-class picnic. Our party got the boat anchored, took all the baskets, ice, a bucket of fresh water, lemons, etc., up the hill to the beautiful grove, and camped down among the bluebells, butter-cups, honey-suckles and the fragrant dandelions, in the shade of the trees. It was too early to "eat the picnic" as yet, so in order to kill time most of us went out to gather ferns and things. No picnic is quite right unless you talk a great deal about how refined it is to love ferns, and how you love, above everything else in this world, to gather ferns and have ferneries about your home—gathering them with your own perspiring brow, etc. Some of the party, however, stayed in camp and read poetry—reading aloud, sawing the air with gestures, and putting in all the flourishes allowed by elocution, and more if they felt like it. Not being particularly in love with verse, we proved our re-

finement of taste by joining the fern-gatherers. The
truth is, we don't know a fern from a red oak bush, and
care a great deal less; but we hunted ferns with a com-
mendable zeal, just the same. After prowling around
through the tanglewood, brush and nettles, for a time
looking for some weed that would correspond with our
idea of what a fern ought to be, we struck it. That is,
we stooped down to gather a clump of vegetation that
averaged a little better for "pretty" than anything we
had before discovered. But, as we were about to pluck
the ferny clump from the pregnant earth, a snake, about
four feet long, hauled itself from beneath those weeds;
we straightened up suddenly, as we are led to presume,
and so did our hair—for we felt that stand up, very distinctly; goose-pimples rose all over our alabaster en-
casement, as big as hazlenuts; we turned our face toward camp, and bounded over or else tore through every obstacle, until we landed heels-over-head across the
dinner basket.

The poetical portion of the party were, by this time,
so busily engaged in picking sand-flies out of their eyes,
shaking big black ants out of their skirts, and the males,
in choking wasps that had gotten well up inside their
pant-legs, that they did not discover our return to have
been conducted in any other than an ordinary manner.
We tied strings around the bottom of our breeches-legs,
to keep out the larger classes of insects, while we sat
down to fan ourself with our hat and enjoy the picnic.

It was not long until the balance of the fern-lovers
reached camp—some with bugs up their backs, others
with green worms inside their collars, and all of them

pretty well eaten into by mosquitoes; one or two had
also "got their hand right onto a snake!" and *they*
were settled. After all hands had gotten most of the
bugs, beetles, ants and worms outside of their inside, it
was agreed that dinner-time had arrived, and so the
good things were unpacked, and the lemonade distil-
lery put under way. Getting everything spread out on
the grass, one person was appointed as steward, while
the party drew nigh and began the enjoyment of that
most famous of all pleasures, eating a picnic dinner,—
The steward's business was to take two little sticks and
keep the bugs out of the victuals; if a grand-daddy-
long-legs got into the butter (and several of him did get
in) he was to get him between the two sticks and spar
him out; when the bugs would run under a slice of
bread, he was to excavate for them; he had to shovel
the ants out of the sugar with one stick, and the dear
little green worms that dropped down from the boughs
overhead, were elevated with the other; the rest of the
party could keep most of the flies and mosquitoes out
of their faces with one hand, and delight their respective palates with the other. The meal over, the party
raked things together in a general pile, dumped them
into the baskets, the steward—that was ourself—hastily
drank a pint of lemonade,—swallowing four large and
one small bug and a measuring-worm—grasped a sand-
wich, and the whole company broke for the boat, and
finished the day "fooling around" on the lake in the
broiling hot sun.

At eventide, just as the sun was throwing his last
shafts of golden light over the enchanting landscape,

the robin was dropping the last worm into the open mouth of her young, and the looing kine came marching homeward, keeping pace with the tinkling bells, our party stepped ashore; that is, they staggered out onto the pebbly beach, what was left of them; then we sort of corkscrewed our way toward the ivy-covered cot, where we may be found hereafter, except in business hours.

The party could not consent to disperse from the beach, however, without " voting *unanimously* that it had been one of the most thoroughly enjoyable, and in every way successful picnics of the season." Of course it was.

AT 15, we imagine ourselves to be about as sharp and cute as a freshly-honed razor.....At 20, we consider our advice and judgment as indispensible to a sufferin' world.....At 30, light begins to break in, and we experience the first glimmer of the fact that we are fools.....At 40, we are sure of it.....At 50, if there be any good in us, we shall have exhibited it, in a modest way, during the last eight years.....At 60, our advice begins to be valuable.....At 70, the only ten years of our life that have been of solid benefit to the world will have been passed.....After that, we go around, picking up pins, and telling what wonderful things we have accomplished.

KILLING WOLVES.

SEVERAL reports have reached us of late that wolves were too thick for the comfort of the farmers' pigs and sheep along the " ravine belt " of country skirting the Mississippi valley in this region. Needing a little exercise, anyway, and wolf-hunting being our favorite pastime, whenever they happen to be comeatable, we resolved to steal quietly out into a few of the neighboring ravines, and spend one day at least in relieving a neighborhood or two from the dread scourge that was nightly making such havoc among the lambs and innocent little pigs, and things. The upper edge of the sun had but barely peaked across the landscape, when we entered the mouth of a densely wooded hollow, with towering bluffs on either side, holes and caves to be frequently seen away up along their craggy sides. We had fixed ourself with all the modern appliances for carrying on a day's warfare against the savage monsters we were anxious to encounter—our old and trusty muzzle-loader, hatchet, carving-knife, a couple of doughnuts, etc. Our path lay through thickets of prickly-ash, over logs and uneven ground, and in fact was as fine "wolf-ground" as we had ever seen. Of course, we had never seen much wolf country, anyway, —not any, in fact—and had never hunted wolves before, except in theory, and our taste for this kind of sport was only a theoretical one; but in theory we had frequently hunted wolves, and slaughtered a large number in the same way. Every thing went smoothly for half a mile, and the prospect of putting into practice our pet theories as applied to ridding a neighborhood of wolves seemed bright, if fortune would only bring on the animals. The first sensation experienced took place just as we were clambering over a big log; an animal suddenly sprung out from beneath it, and the sensation being so suddenly developed, rather jarred our nervous system, and we rolled over and brought up head first in a drift on the other side; our presence of mind, however, never went astray in the emergency—not to speak of—for in less than two minutes we had recovered from the "start," like, and had dug our gun out of the snow and backed up against a tree ready to deal out death in quantities to suit. We felt real queer, like, and our heart, or gizzard, we scarcely knew which, kind of went flippey-te-flop and our hair felt kind of stiff; we concluded the queer feelings, as we stood there watching for animals, with knees knocking together, were occasioned by our stomach being out of order, or by our having forgotten to take our usual dose of cough medicine before leaving home. Peering around underneath the adjacent jungle we discovered the animal that had created such a sudden jerk of our nerves, demurely looking up at us, and to our great relief,—or, no!—to our

9

great disgust, it was no more formidable a creature than
a rabbit. At just about this moment, our ears were
greeted by a long, wailing, rather plaintive howl,
which came down from the head of the gorge, and it
reverberated from rock to crag, and finally died away
on the frosty air of the broad valley below. It was the
musical note of the wolf, and we were soon to be in the
midst of our favorite game! Could we wait? Could
we hold ourself within bounds until we had traversed
the fourth of a mile that lay between us and the scene
of our first carnage, which was to wake the hills with
the dying howls of a bloody monster? We resolved to
try, and so sat down on the log to get rested and fix our
carving-knife. In our fall we had bent it double and
just as we had gotten it put into business shape again,
there was such an unearthly howl emitted from the
throat of that wolf, as actually raised our cap and nearly froze our feet; this time the brute was much nearer
to us, and we actually began to feel kind of lonesome—
lonesome for fear there was only *one* wolf instead of six
or seven; our desire was to slaughter several at once,
because our time was somewhat valuable that day, as
we had just happened to remember that it was the day
one of our subscribers had promised to come in and
settle up his subscription, and it was a stupid thing in
us to have forgotten it—the poor man would come, in
our absence, and meet with a sore disappointment, unless we hastened homeward; another thing, our feet
were becoming colder, and we happened to think how
subject we were to chilblains, besides our stomach being
out of order. Then, again, the weather had turned

more severe, and if we should happen to catch a heavy
cold and it settled on our lungs, resulting in consumption, spinal meningitis, pneumonia, pleurisy, or chapped
hands, terminating fatally, what would become of those
we depended on for a living, and for protection, in this
uncharitable world? Our duty in the premises seemed
plain, and we resolved, for once in our life, to try self-
denial, and resist the temptation of slaughtering that
wolf until another day. And, for fear we might yet be
tempted to tarry—despite our conviction of duty as related to the man who was to pay two dollars for his paper—we turned our face homeward, and struck into a
majestic canter through the groves of prickly-ash. To
still further tempt us to remain among the wolves, and
amuse ourself among scenes of blood, the animal—now
quite near—gave one of his most "searching" wails;
but our inclination to duty prevailed, and to facilitate
our progress we laid our old gun down somewhere in
that valley, took off our coat—our cap had already taken
a rest on some thorny bush—and came right down to a
most effective gallop, for fear we might be too late to
meet our friend who was to pay his subscription—and
the poor man might not have another opportunity, as
we had often known to be the case, apparently, at least.
Our effort was rewarded, so far as being on time was
concerned; for, as we came pacing through the alleys
of the suburbs and the back fence of our own potato-
patch we discovered that the sun was only even with
the house tops. Upon landing in the bosom of our numerous and astonished family, steaming like a portable
Vesuvius, we explained that we had to return home to

see a man, and **that we had** sent our coat and cap to
the grasshopper-sufferers, **and traded** our gun off for a
wolf-dog—the **dog to be** delivered **next fall.** "When
duty **calls 'tis our's to** obey "—and it should always be
done **with all our** might.

<hr>

ROCKING THE CRADLE.

E SHALL believe the scholar when he **as-**
serts that **there is** science in all things. **We**
have only recently made up our mind to receive such an odd doctrine, but have to believe now in
the prevalence of science, or "sleight," or talent, **even**
in so simple a thing as rocking the cradle. This **dis-**
covery was made by the writer only a few days ago.
The "help" was gone, baby cross, dinner behind, **and**
weather hot. Taking in the situation at a glance, we
tendered our services, and volunteered to **appease the**
wrath of the youngster and peel the potatoes. **We had**
often seen mothers rock the cradle with **their toe and**
sew for hours at a stretch, **with no apparent exertion.**
This was our plan, and to **carry it out—so far as rocking**
the cradle and peeling the potatoes was concerned—we
assured wife, was a most trivial matter if thereby we
could assist her any. After depositing the little junior
in the cradle, and getting it all squared around so the
rockers would be lengthwise of the boards, we seated
ourself within easy range, and called for **the** pan **of po-**

tatoes and the butcher knife. No sooner said, than a six-quart milk pan filled with "Celtic lemons" and water was deposited on our knees, and we squared ourself for business. We stuck the knife into the end of a potato, and placed our foot on the rocker just as the expectant youngster was making up his mind that the old man was slower than molasses in January. We tore the skin off one side of the potato and started the cradle on a regular canter; we were a leetle too rash, however, and the cradle slid off sort of diagonally, and we had to put the pan down on the floor and move our chair a little. All set again, we moved on the cradle and cut our right ear with the butcher-knife. Our legs were gradually failing, and the motion of the cradle was becoming very peculiar again, and it was evident that something must be done—either we must take a rest or the baby would have to be lashed to the cradle to keep it from skipping out on the floor. We went around on the other side, so as to "change hands" with our feet, and that was a fatal move to our success. Giving the cradle a lively jump, to make up for lost time, our feet slipped off, we lost our balance and went headlong over the pan, struck the cradle with such a crash that it capsized, and the potatoes flew in every direction. Then there was another little matinee, engaged in by the whole family, and we cut a fearful gash in our thumb, with the knife. Then we sub-contracted that potato-peeling, tied up our thumb, and went out to look at the garden, where we concluded that "woman was an angel," sure enough; for nothing less than an angel could do, for months at a stretch, what we had failed to accomplish, in the face **of** good intentions and a broad and deep determination.

THE SEASON HAS BEGUN.

THE real fact that winter had actually tucked up her white linen, to keep her balmoral out of the mud, and had **emigrated** to her summer home on Hudson Bay, did not seem to be realized by anybody until last Monday morning. But, as old Sol crept from his dewy bed in the east, we could almost feel that something new was taking place in the outer world. At an unusually early hour a neighbor rattled the door of our humble castle, and said he wanted his garden-rake that we borrowed last year, and without stopping to make any great amount of toilet, we said " Don't look," and poked his rake through the crack in the door. A wagon just then went by with a rattle and bang, while the driver cracked his whip and sang, "The beautiful meadows so green." We rushed to the bedside of our family and said to **the other** half of us that **there** seemed **to be** something astir more than common, and it must be that something was stirring that hadn't stirred since things quit stirring in the autumn. We suggested **that** the bulk of our family arouse without the ordinary argument, and as soon as we could get into our two-dollar pants we'd rush out and put on the teakettle and things, and mash up some wood to boil the potatoes. Just as we were waltzing around in an irregular circle, on one foot, trying to strike our center of balance, so the foot that was in the air could be sent home through the twisted trouser leg, another shock was heard at the door and another neighbor cried out, " Where's that wheelbarrow?" That call ruined the effort to even get half of our pants where they would do the most good, and losing temporary control of our anatomy, we fell over a chair. Then we said to the man that his wheelbarrow was out by the dog house; that if he found any part of it broken, we'd fix it with him if we could ever get our wardrobe in a suitable position to appear before the public. We heard him saying something about lending wheelbarrows, as a regular business, and saw him through a crack carrying on his shoulder the remains of what had been an able-bodied barrow at some time previous. After a time we rushed out, and sure enough all nature was animated. The birds were singing "fit to kill," the dog had treed the cat, the hens were singing their morning *lay*, men were going to and fro, the cows were lowing, and spring time was bursting out in all its efful gent effulgency. Every body seemed to have gotten the start of us in the "spring opening," and we resolved to catch up by dint of energy. While the morning meal was being prepared we rushed down street and hired a laborer to engage in the preparation of our garden, bound not to be outdone by our neighbors in industry. We found a man—a gardener—of Irish parentage, by the name of Ole Jughandleson. We spent the day in good honest toil, and at eventide that garden told a tale of labor. We stood faithfully by all day long, holding the hoe while Mr. Handleson used the spade and the spade, while he used the hoe. We also lightened his labor by telling him fairy stories and making suggestions from our store of intelligence as related to gardening. By thus laboring, all our spare time, we feel sure that our summer's work will grow up with its usual results by the time snow flies again. We expect to raise a vast amount of garden truck this season, besides engaging largely in floriculture—comprising a bed of poppies, several stalks of hollyhocks, a row of morning-glories, and a fence-corner of sunflowers.

MONDAY—washing. Tuesday—ironing. Wednesday—baking. Thursday—washing out a few things that were overlooked. Friday—scrubbing. Saturday —doing a vast amount of all kinds of work, by way of preparing to enjoy a little comfort the rest of the week. This constitutes the labor of the weaker sex, who are always expected to look charming, and wear a smile of contentment and happiness.

HOME, SWEET HOME.

E WHO went raving, and wrote "There's no Place Like Home," it has been ascertained, never had a home—he traveled and peddled bedbug medicine. Still, we take considerable stock in his song, anyway—though we presume there are some homes that offer no more comfort than a seat on a hornet's nest, so far as real peace is concerned. But the song didn't mean that sort of a home, any more than "A Life on the Ocean Wave" meant a first-class case of seasickness. It meant the real old sort of headquarters, where at least a fair show of love and affection was kept up—especially when there were visitors around. A home where you had lived so long that everything around the ranch had become familiar; so that you could go out and chop firewood just as well where it was as where it wasn't. Where the old fireplace and mantle always looked the same; and the same old cat would sit every evening and look silly, until a mouse squeaked in the opposite corner; where the old wooden clock ticked once about every three minutes, and where you sat in the corner reading the almanac without interruption, except when a spark flew out and lit on your bare

10

foot, or when wife would inform you that her knitting-needles had gotten so bent that she must have a new set; or, by your boy Zeb telling you that his steers had "turned the yoke" six times in five minutes that afternoon and that he wanted you to say it was all right to tie their tails together—and then he'd stop that nonsense on them, unless their tails gave way. Such a home was undoubtedly in the mind's eye of the author of "Home, Sweet Home," and that's why his song was so homely. Home is a big thing, for a small affair, and it isn't always the biggest that have the most to be thankful for; some homes, the less you have of them the greater should be your thankfulness, and that kind of a home can't be bettered much short of a revolution. It takes more money to make a home than it used to, and you get less home at that. A chimney with a log house, chinked with mud, built on one side of it, a square table, four splint-bottom chairs, a gourd, a skillet, a pair of dog-irons and a family dye-tub used to stand witness to more comfort than the kind they have now, that cost a pile. There is much that might be said about "home," and there has been much said about home that wasn't really necessary, and as it is away past supper-time now, we shall say no more about it till another time, because if we don't report at our hearthstone pretty quick we'll hear something about home that would raise the dust out of a pair of saddle-bags.

CHRISTMAS GIFTS.

A S IT will not be long now before Christmas will be here, and thinking that many of our readers might want to know how to make various little articles suitable for presents, and that will be compara- tively inexpensive as well as useful and ornamental, we have thought of a few articles that might be made at home, during the long evening hours now upon us:

Foot Rug—A very neat foot rug can be made by tak- ing an old gunny-sack, that isn't fit for anything else, cut it into square pieces of equal size, so as not to waste any of the goods; quilt them together and bind around the edge with a piece of corn colored calico or pink flannel. Wash the old sack before cutting it up, as they are most generally pretty dirty; either wash it or paint it a sky-blue, as most convenient.

Match Safe—A very neat match safe may be made by taking an old sardine can, cut a hole two inches square out of the flat side; tie a tow string into each corner—making the hole to put the string through with a nail,—and hang it near the stove suspended from a tin tack. The tack must be a tin tack as a common one would mar the general effect. A match safe made in this way is very pretty and substantial, and can be made at a trifling outlay.

Pen Wiper—A pen wiper is always fashionable as a Christmas present—at least we always see them—and is an appropriate gift to make to any of your friends who can write; if they cannot, you might encourage them to learn by giving them one. Take the top of an old stocking—one the foot of which is hopelessly gone,—scallop the edge all round, and put a handle on it made of speckled calico. This will be found very neat but not gaudy.

Pin Cushion—This indispensible article for the toilet table can be made by taking a red corn-cob and inserting it in a long narrow " poke " of sawdust; or if you wish to preserve its agricultural character, use bran or meal instead of saw dust though this will increase the cost somewhat. The covering of this should also be made of speckled calico, as it will then have the appearance of always being full of pins, regardless of the facts. The cob is only for the purpose of keeping it stiff and substantial. This is one of the neatest things we know of. We can scarcely explain why the cob should be a red one, but somehow we feel that it should be a red cob.

Arabian Slippers—There is nothing nicer for a holiday present to a gentleman friend than a pair of slippers. A very tasty pair may be made by taking a cast-off pair of boots and cutting away all but the sole and the front part of the upper leather—leaving them in a semi-sandal shape. They are always easy to put on or take off, and never chafe the heel; a bow of red ribbon on the instep will be found to add considerably to their appearance, and be a good thing for the cat to play with in the evening. The Arabian slipper is a very popular pattern wherever it is worn.

Smoking Cap—A very attractive smoking cap can be made, at a nominal cost, by cutting a chunk off the leg of an old pair of pants—high or low on the leg as the size of the head may require; gather in one end of the section—which may be about sixteen and a half inches long—and ornament it with a cardinal-red tassel made of little strips of calico torn up and fastened to the top of the cap in a sort of bass-relief. A band of blue flannel around the lower edge will hide the selvage and lend a picturesque appearance, particularly from a distance.

Foot Stool—Take an empty box of starch and cushion it with a piece of hit-and-miss rag carpet on the top; put a deep frill of yellow calico around the upper edge and paper the sides and ends with oak-grain wall paper. This kind of a foot stool will be found very comfortable, and will add greatly to the appearance of a parlor.

There are many very pretty liitle articles that can be made, without cramping your pocket, and the above are only given to indicate a long list that we might name, but which these will remind you of. We believe in making presents to friends when the holidays come round each year. We would rather make a present to any one, than to do anything else—except to receive one. Of the two, however, the latter is our "weakness."

TEACHING SCHOOL.

I'T WAS the first school they ever had in that new region ; there were about thirty children of all ages in the neighborhood, some of whom had lately come on from the East, and were more or less " up " in book learning. The old heads of families convened at one of the settlers' houses, and Joe Bailey —who wore the most dashing buckskin breeches, and a coonskin cap that had two or three more rings in the tail which hung down behind, than any of the rest— was chosen chairman of the meeting. Your " Uncle," who was then a very young man, was designated as secretary. The chairman stated that the objeet of the meeting was to " Take into calkelation the idea of rollin' a school house together an' hevin' a school for the children to go to school into," and told the assembled pioneers that if they had anything to say, to say it then, or forever arter to hold their yawp. The young secretary—who had found a stump of a lead pencil and gotten a newly made clapboard, and bashfully assumed the position of recorder,—made a note of this on the clapboard and during the five minutes of diffidence and silence that followed he drew the picture of a dog.

After a while Bill Simson stood up, and after knocking the ashes out of his pipe, remarked: " Ef we come here to fix things about a school house, I say we'd better fix things; I'll haul as many logs as any other man in the woods, an' I kin send as many children to the school as any body else."

Bob Oles slammed his coonskin cap down on the puncheon floor, and says he: "Thar isn't no man in this settlement, nor no other settlement, as will haul any more logs than I will; I want a school house, ef I can't read myself—an' 'tis just them that can't read that know the good of book larnin'; there's Sam Ames, settin' thar; he can't read no more'n I kin, an' he knows he'd give six months of work ef he could read readin' letters an' write his own name."

Sam said that was so, and said he would rive out the clapboards tor the roof as his share, and Dave McArnaught said he would maul out the puncheons for the floor. Con Wallace said he'd work out the stuff for the door, and the casings, and the sash for the windows; and the old man Gilson said he'd trade off skins enough to furnish the glass. So, very soon all arrangements about the house were made, and it wasn't two weeks until the the school house was ready for business.

Before the meeting adjourned, however, the question of who was to be the teacher was brought up and discussed. There seemed to be but two available candidates for this honor, in the neighborhood—a young girl, and your uncle. It was finally put to vote; the secretary's cap was made the ballot-box, and those in favor of the girl for teacher were requested to vote half acorns, and those in favor of the secretary to vote whole acorns. We got two majority, which result, in the light of latter days, we imagine might have been because we were at the meeting and the girl wasn't.

School opened in due time and we cut four healthy blue-beech gads on our way to the institute. When we arrived we found most of the scholars on hand, including the girl who had been our rival for the position of teacher. We entered with a frown, and stood the young trees up in the corner,.and told the school there wasn't any "bluff" about that, but that we intended to skin the whole outfit if they didn't knuckle tight.

We didn't know very much about teaching school, because we hadn't attended school ourself any to speak of. But we had an idea it consisted principally in showing the scholars who was boss, and in keeping order. We arranged them around on the benches, according to size, because we thought it would be kind of nice to have them uniform, in case of visitors. All the old school-books in the neighborhood had been gathered up, and even then there was only one school-book, of any kind, for every three scholars, and we had to piece out on half a dozen missionary testaments, as far as they would go. These we gave to the boys who looked to us to be best calculated for preachers—and we impressed upon their minds the noble aims they should aspire to; and advised them to strive hard during the term to commit their testaments to memory, and otherwise fit themselves to become missionaries to the South Sea Islands, where they were so badly needed; that although they might be stewed or fried for breakfast by the poor ignorant cannibals, not to allow such a trifling matter to dampen their ardor—because, if they did that with them, their acts would speak louder than any words in the cannibal language to the effect that they were *good* missionaries.

Our lecture to our missionary students had a very good effect on them, for the time being, and they seemed fully impressed with the seriousness and "highness" of their calling. The first day we found it necessary to chastise the whole school, excepting the theological students and the big girl.

The next morning we brought a fresh invoice of gads, and unbuttoned the top button of our red flannel shirt, and thumped our breast savagely a few times in front of the school. Our seat was off in the end of the apartment, and after giving them a very severe lecture on their duty to their teacher, who was suffering so much for them, we retreated to our corner, to "lay low" for the villain who should furnish us with the first job for that day.

We had been sitting for a few minutes engaged in "mending" a quill-pen for one of the scholars with our barlow-knife, when a great black hornet slowly rose from the floor, some place near us. We coolly took our coon-skin and mashed him down violently to the floor, close to our seat, and rubbed him out of existence, and the scholars tittered to see how nicely and how bravely we had disposed of him. About the time we slammed that hornet down on the floor, two or three others came out from somewhere about there and made a pass at us; we told the school not to get uneasy, because we could clean out any four hornets in that section, and with that we went for them with both hands and both feet; pretty soon one of the terrible insects backed up against our lower lip, and we felt as if a ten-penny nail **had been** shot into us. By this time about a peck of hornets boiled out from under our seat; **several of them** meandered up our trowser-legs, and several more got in their work about our head, until within a minute from the beginning of the battle, our head looked like a full-moon in August, and still the hornets kept increasing in numbers. The scholars were piling out at the windows and door, whooping and laughing fit to split. Pretty soon our eyes began to close, and our ears were as big as saddle-flaps, and our lower limbs were crippled beyond measure. We finally made one grand break for liberty, and made out to find our way home with one eye before it went clean shut.

At the end of two weeks we were able to get about a little and then learned, for the first time, how we came to get horneted so effectually: One of the missionary students had become incensed because we walloped a chum of his the first day, and he entered into a conspiracy with the rest, to pay us off. He procured an immense hornet's nest, plugged the hole up, tied a string to the plug, placed the nest just back of our pedagogical seat and had the string run along the floor by the wall to his seat; the rest can be imagined. We resigned our position in favor of the big girl, and our aspirations have never since run in the direction of school teaching, and we don't like young men who only *say* they'd like to study for the missionary **business.**

THE BIRDS HAVE GONE.

E DIDN'T really notice it until the other day. But it is a lamentable fact that the birds have flown, and left our groves and thickets silent and sad. It is really too bad; we love the little songsters, and our heart goes out after them in their long flight to southern climes; we long for the spring time's return, even now; for, in the absence of thousands of birds, our landscape is shorn of its greatest fascination, and even life, itself, seems to bear in it a blank space. As the approach of cold, cheerless winter nears us, they mount the branches of the fading trees, sing us their sweet, farewell song as if to say, " Be of good cheer, kind friends, and when daisies come again, we shall return to your homes and make you glad." Then, in little companies, they soar away, and are " lost to sight, though to memory dear." Life, even in this cold, cheerless, unfriendly and selfish world, has many charms, placed here by the provident care of Him, who even notes the sparrow's fall, and cares for the well-being of all his creatures. One of the most perfect charms in life may be found in the cheery, innocent life of the birds. They are messengers of peace,

and bear tranquility to the **restless,** troubled spirits **of**
humanity. They are types of innocence ; and while
their joyful notes bring good cheer to the heart, their
life is an example which may well be imitated, by those
who call themselves the lords of creation. With the
**birds of song above us, and the flowers of beauty be-
neath** and about our feet—with the mighty loveliness of
the mellow heavens overhead, and the grandeur of Na-
ture spread out upon every hand—men ought to be better than they are, and ought to grow better faster than
they do.

CHARMING.

OW grand it is to rise in the dewy morning,
just as the artists of the air are at work on the
eastern horizon, putting on the " putty-coat "
and getting their paints ready to throw in the colorings
and shadings, incident to a sunrise in this beautiful region; just as the winged cherubs of the sky are sowing,
from **their** fairy baskets, the glinting frost-beams—the
early sunlight throwing athwart its rounds of brightness,
making a jeweled ladder that at least the imagination
may climb from earth to heaven. The earth with its
maiden frost is brilliant and crisp below, the foliage of
the trees hangs in mottled beauty, proving that innocence is always prettiest in death. In life, the green
bowers of Nature served well their day, in death their
beauty is only the more lovely. The busy, fretful and

fretted world has not risen yet, and but few know of the transcendant beauty of the hour. Few realize that there is a time in the day, during which they can rise from their beds, and comparatively alone, thank their Maker for all the blessings and all the mercies showered upon them from hour to hour—from day to day. That time is when morning is distilling her dew upon the parched and care-worn earth; when every leaf is shedding its falling tear in atonement for the day just gone into an eternity of time with its record of human life, and when every blade of grass bears a glistening jewel of purity as an emblem of what God wishes to be our guide during the coming day. The world is hushed, and its troubled sounds have been at rest in buried forgetfulness, and been purified by the holiness of silence. Grief has smothered her sobs, anger has broken its darts, and the heart's best throbs have beaten in unison with heavenly chords, and replaced its venom with love, tenderness and charity. Thank God for the pure bright morning-hour, when all Nature stands drenched from its stains, and a beautiful world invites the tread of man to its dew-damp carpet, and jeweled studio.

HUNTING HENS' NESTS.

THERE was a time in every man's life when all he was fit for was to hunt hens' nests. Every stage in life finds humanity good for something, but fit for nothing else. During the five years of life that a boy is only fit to prospect for eggs, is probably about the most enjoyable epoch in his existence. He knows his business to a professional nicity and he is, very properly proud of his knowledge. He loves to have it said of him that he can flank more eggs, and fresher eggs, than any boy of his age in the neighborhood. To allow a nest to exist undiscovered until the eggs become addled, and brown with age, is an unpardonable botch in the profession, and one that requires years of scientific operation to overcome and wipe out in the annals of the neighborhood. No man can ever amount to much in after life who has not proven himself an expert on hens' nests; and those poor mortals who have never had nests around their homes to hunt, should receive pity from every sympathetic heart—for there has been a long, blank spot in their career. We do not wish to boast, nor intimate that we have accomplished wonders in life; but as the finder of the location of hens' nests, when a boy, we were, briefly immense. We kept a gauntlet lying around loose in our father's barn-yard for five years, and it was never taken up by any other boy, far or near. We could suck more eggs, too, and warmer eggs, than any one of no greater experience. A boy whose father has a very large barn, with a score of mows, lofts, horse and cattle stables, calf and sheep sheds, to say nothing of a semi-underground story, damp, and dreary—meets with a thousand thrilling adventures and hair-breadth escapes whilst plying his vocation. He visits all the nooks and corners of the gigantic establishment that are above ground, once each day, and gathers the " fruit " of his labors into one grand pile; but that dark, cavernous apartment underneath the whole, he explores only about twice a week. This he does on hands and knees, for the most part, but in some portions is compelled to crawl on his belly, squeeze through cracks and holes, and poke his hands into all sorts of places to feel for eggs. He may sometimes get his hand on a lizzard in repose, or a house-snake that is lying coiled up enjoying a snooze. When this happens, he never gallops out from under that barn, because there isn't room to strike that sort of a gait; but he generally uses more or less agility in getting out where he can see eggs better; he rolls, tumbles, and knocks his head against the beams; he skins his nose and tears off both his suspenders, if he has two, which is seldom at that age. When he gets out where the barn stands a little higher, or the ground sits a little lower, he strikes into an impetuous canter, and soon issues from the sheep-hole into the light of day. Just as he gives the last prance through that aperture, he is horrified at getting sight of the snake, that has a fast hold of the seat of his jeans breeches. His blood, when he left the place where he first found that snake, was moderately chilled ; but now it becomes completely congealed, and his hair raises like the quills on the back of an agitated porcupine. He dare not look around, much less *feel* around ; he feels the snake wriggling about the calves of his legs and in an instant he makes one frenzied plunge for a neighboring straw-stack, ascends its steep side at a single bound, runs around the top of it, lies down and rolls over forty times in a twinkling, and then turns several hand-springs down the other side, in order to rub it off; he lands at the bottom all in a pile. He fears the reptile isn't off yet, however, and he begins a mad-waltz around the old wagon in the back yard and, just as he is about to become completely overdone, he gets another glimpse of the serpent, and finds that the object of his terror is nothing more venomous than his bu'sted and dangling suspender.

Jonathan Peter now sits down to rest and refresh himself; feels around to see if that was really all that was the matter, and finally, that he might be perfectly satisfied, he takes off his trousers and peeks down through both legs, and turns the pockets inside out; after climbing back into them again, he clambers up into the old wagon to sit down and think. He finally concludes that he wasn't frightened, anyway,—only a little startled, like. He thinks he will not go under the barn again that day, and doesn't believe there's many eggs under there, at best—that is, not *very* many. After awhile he goes up into the barn, gets the peck-measure, puts into it the pile of eggs he has accumulated, up in the hay-mow, and then goes home. He tells his mother that he obtained nearly all those eggs under the barn, and that it was so close, and smelled so badly under there, that he feels kind of sick at the stomach, and would like to have a piece of custard-pie. Under the circumstances, truthful Jonathan Peter gets a large slice, and goes out and seats himself on the wood-pile, to cool off and eat his pie.

THE OLD MAN.

MEETING an old man—in whose presence we always feel awed with respect—we cannot but try, for the moment, to look out upon life and the world through his vision. We may not behold things in the past, though, as he does; we may not realize as he, how much of moment is in the present, nor see the view that he sees through the vista of the future —however much we may strive to fancy ourself in his place. Nevertheless, we feel sure we can partially group his views, and partially divine his thoughts of the coming time, and his memories of days gone by. Of his early life, but scattering scenes remain distinctly in his mind, but those that do, are more vivid, as seen in the twilight of life, than they were in his noonday of vigor. Fondly does he now review the incidents of his boyhood; kindly does he recall the faces and friends of

early years, and longs to see them again, if living, and
if dead, to meet them in paradise over the river that
flows on the edge of Time; with a sigh of sadness does
he remember the home of his childhood, where the days
of his journey were spent in which he took no thought
of the morrow; when his sharp little griefs were chased
away to the clouds by the jewels of hope and joy constantly flowing in sprays of light from the fountain of a
young and dauntless spirit; how he dwells upon the old
homestead, with its quaint furniture, and colonial surroundings; the pastimes and playthings with which he
whiled away the hours of thoughtless childhood and the
irresponsible days of boyhood; he oft drops a filial tear
when viewing in their benignity, the kind parents who
ever had a care for his comfort, and he lingers with a
fervid memory of love upon that ever watchful, faithful
and toiling mother, who first taught him who the Being
was he must love even more than herself, and upon
whom he must ever lean, and to whom he must ever
look after she had said her last prayer at the bedside in
his behalf.

The present, he regards as fact, not fancy; real, not
imaginary; a time of fearful moment, not a period to be
frittered away amid the thoughtless gaieties of folly and
fashion, and in idleness. The world, he beholds as a
beautiful thing, with heavenly blessings pendant from
every star, that may be had for the asking. He allows
liberally for the lighter pleasures of the young, and still
has ample room for an inexpressible wonder as to why
so vast a proportion of the golden present is totally lost,
yea, worse than lost, by the anxious, surging throng;

and as he gazes out in his mind upon the troubled people who thoughtlessly struggle for might or right in this
pleasant but transient world, he heaves a deep sigh of
sorrow as he realizes, alas! how soon all these hundreds
of millions of human souls will be crumbling to dust;
he breathes a silent prayer in their behalf and turns to
view the beyond for himself, upon whose edge he already totters. The journey marked out in the world
for him by a finger called "Destiny," has been traveled,
and with the world, he has but little or nothing more to
do, to adjust the final accounts of a life for himself, and
pronounce a benediction of love on a world behind, is
all that for him remains; and, with his head whitened
by the light of a dawning eternity he exclaims, "My
work is done, I am ready; Oh, Lord receive me into
thy presence with mercy!" He sees the glowing star
of hope, dazzling in its heavenly brightness, now that
his nearness to its possession has almost given him a
seat in the golden Jerusalem where the King of an un-
fathomable universe sits in love and in eternal glory.
Bless the old man! Respect his years, and revere the
light reflected upon him and into the dark recesses of a
fallen world from a throne he almost views, and which
is, typically, made of burnished gold, studded with diamonds, and rests upon a floor of srarry worlds beneath.

THE OLD WOMAN.

OD bless the old *Woman*—the noblest title ev-er conferred upon the patient, virtuous members of the sex who stand now, as ever, since history began, the light of the world and the salt of the earth. When we meet a kind old lady, and converse with her, we cannot but love the soul that responds in delicate diction, as fresh, pure and beautiful, as when it animated the now aged casket of clay, when it stood 'neath the holly and orange blossoms of young maidenhood. The study of her furrowed brow is one of deepest interest; every sorrow, and every care of years, can be found plainly written in indellible wrinkles; the history of every grief, of which the best of lives are so full, can be read in unmistakable lines; the struggle of three score years, has left a sweet sadness sole occupant of the faded cheek, though the dimmed eyes look up with the frank, confiding look, that is the offspring of a stainless life. Patiently she awaits the call that will summon her frow a life of usefulness and beauty, into the sparkling palace reserved for the blest, whose shining spire is already daily visible on the hazy horizon of her nearly "beyond." She only clings to the world, because of the few acts of good—the few errands of mercy—she can still confer upon those she loves. She says she cannot depart until the last act of love is done, that she can find possible to do here, and when at last her tired hands drop helpless upon her bosom, she smiles a fond farewell, to loved ones, bestows an angel's blessing, and sweetly *sleeps*. Tenderly do we lay the expended form away in a tear-bathed tomb, there to rest until all the living and dead shall stand before their Maker—God. We feel, as we lower the precious remains into the soundless grave, that again we shall meet her; again we shall be greeted *somewhere* by her loving welcome, and again be soothed by her tender presence. **We** *know* that the earth that covers her from our gaze, shall not always **stand** a barrier between us—but that we shall again commune with the sweet soul that has gone away and left **us**, blessed but alone. We plant a tree at her head, from whose branches the birds will ever sing their morning songs of praise to God and **Virtue**; we plant sweet flowers o'er her grave, and seek the retired spot where mother sleeps, when we are worn to grief by earth's sore fight, and **are refreshed by the** balm of a solemn silence, and a holy contemplation. God bless the old woman—the aged mother who carried from the world her full share of griefs, and left, in exchange, an infinite number of priceless blessings.

A LITTLE CHILD.

THIS world produces no other beauty; no other object of interest; no other more lovely nor lovable thing, than a bright, sweet, confiding little child. What heart has not strangely thrilled when a little one came to his knee at the day's close, placed its dimpled little hand in his, and looked up with that sweet, earnest, enquiring gaze, so nearly that of an angel, from another and better sphere? Its clear blue eyes undimmed by tears of sorrow or remorse; its face unwe feel, must yet be bruised and seared by the trials of clouded by the cares and struggles of the life upon which it has scarcely entered; its happy smile and dimpled cheeks forming a picture too strangely interesting to be understood without being studied through eyes of love. When we place our arm around the precious little form and nestle it close to our breast, how a silent prayer, unmarred by feeble words, goes up in its behalf. How we become moved almost to tears, as we reflect upon the possible sorrows that the little darling may encounter in its path of life, and how we wonder where lies the road that these little feet must travel. How well we know, and how sorely we lament, that the throbbing little heart an earthly journey We draw it closely, as if to protect it, in advance, from the ills that experience has told us, beset the way, and that imagination paints, as we follow along, in our mind, the weary road that lies before it. The softest pillow it knows, is the bosom of love, and the only guard from harm is the encircling arm in whose embrace it has nestled. Its clearest canopy of contentment is the smile of affection from its parent's face, and beneath the parental look of tender love, it sinks to peaceful slumber. All is quiet, and a confiding little soul is at rest; we feel that we can almost hear the soft rustle of its guardian angel's wings, as we lay it silently in its bed, and tenderly imprint a good-night kiss upon its parted and smiling lips, and ask God to guard our darling through the silent hours of the night.   May its morning of life be one of golden hues, and every day a little eternity of joys; for, all too soon, it must come to the troubled current; and in the midst of life's surging flood, you will have to bid it a sad farewell, and leave it, whilst you go out of its sight into eternity's great, unexplored ocean. Love the little darling whilst you may.

ECHOES.

E HAVE the finest series of echoes about Duluth that can, probably, be produced in this country. There are many of the glens and coves of Chester Creek, **Lester River and** St. Louis River, where it is absolutely unsafe to say anything, unless it is something you would just as leave have posterity hear, as not. Right here in the city, there are only a very few spots where a locomotive **dare** blow its whistle at all. Because if it did, there **is no telling when** we would hear the last of it. Before they found **out the** peculiarity of this locality, several steam whistles were sounded in the wrong place, and though that was **several years ago, their shrill** sound still echoes among many of the rocky coves of the upper heights. One of the churches, which is favorably located for canyon echoes, rang its bell for Christmas morning service, and the echoes have kept up ever since so regularly that it keeps the faithful members of that church getting up at all hours of the night, and putting on their things at all hours of the day in response to its solemn call; they may be seen at almost any hour going and coming to that church, in the full belief that it is a holy day,

whether it occurs in the night or in the day time. There
are several caves around here, where those interested in
the study of echoes may go and hear about all the
whistles and all the bells that were ever blown or rung
at the head of Lake Superior. It is said to sound a
good deal like a steam calliope when in the throes of
death, or an ancient piano being performed upon by a
pile-driver. We have, ourself, visited some of the canyons along the streams above mentioned, and have been
startled by the conversations going on in them, instigat-
ed by thoughtless tourists. We have learned more of
the true inwardness of the domestic life of a tourist than
we ever dreamed was possible. Some of the sentences
and paragraphs are of a startling character, and we
should never have dreamed of such a state of affairs by
simply seeing them smiling and smashing hash at the
hotels—the very " old boy " is to pay in some of those
families, as we learned, and the old head of the family
who leered across at the brunette at the opposite table,
and the gay young wife who flirted her napkin over her
left shoulder at the young goose-quill, who waxes his
moustache and parts his hair in the middle, at the corner of the room, are both getting the very *divil* up in
the canyons—sure as you live. Some of the revelations,
that are still echoing back and forth among the " hollow
rocks " are just *awful.* Then, mix these up with quota-
tions from Burns, Shakespeare, Mother Goose and other poets, by the tallow-headed fellows who pour into
the echo all they know, then the shout of the ladies and
‘ hullo ’ of the children, frequently interspersed by the
wheezing of the asthmatic and hay-fever victims and

13

the howling of the consumptive, and it makes one of
these canyons a most wonderful place to visit. Next
season's tourists will, of course crowd these last year's
sounds out into space, and we will have a new set of
"funny things" to listen to—but their average is very
similar. Echoes? Duluth and vicinity has more and
purer, louder and more terrific echoes than all the rest
of the world combined; and we wouldn't sell a single
one of them at any price. We are rich, and don't have
to.

———————————————————

WE notice an article in the papers to the effect that
Pennsylvania cannot produce a poet—that no Pennsyl-
vanian ever born could write poetry. Oh, pshaw!
Just listen to your "Uncle" for a moment:

> There was a man in our town,
>   He owned a cat and dog;
> Likewise his wife, a good old soul,
>   Was the onwer of a cow and hog.
>
> The cat went crazy, the dog went mad,
>   And the wife made fun of Reuben,—
> Her cow got choked, her dog died of bloat
>   Then Reub. made fun o' the old woman.

There, now, take it back! thou villainous æsthete
from Boston. We could "keep it up," in verse, by the
mile; but the above is proof enough to nail that lie before it goes any further. Poetry!—guess not.

THE PREACHER'S VISIT.

'T IS probable that **most** middle-aged people who were **raised in the rural "deestricts" of the** old eastern States, can call to mind that longest-to-be-remembered event, in the days of their boyhood, the Preacher's visit to the home of their father. It was *the* event of the season, when the preacher would notify **Deacon** So-and-so, that upon the occasion of his next monthly visit he would make the Deacon's house his home—"no preventing Providence—Amen!"

Though it might be in the very center of the harvest season, the atmosphere in and about the Deacon's residence would become, first cool and then cold, and then freezing, as **the time for** the preacher's visit drew nigh, and when the time finally arrived the boys around the house would feel just **as** though they were **ready to be** cut up, and sold by the stick.

Take an Old School Presbyterian preacher, of twenty years' "practice," and in the particular age to which we refer, and if he couldn't freeze a midsummer sunbeam into an icicle in a minute and a quarter, then it was counted that there was a screw loose somewhere, and he wasn't fitted for the leadership of the quality of lambs that made up the pastoral flocks of those virtuous interior *deestricts.*

How well we remember the visits of old Parson Gildersleeve. He was a model preacher of that day and locality. His consistency was of the purest gristle—he was utterly without a fault as a preacher of the time. In his make-up had been used, dignity, reserve, religion and ice, in about equal parts, and all these had become thoroughly amalgamated and "set" by many years' service in the oldest kind of Old School Presbyterianism.

Of course, his sermons were pretty much all the same thing, and extended, on an average, from "firstly" to "twenty-eighthly," beside from four to six "in conclusions." We never knew of any one who could remain awake long enough to hear the whole story, at any one sitting.

The good wife of the Deacon always had the house in perfect order, days before the arrival of the saintly guest, and a general code was announced among the numerous family, as to what would be expected of them whilst the momentous occasion was " on." Every member of the household was duly rehearsed, and a general impression given to all, that if the slightest digression from the rules of behavior laid down during the presence of the holy man (done in ice) that, as a matter of course, it would be no less than a mortal sin and a whole lifetime's repentance could scarcely wipe it off the slate.

On the day of his expected arrival, a cautious head would be seen peering out from behind some breastwork, gazing down the lane to catch a sight of the "ad-

vance." Punctuality was one of the virtues of those
virtuous days, and in due time the long, gaunt figure of
the preacher would be seen in the distance as, sitting
bolt up-right on his bony old horse, he would draw
near. He would sit up so stiff and straight, as he jogged
along on his wobbling old mare,—who was also well
versed in her duty, as became her momentous position
in life—that it seemed as though he must have swal-
lowed a liberty-pole. His dress was one that had gone
to religious "seed" years before, though the garments
had been brushed until they would fairly shine in their
knapless "ellegance." A "dickey" front to his home-
spun shirt, his neck encased in a black "stock" which
prevented his turning his head even had his profession
warranted a wag of that important member.

Arriving at the front bars, the host would greet him
with almost a sacred silence and take off his saddle
bags, which contained a few dough-nuts, a bible and
half a dozen well-thumbed hymn-books, when the procession of two would go to the house, the preacher in
advance. Jonathan Edward, as he was prepared to do,
would lead the sacred mare to the barn, divest her of
saddle and bridle, give her water, a half a bushel of oats
and bed her down with fine straw clear up to the top-
end of her precious tail.

The decorum of that household during the stay of
the "head of the church," was a spectacle of precision
and frigidity second only to some scene that was more
so, and was well calculated to destroy a boy, who felt
as though he had a great big chunk of something in
him that was just a little too funny for anything, but who

was compelled by the surroundings to perish the thought.

A sedate supper, with the bulk of the family in the background, family prayers and singing by the combined orchestra, then a noiseless retirement of the entire force. The next day, being the Sabbath, the family, headed by the preacher, started for the church on foot at a seasonable hour. The morning sermon lasted three hours; then Sabbath-school, then luncheon on doughnuts around on the fences; then a sermon of great power,—that is, in length,—then home to a cold supper, and to feed the stock, preparatory to attending prayer-meeting in the evening.

On Monday, the good man would pronounce a general blessing on the family, crawl up to the upper-deck of his demure old "bones," and gradually bump himself out of sight down the lane. Then, things would assume their wonted channel again, and the boys would find a relief and a joy in going out into the field to pick up and haul off stones, such as no one can realize who never had that kind of bringing up.

A LAUNDRY sign in a California town bears the name, "Chin Gun." He is probably the daddy of all those peeple who are noted for "shooting off their mouth."

"INDIAN SUGAR."

THE maple sugar days have come, the sweetest of the
    year,
And in the shady sugar-bush, the joyous "whoop" we
    hear.

The "noble red" rejoiceth much as the April winds
    come on ;
He shoveth forth his patient squaw who works the whole
    day long.

With little axe she hacks and cuts until the "sap" she
    finds,—
Her lord lies snoozing in the sun and "hears God in
    the winds."

She gathers in the liquid, sweet, and boils half down, or
    more,
And then she strains and cleanses it down through her
    pinafore.

And then she patiently "sugars off,"—and prepares the
    sweetened feast,—
And 'rouses up her other "half," who gorges like a
    beast.

If any is left, *she* dippeth in, and the papoose "stuffs,"
    as well ;
Day after day, thro' "Maple Time," they eat, and stuff,
    and "swell."

And when the "sugar days" are gone, they "lick" the
    sugar-dish,
And hie them to the crystal lakes, and settle down on
    fish.

NIGHT VOICES.

As now, "I lay me down to sleep,"
The winds about my cottage weep;
The dark and silent hours of Night,
Close my couch from human sight.

Groaning voices, from without,
Tell, in unknown tongue, about
The gambols of unearthly forms
On this sadden'd sphere of storms.

Morpheus touches not mine eyes
Whilst I list' to plaintive sighs,
Borne to my ears on airy wings,
Telling me of heavenly things.

E'en the shrieking, rushing blast
So chains my soul's attention fast,
That awe-inspiring *fear*, is sweet,
As my **soul**, its voices greet.

And, when the storm-wails slowly die,
And zephyrs' voice begin to sigh;
A soft, sweet story, they impart
That sooth's the sore and tired heart.

They speak **of** golden realms above,
Where, dove-like, rests the Queen of Love,—
Bear tidings sweet from *her* who's left
Me here, alone, below—bereft.

When, with eager, earnest strain,
I strive to catch the words, in vain,
I seem to *see* the face, once more,
My angel-mother always wore.

The zephyrs sigh away to rest,—
Leaving their imprint in my breast.
The darken'd world is still and calm,
Bathed in heaven's sparkling balm.

I gaze out thro' the glassy pane,—
Wond'ringly at the starry plain.
I fain would find *her* safe retreat,
Who taught me, kneeling, to repeat:

" Now I lay me down to sleep,
I pray the Lord my soul to keep;
If I should die before I wake,
I pray the Lord my soul to take."

A SYSTEMATIC effort is said to be making to introduce "smelt"—a kind of fish—into our lakes. We side
with the *Inter-Ocean* in raising our voice against introducing *smelt* into our chain of lakes. Lake Michigan,
especially around Chicago, has already too much *smelt*,
and while the waters of Superior are now sweet and
wholly free from *smelt*, we want to keep them so.

A POET WRECKED.

YOU might just as well undertake to occupy the same car-seat with a four-barreled galvanic battery, carrying a hundred pounds of steam, with all the connecting wires wound about your legs, if your nature is at all sympathetic, as to get locked in with a poet; the effect is, or would be, somewhat similar, as we imagine.

We had no idea the fellow was a poet, when we squeezed down along side of him in the car-seat and placed our " grip " underneath our feet for a foot-stool. Then we turned and asked him if he had any objection to our cramming ourself and baggage into the position just occupied. He pushed his long hair back over his collar, so his ear wouldn't get tangled, as he turned and looked us full in the face and remarked :

Nay, plebean, no ill can prove consequent ;
Thine eye seems weak and innocent.

We said thank you, and kept one eye on him. Not being thoroughly satisfied that our seat-mate wasn't an escaped lunatic, we concluded to " tap " him again :

" My friend, do you travel far in the direction in which we are now gliding? " Then he squared for us

again, and we braced well back against our end of the
seat. Says he:

Who'd think so plain a thing, and wiry,
Could hold such vast inquiry?
I yet go leagues, past field and fence,
Thro' hamlet, town, and forest dense.
Be patient, man, and I will prove it thee.

We said thank you, and kept one eye on him. We
knew now that he was real "mad," or else he was chock
full of poetry—about the same thing. We rallied him
once more:

"My friend, didst come from afar, or from 'anear'?"
He replied, with one of his fingers raised,

From beyond the Rockies' gilded peaks,
Where the golden ray it's good-night seeks;
Where the canyon splits the earth in twain,
Where the rivers are spread o'er fields for rain;
There is where my hearth is spread—
There's my childhood's rocking bed.

We said thank you, and kept one eye on him. Yet,
we began to feel that he wasn't dangerous, and commenced taking on much "poetic sympathy;" still, being an old frontiersman, we felt bound not to give him
the "drop" on us. We said:

We'd like to hear more, my earnest friend,
Of this grand continent's other end.

Whew! Jemima's aunt! We were getting the "power" ourself; we began to have a queer sensation running all through our frame clear down into the grip-
sack. In short, we were beginning to "strike it," and
felt like doing the whole world up in poetic parlance,
ourself—bound in "calf," price seven dollars, sold only

by subscription. When we gave him the "breeze,"
above, he fairly broke himself in two turning upon us,
as he exclaimed:

> Thou weezen, wistful short-capped " Pan,"
> Whence comest *thou*? —speak, strange man!

We said thank you, and kept one eye on him. His
manner was now an intensely excited one. We replied:

> Marvel not my good friend of kin,
> For, knowest thou, if any man kin, I kin?
> 'Tis not a " fool verse," or "taffy" thing
> I give thee—but lines with true poetic ring.
> I come from Alleghany's sun-lit crest,
> From the lucky horse-shoe's sloping breast;
> I'm a poet, real, and to the manor born,
> I know no such word as "boor," or, "in a horn."
> Pray tell me more of that far off State,
> Whose portals ope' through a Golden Gate;
> Where mountains hold the back-door key,
> And bathe their feet in the billowy sea.

About this time he crawfished and sat on the back of
the seat, and gazed down on us in amazement. His
actions were those of a sensitive and poetic nature when
enjoying a first-class scare. He didn't discover that *he*
had imparted to us our *sudden* gift. With a tragic mein
he replied:

> Such a kindred spirit, I'll be bound!
> In such a castle ne'er was found;
> A *thing* that gives me converse sweet,
> Like golden grain in chaff of wheat!
> Thou'st not the semblance of a bard—
> More like the cleaner of a yard.
> But now that thou hast ably proven

That in thy soul a bard is woven,
I will no longer look askanse
But on thee take a double chance.

We looked at him and continued:

Aye, thou poet with soft brown hair,
Eye so sharp, and cheek so fair,
Inside this shell of commonest clay,
Lies a sentiment, refined as day.
My name and fame thou fain wouldst know—
Though in this coat is wrapt your foe.
" Diamond cut Diamond " is my name,
And jealous are both, of each other's fame.

About this time the fellow began looking for a place
to jump, and it was surely true that he was greatly
puzzled as well as actually frightened—no doubt thinking that we were a madman, or else a rival poet on his
track and bent upon his ruin. He fairly screeched this
response:

Hold! Thou scraggly chim-pan-zee,
I would I could make friends with thee!
I give thee here my solemn word,
No curse from me was ever heard,
'Gainst other poet far or near—
Much less the one who meets me here.
I'm a simple bard, from the western slope—
Where I struck an easy, poetic ' lope '—
And thought I'd to the eastward fly
And mash all bards beneath the sky.
Thou art the first of all I've met,
Already, as a bard, my orbs are set;
I acknowledge, the first and only test,
Admonishes me to again go west.
If thou wilt spare me further pain,
I'll again turn back whilst yet I'm sane;

And nevermore leave my Rocky den;
To mash the world's poetic men.

We found that we had given him a zephyr that had jarred him worse than ever one of his Rocky Mountain winds had done, and yet he never dreamed that we, in tapping him so persistently, had gained all we knew *about it.* We now neared the station where our journey ended, and having found out from another fellow passenger that it **was** Joaquin Miller with whom we **were** striving, we determined to give him one **more** *twist* ere we left the car, and while the spell was on. Says we:

> 'Tis well, thou long-haired, sleekly cuss,
> Remember long 'tis 'we'—'tis 'us;'
> 'Tis 'we' who stands on picket line
> To vanquish such poetic swine.
> 'Tis 'us' thou'st come to tease and quiz,
> But, seest thou' we know our 'biz?'
> Face once again the setting sun,
> **And as you go, count on your thumb,**
> The eastern poets thou hast slain—
> A 'sum' you see that's all too plain.
> **If a** common poet from 'Horse-shoe's' breast
> Can mash a nit from 'Rocky's' crest,
> Then, how would Whit. be, for a filler,
> To a one-horse bard like Joaquin Miller?

As we backed out of the door at our station, he was hanging over the back of the car-seat, limp as a superannuated dish-rag, and if we ever hear again from Joaquin it will doubtless be as a joker, not as a bard.

Before we reached our hearthstone, we had our jaw all straightened around again, the spell was off, and we can't talk now only in the common way. But we **are** likely to 'go off' again, whenever we strike real poetic

genius. Joaquin Miller has it, and has it bad, too, as
the above will testify; and anything herein that may
seem as though we were actually bent upon belittling
Joaquin, our readers must take only as a joke on him,
and not meant in earnest.

DOGS, *AND THINGS.*

A DOG isn't the most reliable creature in all the
wide world, excepting as a dog. You may cut
his tail off, pull off his 'bark,' harness him up
and *play* horse with him, but the only way you can possibly make anything else out of a dog, is to work him
up into sausage; and even then, the dog *will* stick out.
A dog *has* a legitimate place in the world, though, and
can find a good deal to do that no other animal can do
—but we are now speaking particularly of the average
dog; the class that have so many breeds, and so many
kinds of blood into them, that any kind of a bet can be
made as to breed, and both parties to the bet may win
every time no matter if they bet in clubs of a dozen or
fifty. He becomes, at this stage in his evolution, a
'quicker dog'—he would quicker lie around and snap
flies than to attend to any kind of business. These are,
with a few honorable exceptions, the kind of dogs the
boys of this town 'work to sled.' They can, after a
good deal of patient training, do a tolerably fair stroke
at 'horse,' because they have no particular ambition and

will consent to be mauled into almost anything; although it takes a boy with a rugged constitution to maul one of them into any remarkable aptitude as the puller of a sled. There is only one thing that will stir up one of these dogs *worse* than half a bushel of fleas, and that is the sight of a cat; a cat is about the only thing left that they fully *realize*, so to speak, or have any passionate taste for. Of course, after enough pounding, even the sight of a cat doesn't disturb them much, but that idea cannot be fully mauled out of them until about the last season of their usefulness; so, that the only way a boy could always have a safe and reliable dog-horse, would be to keep a few pounded ahead. One of them was leisurely trotting down one of our avenues the other day, and the driver, with lines in hand, was enjoying the fine scenery at the head of the lake, breathing in the health-giving morning air, and occasionally staining the snow with a liberal expectoration from the last plug of tobacco his father had left exposed. When about half way down the hill, however, something took occasion to occur. The occurrence that occurred proved conclusively that this particular dog, so far from having the 'cat' all mauled out of him yet, was just ripe for cats. One of them came jumping along out of a side alley, and though a cat usually uses great precaution, and seldom leaps before she looks, this one bounded into the avenue just a few feet ahead of the dog. About this time the boy's *regular* sleighride commenced. He didn't have time to tell the dog that he needn't be in a hurry, nor to say anything, in particular. The cat had occasion to go down across the railroad into 'fisher-

man's alley,' and it seemed to strike the dog that he also had a little business down that way—so, they both
commenced to go immediately, and the boy also started
down in that general direction—like-wise the sled. The
whole establishment seemed to have been behind
time and was bound to reach the next station on time,
or tear up the track. The boy took a death-grip on the
sled, attending to nothing, whatever, except his regular
holding on, and exhausting tobacco juice. The cat attended strictly to business, and the dog pursued his way,
reaching for the cat's tail every time they both happened to touch the ground at the same time. The light
snow disturbed along the route by such velocity, finally
assumed an appearance of a horizontal pillar of fog, for
half a mile, and hollow ; finally, the only way we could
see how they were making it, was to run and look in at
the end. At last, they turned a corner down on the
Point, all well together, the boy's legs flying around like
the arms of a wind-mill. We are sorry to say that although we went down to that part of the city as soon
as possible, and spent several hours in investigation and
inquiry, we failed to ascertain definitely where or how it
all ended. The people, until we explained, thought it
was a heavenly stone, or meteor, that had gone through
them in that quarter, and were very much agitated. All
that could be found was some cat-fur, a dog-collar, a
demolished outhouse, a sled-runner and some pieces of
a boy's coat. It is probable that the whole train went
into one of the fish-holes out on the lake, and we should
advise every family in town to take a fresh invoice of
their children to see who it is that has lost a boy about

15

twelve years old, wearing a peaked cap, a blue wamus, and a brindle dog.

~~~~~~~~~~~~~~~~~~~~~~~~~~~~~~~~~~~~

A "CLOSE CALL."

UPON entering our ivy-clad and fern-embanked cot the other evening, our large flock of little folks proceeded to inform us that a man had been there during the hours in which we had been absent, toiling like a slave for means with which to fill the mouths of our little home-birds. The toil consists chiefly in prying out one-horse ideas with a five-cent lead-pencil, as our crow-bar, in a cool and elegantly furnished office, a few hours each day; three-fourths of those hours, even, are spent in sticking our number elevens up on the table, leaning back in an easy chair and thinking deeply about nothing. The man who had been there was the tax-gatherer—the *poll*-tax fiend. He left a notice which read: "Sir—You are hereby notified to appear on Saturday next at 7 o'clock a. m., at Lake Avenue and Superior Street, provided with pick and shovel, to work on the highways of the village," etc., signed by the street commissioner. Now such a notice was rather startling to a man who thought he had nothing to tax. But it seems as though a man was born to be taxed. This poll-tax is hard to understand; it seems to strike a fellow about so often, whether he owns a palace or a dog—or nothing. It seems they charge a man for walking around on the ground—the

earth which was made for the free use of man, likewise
women and children. Or, for the air he breathes, which
is so plentiful around here that no reasonable man
would think of charging us for the little we used; after
a person breathes up all he can of it, there is a whole
sky full of it left, that has never been touched—enough
to supply Chicago for a week, without warming over—
and *such* air!

But, the street commissioner evidently didn't know
that it would have been dangerous, if not positively dis-
astrous to the city, had we responded to his call—which
we did not. There *are* men who can safely be let loose
with a pick and shovel to work out their poll-tax; they
are moderate workers, who work as though determined
to leave a whole lot of the 'poll' for the next year—
they are not inclined to be piggish, and turnpike the
whole country, for an imaginary dollar and a half.
They labor moderately, so as not to deprive future generations of the enjoyment of working on the roads for
imaginary shekels. *We* are not that kind of a man,
however, when yoked in with a pick and shovel. We
don't *mean* to be mean, but when once we grapple the
business-end of a pick or shovel, it is just awful to see
the dirt fly. Of course we didn't respond to the commissioner's call, because we knew he didn't know who
he was fooling with. Having no grudge against the
town, we forebore working out our tax. It could not
but prove calamitous to let us loose on Lake Avenue.
When once started, we could not be shut off until the
whole hill for several blocks, up and down, would be
shoveled into the bay; the houses would be wrecked

and many of the people probably killed, or maimed for life, the rocks rolled over into Wisconsin, and the copper veins that underlie the city would be pulled up by the roots and shoveled into Lake Michigan. There would be an awful trouble all around this region, and though we would make beautiful roads and a level country out of it, the town would be entirely destroyed. There's no use in the street commissioner urging us, because we cannot consent to *work* out our tax; *we* are better acquainted with the notified party than *he* is. If he would see us pull up a cistern or a well and throw the hole over into another county, he would at once see that it was not proper for him to talk pick and shovel business with us. If his honor is a fit man for street commissioner he will take due notice of this warning, come around and get his dollar and a half, and hire some man who is in the habit of working moderately when working out a poll-tax.

A DISTRICT attorney out in Dakota has sold his saloon to Young-man-not-afraid-of-his-aquifortis.

A MILK-WAGON ran away in St. Paul the other day, and the pump-water flew so that the driver was nearly drowned.

YOUR RIGHT-HAND POCKET.

DID you ever just notice your right hand vest-pocket? That is, did you ever take everything out of it, all at one time, and spread the contents out on the table and look 'em over? If you never did, just try it, and see if you aren't a boy, the same as when a ten-year-old. The only difference is, you have changed pockets. *Then* you used to go about with your left-hand breeches-pocket hanging down like a pair of saddle-bags with both ends on the near side. It was *more* than full; leather strings and tow-ropes dangled from the extended mouth, while the ends of nails stuck out into daylight from the bottom of the great poke, and your left knee was blistered from the chafing of the heavy receptacle. A boy with that kind of a pocket was considered, among the boys, as being tolerably forehanded in the matter of valuable personal property. He could show a miscellaneous stock that would put in the shade any ordinary variety store of to-day—everything from a rusty gimlet or wooden clock-wheel down to the running gear of a flutter-wheel or a dozen spotted beans. The immense weight of the menagerie stretched his single yarn suspender until it was about two feet

longer, and correspondingly narrower, than when his
mother knit it for him, or before he lost his other one.
It made him stoop-shouldered, and hauled him over so
far to leeward that he walked with his right arm thrown
out, to balance the center of gravity—his gait being still
further "oddified" by walking only on the toes of his
left foot, in order not to crowd the great blue stone-
bruise that overpowered his left heel.   That was about
the shape of it when we were boys, and we often laugh
when we think of it.   *We* did think of it the other day
when we cleaned out our right-hand vest-pocket, and
beheld the accumulation since the old vest was new.
Among other things, we found half a dozen scraps of
paper with memoranda on each, three big screws, four
matches two tooth-picks, two stubs of pencils, a pencil-
holder, button-hook, three shirt and one pant button, a
four-penny nail, a tin tack, a nickle, a printer's rule, a
row of pins, a small piece of tobacco and a *little* dirt.
About the only *vital* difference between now and thirty
years ago was, that we found no "slings," no assortment
of strings, no second-hand horse-shoe nails, none of the
machinery of a wooden cart, mud marbles, or broken
hen's eggs, as we used to in those days.   But, we found
enough to forcibly remind us of that happiest period of
life when we didn't care whether school kept or not,—
only a good deal rather it wouldn't—or whether General Scott killed the last Mexican greaser in existence—
only a good deal rather he would—or whether the put-
ty market in Antwerp fluctuated up or fluctuated down.

SLAVES TO FASHION.

THERE was one thing, during our boyhood, that we boasted of; that was that a resolution had taken hold of our soul, heart, gizzard, and the rest of our body, to the effect that should *we* live to the age of even a thousand years we should never become a "slave to fashion"—no, never, *never!* Often have we sat on the fence of our father's farm, and made faces by the hour at the dandies and belles who passed on the road, holding them in the most utter contempt because of their frivolous character. With our "pepper and salt" breeches, held in position by one yarn suspender, our hickory shirt, and a first-class stubbed toe on each foot, we felt good and noble and Christian, and looked with profound derision upon those who wasted any more dry goods than we did in the protection of their anatomies. We stood manfully by this noble resolution for several years—until we had an opportunity to do differently. But, as time rolled on, and we became "our own man," at the age of fourteen the temptation to "pile on the agony" in the way of dress became very, very strong; it wasn't long, in fact, until we commenced getting everything possible with our limited means with which to fresco and adorn our anatomy, until we soon found ourself as big a fool as anybody else—as frail, in fact, as a stalk of the tenderest asparagus. From one thing to another we have passed, until now we actually wear a great standing collar, just because other folks do. As a luxury, we consider these "latest collars" equal to any fashionable misery that has come out for a long time. Of course, a man's head is made to feel like a pumpkin in a cheese-box, but never mind—they are the style, and that ends it. Their shape is admirable for scoring one's cheek or cutting his ear loose; a man in turning a corner has to commence stern-wheeling himself around half a block away so as to make his body conform with the corner simultaneously—make it straight with himself—or he will be certain to cut his throat. It is awful to see a short person with a short neck wearing one of these double-bitted throat-cutters; he looks like a toad on parade—that's the way we look, and we *feel* like a boxed codfish. We dare say, however, that our appearance is perfectly stunning to the average beholder, and with our collar, we become admissable to "the best circles." If a man has a good deal of cheek, he will last longer and win more favors than one with a scarcity of jowl; ours is not particularly "big," but it's awful tough, hence we expect to hold out with many a "fatter fool," and we defy fashion to produce any damnable thing that we won't wear, and wear with the same ravishing grace that we do this blessed collar—that takes our life every time we turn our head around to "see a man." Fashion!—a slave to fashion!—what is life without fashion?

That's what life is for—to "pile it on" and learn how to get the most fashion out of the most misery. Philosophers, wise men, eminent Christians, and so forth, tell us that this life is intended as a preparation-room for a better life; that is all nonsense! Keep up with the fashion, young man; if it takes all the money you can earn, and all you can borrow, go for it. What everybody does, must be right—and they all do it. Just at present, the chief end of man is a high collar, and a heap of cheek, backed up by a fool, just like we are. Let eternity look out for itself; a fashionable collar is all a man, these days, can handle.

A MAN should strive hardest to acquire those things which he can carry with him when he dies. It will be a light class of baggage, but very valuable.

ANOTHER sea-serpent, about 300 feet long, has been seen off New York harbor, by the captain of a vessel. Some of these sea-captains must drink awfully strong 'booze.'

AN exchange tells us that a Maine man has regularly received the Congressional Globe and Record for the last thirty-six years, and has read every copy. We have often met men who were 'walking dictionaries,' but we never heard of a traveling waste-basket before.

MEETING A CHAIR.

EAR reader, did you ever arise from your couch during the stilly hours of night? If so, did you ever find a chair in the very exact spot where you could have sworn that it wasn't? We did. It was not a hundred years ago, either, when we had occasion to slide out from our downy couch, just as the "faithful clock" was about to toll the hour of midnight. The principle object of our night-tour was to reach the rear door of our humble cot. Our business there, was to gently toss a stick of stove-wood at a brace of "feline cats," that were indulging in the devilish work of keeping us awake to the great detriment of our needed rest. We had stood it just as long as we possibly could, and blood was all that could satiate our parching thirst for vengeance. We arose vigorously, nor bated in our vicious march for the front door of the back kitchen; that is, we didn't halt until we stopped. An heir-loom, in the form of a heavy, hardwood chair, which had been handed down through our family from the days when Marc Anthony dandled Cleopatra on his knee, met us in the blackness that prevailed in the rear apartment, adjoining the wood-shed where the cats were located.

We could have testified, on a stack of Jayne's almanacs as high as the Pyramids, that that old oaken chair was in the garret. That is, we could have testified in that way before we met it in the kitchen. Immediately after we had interviewed it, however, we could have *sworn* it *was not* in the garret—in fact, we *did* so swear; our testimony was emphatic on the question of locality. We met the chair directly on the end of our second-best toe on the south foot. The impetuosity of our vigorosity of motion, made it very bad for that toe. We saw stars— the "bear," "dipper," "Jacob's ladder," everything but cat. Our remarks, as we stood on our head just north of the wood-box, would have been highly credit- able to an important meeting of the bulls and bears of Chicago, when wheat was on the decline. **We finally** got our centre, and yelled for a light, which was instant- ly brought forth by the next-best member of the family, who felt sure that the house had "settled," or the cellar caved in. Upon examination, we found the toe in question, completely telescoped, with not enough of it sticking out of the "bumper" to make a coupling on. In fact, there was only a *place* for a toe; it had been driven up worse than the tail of a butcher's dog. It re- sembled a turtle's neck, when the turtle wasn't "at home." After getting it pulled out by means of a pair of nippers, and splintered into place again, we went to bed, and were rather grateful the rest of the night, be- cause the cats kept us from getting lonesome, while we laid awake and nursed our toe.

ANSWERS TO CORRESPONDENTS.

JULIA—You are in a pickle, sure enough. You say you gave your 'adorable' the 'mitten,' and now you are sorry you did so, and want us to tell you the best way to win him back without having to go through too much humiliation. Well, let us see. You had better write him a note, perfumed with sasafras, and things, and tell him you were only joking—that you are just as much his as possible, without the aid of a parson,—that your heart is in his vest-pocket, or in that vicinity, and he ought to know it. If this doesn't work, just write him again that you are anxiously awaiting his reply to your last, before yielding to the persuasions of another chap, who is absolutely turning yellow for the want of your smiles. This will bring him, if he isn't a fiend, and if he is a fiend, it will be dead sure to fetch him.

"Finance"—You ask us "what is the difference between a greenback dollar and a gold dollar at the present time." Well, as far as we know, there is just the same difference that there always was: A greenback dollar is a paper concern, about three by six inches in size, and has several nice pictures on the front side, in-

cluding a portrait of some one of our lamented old patriots who *fit* in some of our American wars,—the backside being green, and ornamented with a lot of neat
curlemacues. A gold dollar is a little yellow contrivance, about as big as a cat's eye, when the cat is working a mouse-hole, and is made of gold—in most cases.
On one side it has the goddess of Liberty's head, and
on the other side it hasn't. We saw one of each kind
last summer, and made a note of how they looked ; had
we not been favored with the opportunity, your question would have been to hard for us.

" Pap "—Your question is one that has puzzled the
philosophers of all ages, and we give it up, of course.
Like yourself, we could never understand why the hind-
wheel of a wagon did not overtake the forward wheel,
it being so much the larger.

" John "—The nearest approach to perpetual motion
that has ever been attained, is by the tongue of an agitated mother-in-law. It runs without greasing, and with
the regularity of an eight-day clock, that is wound up
every twenty-four hours.

" Inquirer "—Yes ; it is always the very smartest men
that can be found in the State, who are elected to the
Legislature. Their pictures show that, or if they don't,
the laws that they pass give conclusive evidence of it.

" Eliza "—We have forgotten some of our geography,
including that part that treats of the earth's axis. If
our memory serves us, however, the said axis sticks out
a bit, at either pole, and rests in a forked stick. How
nearly it is worn off, we are not informed ; and what

will take place when it does wear off, is not exactly certain. The probability is, however, that somebody will get left.

" James "—No ; it is in very bad taste to whistle in company. To break yourself of it, wear a very tight collar, and stay at home.

" Mary Ann "—You say your old house cat has sort of crazy spells—you fear she is threatened with hydrophobia, etc.,—and want us to tell you what to do for her. Certainly ! Although it has been some time since we left the cat " practice," yet we remember that these symptoms indicate a very common complaint among house-cats. But, we should have had a lock of your cats hair, in order to tell the exact phase of the disease. You need not fear hydrophobia in the case ; she may be somewhat angry, but not necessarily ' mad.' Her complaint is what is technically termed by the profession, ' worm in the tail.' You should diet the old pet ; give her less oats and more chop-feed, with a spoonful of saltpeter mixed into the chopped straw and bran ; bathe her in turpentine, and rub her down with a stick of stovewood. After a reasonable time, if she does not improve, lash a stone to her neck, and make her drink a barrel of water, without stopping to take breath. This latter remedy is a sure cure for ' worm in the tail,' or for almost any other disease in cats—as many scores of cats, that we have had the treatment of, could testify, if they were alive and could speak.

" Farmer "—The only way we know to cure your " valuable breeding sow of breaking through the fence into the corn," is as follows: Go to the woods and find a large tree that is crooked and hollow. Cut it down, cut it off each side of the crook or bow; take it and build it in underneath the fence, at the point where the feminine swine generally breaks through, leaving the bow of the log *inside* the field, but both ends projecting *outside.* Then, hide yourself near by, and enjoy the circus. The gentle creature—all old sows are proverbial for their gentleness—will come along after awhile, discover the extraordinary facilities offered for entering the field, and after looking the thing over for a minute or two, she will proceed to go into the field through the hollow log, with several grunts, evincing rare satisfaction. After a little, however, she will "issue" from the other end of the log but, of course, on the same side of the fence. She will elevate her nose, wriggle the little pancake on the end of her snout, and smell around for the crop, vigorously, for as much as half a minute. Then, she will throw a hog-eye around to the rear, to see where she came from, and turn about and smell the end of the log; she will eye the crop through the fence, and wonder how it got over the fence so soon. After taking the bearing of the hollow in the log, and seeing that it certainly leads directly through to the corn-side of the fence she makes a lively entrance, and waltzes around through the log on a trot so as to get there before the corn can hop over the fence again. She comes out at the other end of the log with a tread and a grunt that says, "Now, I reckon I'll have some corn, alle samee!" Then she sticks her nose up into the air again, and wabbles the little "graham gem" on the end of her nozzle, around in more directions than characterize a "dying" top, and tries to imagine that she sees "dead-loads" of corn, and things—but she doesn't, and will soon "give it up," and start into the log-hole again, with the same result. After you have enjoyed the menagerie as long as your sides can stand it, you can go away to your work contentedly, and stay a week, if you want to. She will never leave the spot, but will travel back and forth through that log all summer, in her effort to be a little more "previous" in getting *through* the fence than the corn is in jumping over it. This is an old cure for breachy sows, but it is the best we ever tried when we were in the business.

The "civilized" Indians around here *do* show wonderful signs of forsaking their barbaric state and embracing a sort of Christian style of doing things. But, when one of these new-made Christians goes into a grocery store, with his wife, and buys a sack of flour, he suddenly remembers that he is a noble red-man, and at once determines that he will "toil not, neither will he spin." Hencely, he invites his squaw to shoulder the bag while he starts up street, a few steps ahead of the flour, walking as stiff and straight as a Roman gladiator —or a lazy Indian.

THEY'RE ALL ALIKE.

SOME one asks: "Wonder if it seems just the same to a king and queen when they get married, as it does to other folks."

To be sure it does. In all probability Alfonso of Spain and his bride had about the same sensations playing around under their vest and corset, respectively, as common people do when they "git spliced." We suppose they got together after the subsequent tom-foolery was ended, and talked things over as to their domestic affairs just as everybody does—how many rooms they could put up with, whether she couldn't "do without a girl" *for a while*, anyway, and just hire her washing and ironing done, etc. They talked "economy" to death. He proposed that he was willing, when he went down to work, on his throne, to take a cold lunch in a tin bucket and just step out to a beer-foundry and get a glass of beer for five cents to wash it down. He would wear his best clothes only when he expected callers, and in the meantime she could darn up his pepper-an'-salt coat, patch the "heel" of his pants, and draw the grease-spots out of his every-day hat with ammonia and a hot flatiron. Oh, yes; kings and queens are just as

fond of all this kind of talk, after marriage, as anybody
else. What would this life amount to, anyway, it young
married folks couldn't talk over their plans? It would
be a desert waste. If we were to be offered a kingdom,
with this *green* spot in life left out, we'd tell them to
take their old kingdom and go to—and do what they'd
a mind to with it. We wouldn't take a half a dozen
kingdoms on such terms, and we dare say Alfonso and
and his young wife wouldn't either. We can almost
hear the young queen telling Al. that he must put
her up a lye-leach before spring, and she will save up
her grease and make a whole barrel of soft soap; and
that he must get a pig to eat up the tater-peelings, and
things, and a cow and some chickens—regular layers—
and she'll work up the rags during the winter and have
enough for a carpet by spring. Oh, yes. And then
she counts her fingers to see how many balls it will take
to make twenty-five yards of rag-carpet, while Alfonso
gets down to his ciphering to see how much it will cost
to get it woven at ten cents a yard. And Al. he delights her by enumerating how many nice little things
he can make for the house during odd evenings when
there's nothing to do down at the throne—such as
brackets, flower-stands, a bread-board, potato-masher,
a cradle, and ever so many things that will *save*, you
know. Yes, indeed. She will fix over her old rep
dress, put on a polonaise trimmed with a shade darker,
and that will do all winter for afternoons, and she can
"turn" her fall hat, and get her old shoes mended.
Economy? That's the way it always begins, and there
is no other time in a woman's life that can compare

with right after marriage, in the amount of solid happiness to the square foot, unless it is when she is dressing her first doll; and, as for a man, he cannot deny but what it fully equals in pleasure the days when he used to go to mill on the old horse, with corn in one end of the bag, and stones in the other.

THE WOOD-BUCKER.

HE that bucketh wood, on a buck, with a bucksaw, bucketh from out his saw-buck an honest living. There is a greater quantity of buckness to a buck in a buck-saw and to a saw-buck, when faithfully bucked, than is found in any other way of bucking for one's daily bread. Bucking a buck-saw, on a saw-buck, bucketh much perspiration from the brow of the buckee; and, the buckor, for whom the buckee bucketh, pays very stingily for the bucking of him who bucketh it. Whenever we see an aged buckster bucking away with his buck-saw and his saw-buck, we always get the "buck-fever;" and feel as though we ought to contribute to his task of bucking, whatever of the bucking ability we might add to his buck. Being very conservative, however, as a bucker on a buck-saw, we seldom, or hardly ever, mention our inclination to buck. Hence, when we sit in our warm office, and gaze out with tear-dimmed eyes, upon him who bucketh his buck, we feel that our tears availeth much, and that the only real difference, after all, is, that for bread, he

bucketh his buck-saw, on his buck, whilst we buck a
lead-pencil, bucking out editorials and things. Nevertheless, we mourn for the aged bucker.

THE "YALLER" HORSE.

E SAW a team and a dog on the street the
other day. This of itself, however, is no very
extraordinary spectacle, because there are lots
of horse-teams, and also several dogs to be viewed in
and about this town nearly every day. The team in
this instance had been unhitched and was feeding along
side of the wagon. They were country horses, and
were dressed in harness that seemed a sort of compromise between a lot of old ropes, odd pieces of straps, tow-
strings, and nothing at all. The harnesses were an average set, in the rural districts common to the ragged
edge of civilization, and matched the wagon perfectly.
The vehicle had seen service regularly, on mighty rough
roads, since about the time that Fulton's steamboat first
wrestled with the Hudson River. It was extremely
aged, and every wheel on it was bow-legged with the
weight of years, while the pole was worm-eaten and
"humped down" through a weakness of the backbone
—an evident case of "spinal-maginnis" which had become chronic. But, we are forgetting the team, and
also neglecting the dog. As we remarked, the two
horses were eating their noon-luncheon; it was a frugal
repast and consisted of an armful of wire-grass, sprinkled

with weak brine, so they could worry it down, and imagine that it was the timothy of their childhood. Their general appearance told, in thunder thoughts, that wiregrass had constituted their "stuffing" for the last score of years. One had been a black horse when he first began his career, but time had faded him out until he was of that rare shade known as no color in particular. Three of their ears had been frozen down to the first limb, and the remaining one hung limp. The other horse was a pale yellow in color, and had bright eyes that indicated great force of character and energy—a horse that made the most of everything, and was bound to be cheerful no matter what the surroundings. He was thin almost to atenuation, and resembled a pipe stem on a couple of clothes-pins, with a stomach in suspension. The long hair looked as though it grew clear through; his lip hung down carelessly, while his tail seemed to have been eaten off by the calves. As he leisurely chawed away at his repast, a city dog happened along, and observed the "establishment." He evidently was larking around in search of some sport, and he rightly judged that he had struck a rich lead in the yellow horse, and he began to caper about him and bark in the most gleeful manner. The yellow horse didn't seem to scare to any noticeable extent, and only seemed to enjoy the racket as he kept on munching his wiregrass. The sleek city dog warmed up in his enjoyment of the sport, and after a quarter of an hour's rollicking about the front of the horse, he went to the rear and began jumping up and toying with the remains of what had once been a horse's tail, and barking for very joy.

The old nag, however, kept one of his eyes rather on
guard in that direction, as any close observer might have
noticed, though showing no sign. At last, however, the
scene suddenly changed, and a fat city dog might have
been seen flying through the air, landing part way down
on Lake Avenue bridge. There wasn't very much *seen*
of the dog after that, though he was not out of *hearing*
for ten minutes. The " yaller " horse from the country
kept on eating his dinner.

AN EGG.

AN EGG is a very eccentric animal. When it is
good, it is allfired good ; when it is bad, it is in-
fernally that way. There are no middling good
eggs, nor are there any tolerably bad ones. An egg
never occupies a middle-ground, nor is found " on the
fence," like David Davis. It will, or it won't. When
it is barely ripe, it won't do to put it away in the bureau
drawer to get mellow, or to give the drawer and its contents a nice scent. It isn't that kind of an apple.
Strange as it may seem, when an egg contains a chick-
en, both the chicken and the egg are worth less in the
market, than the egg, without the chicken. When eggs
rise and fall in the market, the eggs are not broken ;
but when they rise and fall anywere else, they become
a total wreck. The way to eat an egg, is to drink it—
right out of the shell. The bark of an egg isn't good
for anything at all—not even for tanning purposes. As

good a way as any to appreciate an egg, is to fill your trowsers pockets full of them, and then climb a high rail fence on your way from the barn to the house, and after you have forgotten you had any eggs about your clothes. We have often appreciated eggs that way. Eggs are good, though, if absorbed before they get sort of "funny looking" inside.

THEY are playing "One Hundred Wives," in a Chicago theater. We know of instances where men have had only *one* wife—and there was mighty little *play* about it, either.

"I WILL raise you one," as we heard the sun remark to the thermometer, the other morning.

To TAKE a good hind-sight, is as important as to take a good foresight; like those on a gun, the hind-sight should govern the foresight.

AMERICANS are physically frail, because they have too much brain, and too little balance-wheel—or too much balance in their wheel, or too much *wheel* in their balance.

TOUGH STORIES.

THE Russians, says a certain writer, live in their cold country in great comfort. Among other items, he tells us that they can stand more heat as well as more cold, than "any other man." That even in the humblest cots, a large stove is the principal article of furniture, etc. His whole sketch, barring the concluding paragraph, bears the marks of a perfect plausibility. When he winds up by saying, however, that the humble Russian very frequently sleeps *on top* of his stove, we begin to limber up as a believer; and when he further asserts that, "indeed, they very frequently sleep *in* the stove," we desire him to understand that there is a limit to even a Yankee's credulity. It is as hard on us as the story told us once, by a fellow, concerning a wild Indian he met away out on the plains. He went on to relate what a magnificent specimen of the "noble red man" he was—tall, always beautifully dressed, gorgeously and tastefully painted, the gaudiest feathers adorning his head, wonderfully intelligent, and *so* scrupulously clean and tidy in his person. We drank in all the details concerning this grandly beautiful wild man of the plains, with great relish, though he certainly

discounted anything *we* had ever seen in the line of
Indian samples. The narrator, however, went just one
step too far, and we suddenly became a mass of ruins,
as a believer in the recital. "Why," he exclaimed, "this
Indian was so neat that he would *no more think* of sitting down to a meal, without first carefully *cleaning his
finger-nails*, than he would think of cutting his head
off." That bu'sted the entertainment; and we have
always believed since, that he never saw an Indian in
all his life—not even a tobacco-sign—and knows as little about an Indian, or the "Indian problem," as a
Philadelphia Quaker.

THE OLD SETTLER.

EVERY community is blessed with its "old
settler"—the old chap who can tell you how
many deer and bear he has killed "not twenty
rods from where your house now stands." He delights
to tell how many hard days' work he did with only three
small potatoes and a roasted chipmonk to eat; and who
was the first baby born in the town, and how they sent
for him to preside, because he happened to be the only
man in the region who knew what was good for babies.
He walks around among the modern settlers with all
the airs possible for an original "developer" to have,
and carries the conviction to every heart that he, the
old settler, is ever so much more than an everlastingly
"wise injun." He can kick a neighbor's dog clear across

18

the street, and it's all right; **because** he is the " old settler," and emphatically the privileged character.   When
he comes into a town meeting, **everybody**, for a moment, dries **up, and** grabs onto a more respectful run of
sentences, and when they presume to advance an idea
they involuntarily turn and address the old settler in the
hope **that he may nod** an approving smile, or smile an
approving **nod; if they get it, they laugh** right out; if
his countenance **clouds over, then the speaker** very
quickly sits down, leaving an **impression that he** "didn't
say anything, nohow," and **didn't try to.   An** " old settler " **can tell one story over more times,** successfully,
than anybody else.   He has but a small stock, gener-
ally, because a story without **himself as the hero,** isn't
any story at all; and in order to be plausible, he **dare
not hero himself too often for** fear it might get what
this age terms " thin."   Even **the** naked truth gets thin
enough after you have listened to it four or five thousand
times.   There will be a terrible vacancy in our western
communities when all the first settlers die; there will be
a happy lonesomeness prevailing for a long time, but
after awhile it would seem sort of good to have them
come back again—just to get off that story once more;
it would seem so old-fashioned, like.   The " old settler "
is happy, because he knows if it hadn't been for him the
country would never have developed; hence, he can
afford to be arrogant, uncivil, and imagine himself a real
actuality, and everybody else mere accidentals.   He
nearly always says " no " to every progressive movement, because it shows he has a mind of his own, that
he is the only man who " *knows* to the contrary," and

besides he wants things kept just as near the "good old way" as possible. All in all, the "old settler" is an eccentric old gimlet, and aside from keeping up a perfectly freezing dignity, and being perfectly harmless, is of about as much public use, as a bull is a private success in a china shop.

RIDING ON AN ICEBOAT.

F YOU never rode on an iceboat, dear reader, an iceboat with a big sail, we sincerely lament your condition—you must be as miserable as a bee without flowers. As for us, we have stepped away from you; we have climbed aloft into a new sphere of contemplation, to which you, poor mortal, are a total stranger—we have had our ride on an iceboat over the broad bosom of the Lake. We can now look back with contempt upon the commonplace enjoyments of life, and wonder how we ever could have been amused with Fourth-of-July celebrations, circuses, picnics, sleighrides, railroad life, marbles or base-ball. We can scarcely conceive that we ever took delight in a minstrel performance, a political campaign, or in pulling the legs off of flies; because, you see, we have "rid" on an iceboat. We had an invitation to sail with a couple of friends, and of course accepted it, as it had long been our desire to take a trip on an iceboat. We descended to the shore of the beautiful lake—now solid in its icy grandeur—and found the boat just having her sheets

spread to the zephyrs, which, in next the shore, barely
wafted our Byronical locks from behind our ears around
and across the bridge of our Grecian nose.   An iceboat
is a wonderful craft, in its way, and in general appearance resembles an old-fashioned harrow; it doesn't look
like a harrow either; but like a "lizzard" upon which
logs are hauled out of the woods; and yet, that isn't
what it resembles, either—it bears a resemblance to an
iceboat more than to either of the other articles.   This
one was clipper-built, with mutton-chop sail, and iron-
clad stem and stern.   We being the invited guest were
given the position of honor, at the nose, or on the corner that went first.   The establishment moved in obe-
dience to the pulsation of the breeze, and we glided
gently out toward the central portion of the lake's bosom.   Though the brave old "salt" who sat at the helm
said, in response to our question, that the boat was going very slowly, we felt a little nervous, like, and the
ice-scales were flying up into our faces; as the wind
freshened, the craft flew ahead with such a velocity that
we lay down, head to the wind, and only kept one eye
open at a time.   The ice chunks began to fly down inside our coat-collar, and never stopped till they landed
inside our socks, and the packing of our body in chopped
ice went steadily forward until we were chin-deep in it,
and we felt like an ice-cream freezer on a bu'st.   We
made out to twist our left optic around until we sighted
the engineer at the helm, when in an agony of fright
we shouted that we thought she had sprung a leak in
the bow; but the old fiend of the deep only smiled as
he closed one eye and said, "Keep cool, yer lubber, we

haven't commenced to go yet." "Let us go ashore, then!" we shrieked. But he only changed eyes, shifted his quid, and took his bearings for a point at the other end of the lake. We now hugged down like a toad to a warm brick, drew our head deep down inside our coat-collar, and muttered, "Mercy on us!" The ship leaped before the gale, scurried right and left, rocked over and flew along like a comet, first on one corner, then on another, and anon settling flat down and making the ice fairly bellow with the friction below, while the air above was full of congealed scales that cut like wire. The Point was reached and left behind, and the winged devil to which we had, in an unlucky moment, tied our fortunes, doubled the head of the Lake, and started on the southern track as if swept ahead by all the Furies, We felt sure that such a velocity could not be overcome this side of the Gulf of Mexico, or possibly we were entering upon the initiatory movement to form the nucleus of a gigantic meteor that would at no distant day appal the astronomer, by our fiery passage through space—a fiery body done in ice. As we lay there hanging on like grim death to the cross beam, speechless, motionless, almost senseless, in our enjoyment of a ride on an iceboat we reflected upon our only remaining desire in life ; to live, that we might slay our friends who had inveigled us into this indescribable peril, and unutterable enjoyment, to be found on earth only when taking a pleasure excursion in the forward hatch of an iceboat. We live, thanks to a tough constitution, and the balance of the programme would be faithfully executed, only that the friends who treated us to that ride have left the country. We are barely able to sit up, and keep poultices on the innumerable places where the skin is torn off, and rub Russian salve on the frozen spots.

HUNTING PRAIRIE CHICKENS.

ANY one who desires to go in search of prairie-chickens, and have more than a bushel of fun— the same as we did a few days ago—should go prepared just as we did—that is, if he wants real pleasant excitement and recreative hilarity. Get your gun and equipments, and two dogs, that know less about hunting chickens than the Old Harry knows about a hymn-book, and then start out with your eye sharply cocked for a "flush." You go north two miles, south one, west three, and east a reasonable distance, by which time you will most likely strike a covey of chickens; you may know it was the first covey, because the dogs have, up to this time, scoured the entire country, clear to the horizon, in every direction, and are just coming to you about noon for their meat, that you are packing for them, when they scare up chickens all around you. Now is your time, or never, and you blaze away—both loads at one bird, and down he comes; the dogs are just charging in all directions, and when the chicken falls, they make a grand rush for it and frighten the whole living covey half a mile away. As they start for it you begin yelling for them to " Git eout!" at the very

howling pitch of your voice; but, it's no use, they have
it—one by the head, the other by the tail. Just as you
have rammed your two loads down—all the shot in one
barrel and all the powder in the other—you start on a
dead run to get the chicken away from the dogs, yelling
bloody murder at every jump—to say nothing about the
"irregular" sentences that are meant to give relief to
your inmost feelings, and emphasis to the admonitions
being addressed to the dogs. On the way to the scene
of the struggle, that is almost hidden by a cloud of feathers, you step into a badger-hole and turn several somersaults, and fetch up with your head and both barrels of
the gun rammed deep into a neighboring ant-hill; all
intent, however, upon getting that chicken from the
dogs, you start again on the run, scraping the ants and
dirt out of your eyes on the way, and of course, keep
on saying something to the dogs. You arrive at the
scene, and amid and over the carnage, begin to pour
out the vials of your wrath in relation to the two dogs,
and kick first one and then the other till their ribs crack,
but it is of no avail; they pull and howl for the victory,
one over the other, and when they get the chicken torn
into a thousand pieces they go for each other. Being
borrowed, and highly valued as bird-dogs by their proprietor, they must be parted ere they kill each other.
Taking hold of one by the heels, and placing your left
foot on the tail of the other, you finally get them pulled
apart, and they go in opposite directions to lie down
and rest, whilst you sit down to recuperate and finish
the stanzas you have only commenced, and repeat, over
and over, others of the more emphatic kind relative to

the proceedings and the result of the whole effort. You finally gather up five toes, a hand-full of feathers and the head of the very deceased chicken, and deposit them in your vest pocket as relics of a first-class hunt with bird-dogs that know how to "work." You hunt up your gun, find both barrels full of mud, turn about and say something more about bird-dogs, and start for home. Although this class of hunting is not calculated to bring in any great amount of meat for the family, yet, as a matter of "fun" and good, wholesome recreation, we recommend it highly.

MARRYING FOR MONEY.

THERE is nothing so dangerous to the happiness of married life as for either party to marry the other for money. We tried it, and know. When a young man, and at the age when we thought all honest people ought to be married, our capital was small. All we possessed in the wide world was two dollars and fifty cents and a handkerchief full of clothes. To cast about for a wife who had some filthy lucre with which to commence life, seemed to us our first and plainest duty—to ourself. Our search was speedily and richly rewarded; we found a young heiress who "couldn't tell a lie" by saying "no," and so the matter was focused at once, and we set sail together most auspiciously. She possessed three dollars, and a new spring hat—raising our wealth to the extent of fifty cents. Life, since that time has been fully as blissful as might have been expected, we presume, and but for that unfortunate difference in moneyed wealth at the outset, no grim demon of disturbance would ever have been discernible about the ranch of which we claim to be the principal head. But this idea of superior wealth can never be fully eradicated from the system, even in the face of good intentions. Hence, we say: young man, never marry for money!

OUR recent article on *how to commence* farming on a new place, seems to have proven very valuable to several thousand of our readers, and we have received a number of requests asking us to give our own experience on a new farm, hoping thereby to elicit something further that may prove beneficial to them—which is to say, gain something from our experience. Of course, we gladly serve our friends in any manner possible, and as we had about six months' experience on a "homestead," once upon a time, we feel perfectly sure our experience must prove beneficial to all contemplating that course of life for the future.

Our outfit consisted of a yoke of six-year-old black oxen—but we advise white ones, as they will not "draw the heat" like black ones—a cart, a cow and calf, four hens and a rooster—the brama sort—two pigs, one 12-inch breaking plow, a set of harrow-teeth, and three dogs. Of course we had provided for the family by

laying in a bag of flour, a hunk of bacon, two quarts of
castor oil—in case of sickness in the family—a Dutch
oven, some morning-glory and sun-flower seeds and a
pair of flat-irons.   As we sat on the dash-board of our
cart and turned our back on the last town, with our face
set straight for the frontier, we lighted our pipe, and a
thrill of confidence, independence and joy coursed up
our spinal column, as we turned and remarked to the
second best member of the family, that, as a successful
farmer, we felt sure we would prove a "terror."   The
dogs sportively ran hither and thither, in search of anything from a fly up to a mosquito, and seemed to say,
" Go it, old man, and we'll keep off the animals!"

We were very happy.   After some years spent in a
" work-shop," the freedom of the plains, the absence of
crowds of humanity, the bracing air and the wildness of
the scenery, raised our soul—our very being—mountains
high in the scale of jubilant joy, the like of which we
never had before experienced.   Talk to us about your
brown stone fronts, your gilded halls and your palatial
homes!   We would not have traded our " homestead "
on the wild frontier of Minnesota for forty thousand
brown-stones, nor our oxen for a gilded hall big as the
prairie over which we traveled.   We sang out, as we
snapped our whip over the backs of our team, " Oh,
for a home in the wildwood," and the chorus was entered into by the whole family.

At last, after a two days' ride, we arrived at our homestead, where previously a house had been provided, in
the shape of a log cabin with a bark roof.   After getting
settled, and putting a bell on the cow, we completed

arrangements for a first crop by putting in two acres of
breaking to barley and the other five to turnips—re-
serving half an acre for a garden. Things went on
swimmingly for a time and we voted the enterprise an
entire success, and our ability to manage and carry on
the farming business, A, No. 1. So it would have been,
if "nothing had happened." The first reverse occurred
with the calf: In an anxiety to take in a little sustenance during the night, it had rammed its head through
a crack in the fence, and in the morning there it hung,
as inanimate a young bovine as could have been found
in any country. The potatoes came up finely, but were
taken entire charge of by the bugs; the corn made one
or two partial breakfasts for the blackbirds in that vicinity, and the cow ate so many wild leeks, or something,
that she was sick most of the time; the flies wore the
oxen out so badly, that we had to sit up with them
nights, and finally they "passed in their chips." The
badgers and things had, in the meantime, gotten away
with the poultry department, and the dogs were rapidly
emaciating for want of the substantials necessary to keep
a dog effective. In fact our property became rapidly
absorbed by the various kinds of demands made upon
it by that new region; our two pigs grew so thin that
they walked out at a crack in their pen, and we never
knew anything further of their history; probably if the
bears that infested the neighborhood could speak the
English language they might be able to contribute
something as to the closing scenes in the lives of those
two hogs. At the end of six months we walked out of
that country, with our family, all the members of which

had been spared by a merciful providence, though in a considerably demoralized condition—and headed our domestic procession toward the nearest settlement. With the baby on one arm, and the grindstone under the other—all the property that remained, as the cart had fallen to pieces through the influence of the dry atmosphere—we finally reached civilization. The oldest boy led the remains of the last dog with a piece of bark attached in the vicinity of where the dog's bark was located in his more palmy days, and previous to his losing so much of his wonted vigor. It is impossible for those not knowing how it is themselves, to appreciate the soul-soothing comfort enjoyed since, by that family, in the full consciousness of having made so liberal and useful a contribution toward the noble work of opening up a new country. And we say to all desiring free homes in the West, and especially if you are a discontented mechanic and know nothing about farming, go thou, and you'll do likewise.

THINGS HAVE CHANGED.

THERE they go, and we are reminded. The things that are going are two horses—loaded with bells—a big sleigh loaded with youth and beauty, or, in other words, shouting, laughing boys and girls. The bright moon-beams glitter on the frosty snow, and the bells chime out on the clear winter air, while the passengers—if they only realize it—are in the midst of one of the few rollicking, careless, happy acts of life. They will pardon us if we sit back here on a nail-keg, in our dimly-lit sanctum, and just merely intimate to ourself that they are a pack of addle-headed, giggling ninnies, running out the life of the poor horses to serve their foolishness. You see, the writer has been there, and knows how it is himself. We thought it was perfectly enchanting then, and the most proper thing on top of earth—or under it, for that matter. But you see, when crows-feet begin to cluster about one's eyes, forming festoons of dignity and staidness, things seem different. We can scarcely credit our senses when we say we have been there and actually enjoyed it. Just crawling into the back seat, on the bottom of a sleigh, snuggling **down between two robes,** with Deborah Jane

Smith close to us on the south side and right between the same identical coverlets and blankets. Whew! And when the sleigh runner would strike even the smallest obstruction on our side, how it would set us over southward, and the same with Deb. on the other side. How we would finally just slide our arm around her waist, for fear the sled would strike some little frozen thing in the road, and that sweet creature, D. J. Smith, Esquiress, would go up in a baloon, and leave us forever; such a mishap we knew to be entirely improbable, but you see we were animated by an innate desire to leave no stone unturned to avoid the most remote possibility in the case, and Deborah always seemed to coincide as to the wisdom of our precautionary movements, and so we hung on. The bells jingle now just as they did then; the five miles to the taffy-pull, apple-cut or spelling-school, seemed to be only as many rods, and at that time we were about the same quality of fool as those who just chased by our door; running chiefly to "girl" and the cultivation of a sickly mustache. Alas! for those days. 'Tis ignorant to be bliss, when 'tis wise to be foolish. Poor Deborah; she thought "a heap" of us, and at that time would have contracted to do our washing for life, at a very low rate; and we longed to cut stove-wood in the back yard, for her comfort, just as long as we were able to shoulder an axe. But it was of no use; we never made the "set-off," and now Deb. spanks another fellow's babies, and we cut wood and pack wash-water for another person. But, as we remarked at the beginning, things have changed. Sleigh-bells have no charm for us now; they have been displaced by rattle-boxes, and sleighs, by hobby-horses. Instead of riding now, we go on foot, because it is more within our means, and far healthier, you know. Instead of spending our evenings at taffy-pulls, etc., we do all manner of chores about the ranch where we reside, trot baby on our knee till it aches, shave kindlings, rock the cradle, look after the paragoric department, and any such harmless and exhilerating pastimes as may be lying about loose requiring attention. And, while rioting amid such tangible sports as these, is it to be wondered at that we should vote these sleigh-riders a pack of silly creatures?—Sour grapes!

NATURE'S DECAY.

AS WE sit in the seclusion of a viny bower, in the twilight of a dying day, a feeling of saddest melancholy steals unbidden o'er our heart. All Nature, save her warning sentinels, is hushed to a silence that weighs heavily down upon mind and soul. The tide of human struggle has sought its harbor for the night, and now, in the repose of eventide, the little stars peep out with modest twinkle from behind their veil of blue. Even the last warble of the songster has closed, and the sweet singer has sought his leafy bower to await the approach of a new-born day. The silence of the time is worse than broken, however, by the rasping rattle—the mournful creaking—of the night harbingers of the season, and the cricket and katy-did tell us again that the green **robe of the earth** is fading, and life in **all** of Nature's beauty is drawing to a close. The foliage is already changing with the palor of death, and soon all will drop, fiery-hued, to enrich the mother earth with their decaying fibers. The sounds of the insect warners of approaching death is grand **in its** monotonous melancholy, and the heart is filled with sadness as the mind reflects upon the end of life. By eye and **ear we are** warned of the near and speedy approach of that dark chamber which will receive our expended forms, and hold, for perhaps ceaseless ages, the very forgetfulness of our souls. How near it is we know not, we only know that it is near. All this dying beauty about us is but a warning; we sprout up in childhood, bloom **in** youth and, in faded semblance of our former selves, **are** quickly plucked from the bough of life, and **laid low in** an earthy receptacle; as quickly to be forgotten and succeeded **as the** crimson leaf, that pleases the eye for an instant, in its passage from its parent stem to its grand-parent earth. The early-autumn evening is inexpressibly sad in its melancholy silence, and in its dying beauty and sounds—passing, passing **away.**

THREE OLD GENTLEMEN.

HAPPENING into a store the other evening, we discovered three venerable old gentlemen engaged in a regular old-fashioned confab, in which they were living over the days of their boyhood and young manhood. All being intelligent men, with lives brim full of "scene" and "event," we became intensely interested as we quietly listened to the stories and experiences of men who were men before we were born.

One old gentleman was descanting upon the characteristics and peculiarities of the various peoples of the earth, and he asserted that the Laplanders were the most honorable and honest people in the world. At this, another of the trio became a little nervous, and as he looked over his spectacles very sharply at the speaker, he remarked:

"Now, friend A——, be a leetle careful when you say the Laplanders are the *honestest* of all people. I think there's a heap of honest folks that ain't Laplanders—I b'lieve Americans average tolerable, like, with any body else, you know."

"Oh, yes, neighbor B——," returned the first speaker, " I ain't sayin' anything against the Americans—I believe my own people are good. But, neighbor, let me tell you how honest the Laplanders are. A friend of mine was traveling in that country once, over the eternal fields of snow, in a sledge drawn by dogs; it was a day's journey sometimes from one settlement to another. This friend of mine stayed all night with a family of them, and the next day made a very long day's journey over a dreary waste of country, arriving at a settlement very late in the evening, having traveled nearly a hundred miles. After he had become settled for the night, had eaten his supper, and was about to lie down on his robes, in the hospitable hut, another arrival was announced at the door, and in a moment more the Laplander woman at whose hut he had spent the previous night, entered. Of course, my friend was greatly astonished to see her, and inquired what ' in nat'er's name ' she came so far after him, and what could have induced her to brave the perils of such a trip. She smiled, and after seating herself on a rug before the fire, she asked him if he had not lost something. He said he hadn't missed any part of his effects, but suddenly thought of his money, and felt in his pouch, and found that a bag, containing several hundred dollars, was gone, when he excitedly assured her that all his gold was missing. She smiled again, reached into the bosom of her fur wraps, and drew forth the bag, saying she had found it shortly after his departure; that she had hastened to overtake him, with her own sledge and dogs, that she might restore to him his lost treasure—and she handed my friend his money-bag, with not a coin missing. My friend, as may well be imagined, was well nigh over-whelmed by such an evidence of honor and integrity, and hastened to offer her a share of it as a reward for her honesty and the hardships she had undergone that she might restore it to him. But—would you believe it?—no amount of entreaty could induce her to accept of a single piece of it. She modestly said that her people never accepted pay for being honest—that their belief and practice was to be honest because of the beauty of honesty alone; and all the reward he was permitted to bestow upon her was a warm kiss on her forehead—which is the manner in that country of acknowledging a courtesy or favor. "Now," continued the speaker, with a slight air of triumph, "how many Americans are as honest and Godlike as that poor Laplander woman, neighbor B——?"

"Well now, I acknowledge that *was* a really noble act; but I insist there's lots of Americans who'd be just as honorable as that—I b'lieve I'd do it myself; wouldn't you, friend C——?" addressing the third old gentleman, who had been quietly listening.

"Well, no; I don't think I'd have followed him so far—but I might have kept it for him," he replied.

"Well, now," continued the defender of American honor, "I know of an instance that will go to show that Americans are just as honest as Laplanders. It was the time of the Revolutionary War, and my father knew the man well. He was a man who had been pressed into the British army; he got a chance to desert and made his escape to the little American army, an' it was just before the surrender of Burgoyne. As he was making his way along to the American lines, he came upon a monstrons canvas bag of gold lying right in the road; it was so heavy that he could scarcely carry it, and so he dragged it along to a neighboring field, where plowing had been done, and he just lifted up one of the sods, laid the bag in, and tipped the sod back, covering the money completely from sight, and, after making an observation or two, so that he might find it again, continued on his way. After traveling an hour or so, he met a man on a powerful horse, coming like mad along the road, the animal white with foam. As he came near he shouted to the footman:

" My man, have you traveled this road far?"

" A considerable distance," he replied.

" Did you find anything?" he nervously asked as he drew up his fretful and prancing steed.

" Have you lost anything?"

" Yes, indeed!" he almost screamed; "I am the paymaster of Washington's army, and I was on my way, with a bag of gold, to pay off the soldiers. I have lost the gold out of my saddle-bags somewhere, and if I cannot find it I will have to fly from the country."

" 'That *is* a sad thing,' replied the footman; 'come, and I will go back with you and assist in the search, and we may be able to at least find some trace of the missing treasure.' "

" After a careful march of several miles, watching for even a sign that might indicate where it had been lost, the footman suddenly stopped and said:

" 'Here! This looks like a mark in the dust where it had been dropped, and dragged away.' Then he

went away over into the field, turned back the sod,
dragged out the sack of gold, and lifted it up to the
horseman, who was in a perfect and trembling ecstacy
of joy. He nervously tore open the mouth of the sack
and handed down to the footman a handful of the shining gold, but he met with this reply :

"'No, sir; I want none of it; I am an American, and
have just fled from the British army, and am making
my way to the Americans to give them my assistance
against the oppressors of our country; take the gold
and pay it all to the poor suffering soldiers, who need
it far more than I do, and I will follow you on foot as
fast as possible.' There now," remarked the speaker,
"isn't that a parallel case of honesty?"

"Oh, yes; but in *those* days there were *patriots* in
America!"

"Well, there are plenty of patriots in this country
yet. Look at the heroism that was displayed in the
war of the Rebellion! I know there are piles of rascals
in the land; but I tell you there's an army of honest
patriots, too."

"Oh, yes, that's so, I'll allow. How's your apple-
trees coming out this spring, neighbor B——; were
any of your young trees killed by the frost and sunshine?"

Thus ended a pleasant little scrap of conversation between three noble old gentlemen, in which was blended
both interest and history. Men who can speak of such
events from personal knowledge are growing scarce and
the interest and value of their recitals are correspondingly increased.

A QUIET WALK.

A MORNING or two ago was a quiet, monotonous kind of a morning; a morning when one could feel sort of sad without singing any. We felt constrained to take a walk, and so we did. Solitude is good, when one feels solitary, and so we sought the seclusion of the groves. As we remarked, it was a singularly singular morning; a quiet, damp air stirred the boughs overhead; all nature seemed in repose; everything acted as if waiting for something to happen. The little birds sat quietly on the limbs, some of them engaged in making their morning toilet, by stroking down their glossy feathers, or picking fleas and things out from under their wings. The untiring grub worms were the only creatures that seemed to be full of business. As we would pass a dead tree, several of them could be heard inside the decayed trunk, their saws cutting away with regular and unceasing energy, just as though they had a government contract in war time. Pretty soon the quietude of the time was broken by a loon which passed over screaming as though some great convulsion of the elements followed in his rear. From over the stream came the sad, plaintive lullaby of the

Indian mother, as in its barken cradle she rocked the infant to and fro, for the purpose, no doubt, of distracting its attention from the pangs of an early attack of the stomach-ache; the murmur of the river, the moan of the zephyrs among the tops of the pine trees, all conspired to make one feel as though it were " a fearful thing to live." We felt the force of this quotation to almost an oppressive extent, and agreed with ourself that there was only one thing that could "raise it" in the way of fearfulness, and that was, to die. We would stake our money on living, fearful as it is, at all times and under all circumstances, however, win or lose. Our soul seemed sad; and the reflections incident to solitude crowded in upon our mind to such an extent that we seemed transported to another world, for the time being, and were unconscious of everything save the most sublime meditations as we gazed away up into the blue vault of heaven; so deeply intensified had become our whole being that it is very difficult to decide whether or no we should not have been actually taken away from this cold earth then and there, had it not been for the timely relief brought to us by a neighbor's dog. He had probably seen us through the trees, "mooning around" in what seemed to him a most idiotic manner, and deemed our case one that demanded immediate and earnest consideration,—his earnestness was praiseworthy; the first pass he made carried away our rear guard altogether, and had we not been fortunate enough to find a club near at hand, his next assault would probably carried our rear bastion completely. Fortunately, however, we dissuaded him from any further advances, and being fully brought to consciousness again, we sought our ivy-cot, by the back way, arriving just in time for breakfast, and during the breakfast-hour we explained how it all happened, and got our trousers mended.

***

HIGH GATES.

PARENTS who have any regard for the comfort of young cooing lovers should remember to construct their front gates only high enough for young people to enjoy a cozy lean-too over the top of it. A few evenings ago *he* called upon the object of his affection; and after tarrying within, until an advanced hour in the evening, she accompanied him to the gate to take a last little leave of him, and have a last little talk thereover. It was at a residence up on ——street, and the gate to that place is very high, and the lovers could neither get elbow rests, nor could they reach over the top to get a little "smack." So, as they just happened to remember that there was one little point that they hadn't talked over quite enough, they slid along to the gate of the next neighbor—a few feet to the left—which offered all the conveniences for such a momentous occasion, and we leave them, for a moment, to see what the owner of the invaded premises was doing. He was a very wakeful old gentleman, and hearing his gate creak he rose from his bed and peering out from behind the curtain he distinguished, in the very uncertain light without, what he took for two robbers, making their final arrangements for a descent upon his home, and his spoons, and his Brittannia ware. To nip their infamous plan in the bud, the venerable gentleman slipped out to the back shed, where Carlo was tied up, and unbuckling the collar and opening the back door he remarked, "Seek 'im Carlo!" and then hurried through to the front window to take notes. He arrived just in time to see a cloud of crinoline sailing for his neighbor's door, as Carlo came tearing round into the front yard; and in less time than it takes to tell it—yea, less than it does to think it—Carlo had struck a point on the remaining robber, and proceeded to flush him in the most impetuous manner. About all the astonished old gentleman could observe, in short, was the screaming object rushing toward his neighbor's, a white streak —Carlo—shooting toward the gate, and a dark column going down street like an avalanche, yelling, "Git eout!" at the end of every distinct canter. The next morning, however, the old gentleman found, out at the gate, a white handkerchief, and an irregularly square piece of steel-gray cassimere, a remnant of shirting and a cardinal red necktie. It was really a stirring moment and although the old gentleman is one of the kindest and best of men, he is worse than a run of smallpox on "robbers," and so is Carlo.

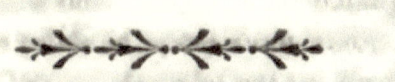

WASHING DAY.

THIS is a day of great celebrity, more ancient than St. Patrick's day or Washington's birthday. In all well regulated families, this holiday occurs fifty-two times in the year, and Monday is the day set apart for its observance. But as the Jews and Christians disagree as to which day of the week Sunday comes on, so, different families disagree as to which day washing day comes; some even stave it off until Saturday afternoon, and do their ironing the next week. In families that are well put together, however, washing day comes about four a. m., on Monday morning. The first intimation the head of the household receives of its coming, is a sharp nudge somewhere in the vicinity of the fifth rib, just as he is indulging in a fine feast, or attending a wedding, in his dreams; he is informed that it is wash day, and, as the washing is peculiarly heavy that week, an early start is indispensible; he is called "Dear Albert, get up," several times, and at last, in a fearfully agitated state of mind, and stupid for the want of just two hours' more sleep, he slides out on the floor, and sits down on the oil-cloth to cool off till he can wake up. Finally he gropes about and gets his pants

and stumbles into them, but does not discover that he
has them on wrong side in front, until he goes to button
on his suspenders. Wife tells him about this time to
build a fire, put on the boiler, carry a tub full of water
and separate the colored clothing from the white, and
if she can get the baby to sleep, she will be out by that
time; of course you are to put on the tea-kettle, grind
the coffee, cut the meat and split up some wood in the
meantime. After a while Albert comes to the tub and
puts his first turn of water into the thing, only to see it
spurt out of every crack and go toward dampening the
vegetation just outside the door; it has been left in the
sun since the last similar holiday, and the staves are
standing around in rows like a platoon of drunken soldiers. There is only one way to mend that tub, and
that is to keep it damp till it swells shut. He pushes
the upper hoop up a little, gets some more water, and
with the dipper keeps the thing damp all around while
he reclines on the floor, his legs on either side of the establishment, waiting patiently for the swelling to develop itself. Wife gets the baby asleep about seven a. m.,
and comes out to find the fire out, the kettle boiled dry,
the flies all over the meat, and the dear husband she
routed out at four o'clock, in happy unconsciousness
of passing events, leaning over the tub fast asleep.
"House-warming" commences about this time, by
building a fire and introducing a series of lectures more
animated than classical. Albert responds but feebly,
but is encouraged a little by seeing that the staves of the
tub have in the meantime waltzed together, and the tub
ready for any reasonable amount of moisture. He strikes

out for the well, while the chairs, table and dishes are dancing merrily inside, and things about that particular kitchen are emphatically lively; for, lost time must be made up. Albert, thoroughly aroused by this time perfectly deluges every hollow vessel in the house, and winds up by kicking the cat clear into the next room, and giving the dog an "early start" by sousing the last bucket of water all over him. Finally Albert gets through with his part of the observance, and, after an extremely frugal repast, he betakes himself to business, thinking that an early start on washing day, and a pleasant wife, are among the prime blessings of earth.

AN EDITOR AS A DEER HUNTER.

FOR twenty or thirty days, as we passed along the street, or happened into the village post-office, during the prevalence of the first snows, we could hear but little among the leisure men save broken sentences, such as "Good tracking day,"— "Deer"—"Fat now"—"Two every day," etc. At first we did not notice these mutterings that might be heard around the bar-room stoves and the street corners, because the subject was one out of our line, and but Greek, in phraseology to us, at best. But after hearing such talk for a week or two, it began to sound like the tick of an ancient clock, or the endless rasping of a grub-worm in a fence-post. These were the premonitory symptoms. The third week we began to dream of parks filled with deer, and of ourself roosting on the fence shooting them down with a squirt-gun and skinning them with a candle. Every night we were at it, until hunting deer became our nightmare, and we actually became possessed of the buck tremens. We finally told wife how it was, and that nothing would appease us save blood and venison steak; we felt it to be our duty to go forth and bring forth a buck, and so forth; because, our children must have meat, and there was nothing that would prevent an attack of scurvy in the family like good fat venison. Sure enough, that very evening the snow clouds rolled up in the west, and a fresh fall of that article sufficient for good tracking **was** inevitable. During the afternoon and evening all was life and animation wherever we moved—for you see we had it bad. At the office we fixed things to admit of our absence a day or two, and purchased an ample supply of the munitions of war. We sat down and wrote several very vigorous editorial articles—one on the financial condition of the world previous to the flood as a sort of an excuse for the present hard times for money; one, giving our opinion as to what the hieroglyphics on the inside of the Pyramids of Egypt meant in English; an exhaustive article to the effect that the sheep over which King David presided, when a boy, were nothing more nor less than the deer of the present day, and a treatise upon the most successful manner of hunting the wild deer, which we wrote up for publication in our paper for the especial benefit of amateur sportsmen. We left plenty of "copy" so that our office boy might not run short of business, while we went into the adjacent forests to take a supply of venison for the winter. When tea time arrived we reported at our domicile, loaded down with supplies, including a hundred cartridges which had to be warmed, and the tallow wiped off them, during the evening, besides an immense amount of other fixing up, so as to be prepared for a large amount of slaughter, and be as well fixed as the fifty other hunters who would be sure to be out next morning. We had to grind our tomahawk, whet the knife, oil up the rifle, test the compass with the poker, provide matches, get a hunting suit prepared, and a four o'clock breakfast set at half-cock in order to facilitate matters in the morning. But, upon entering the rear door of our cot, wife met us with a reminder that the neighborhood "sociable" met that evening, and as it was the first sociable of the season it was our bounden duty to attend; it would never do not to go to the first sociable, she continued, as she seated herself and worked away at darning up the various places in our best pants that had been rented, like. After disencumbering ourself of our cargo, we sat down on the edge of the washtub to think a little. We had clean forgotten the sociable; wife was right—we ought to attend; she was always right, and we knew it. Accordingly we vigorously went to work rubbing the grease off the cartridges up to "sociable" hour, and after we came back labored faithfully in our preparations until after midnight, in the interest of deer and on behalf of a meat hungry family. Daylight found us in the wilderness, and sunrise revealed to us a "fresh track," and we vigorously and watchfully pursued that deer most of the

day. Although only an amateur ourself, we felt sure
our operations in rear of that animal bordered closely
on the professional; whenever coming to an "opening"
we would strike an animated canter, and when in the
thick brush we elongated our neck, ever and anon
creeping on hands and knees through the tangled brush
wood, straining our eyes, and maintaining a ceaseless
cock on both ears for sounds. We had often heard old
hunters telling about "close hunting;" and we resolved
that if close hunting would overhaul the venison we
had followed the livelong day, he was bound to become
our meat before nightfall. Just as the sun was settling
down behind the jack-pine forest in the west, we ran
across another hunter, who had a fine deer on his back
and was trudging toward town with the result of *his*
day's chase. We conferred with him as to what was
necessary in order that we might get *our* deer similarly
located with his, and showed him the beautiful fresh
track we had been following, round and round, all day.
He gazed at it briefly, and then, as he smole a smile,
he informed us that it was quite unreasonable for us to
expect to find a deer by following a rabbit track—no
matter if we followed it for six months. For about a
minute or two we felt like a victim of the yellow jaun-
dice; our legs got weak, and we commenced perspiring. We felt homesick, and wanted to go home if we
could do so, and feel as though we hadn't been gone.
We got the man to promise that, if we would carry his
deer home for him, he wouldn't say anything about it.
We did, and he didn't.

A STROLL.

WE STRAYED away from the "din," the other day, and after a due amount of manual labor and leg-weariness, we found ourself sitting on the highast peak that *peaks* in this vicinity. Talk about high, too, that peak was high, you better believe. We sat with our legs—our limbs, pardon us—dangling over the crags, and our soul soaring aloft o'er the world below—our boot-sole, we refer to—while our perspiring and manly brow was softly wiped by the hands of fairies with the silken cobwebs of the skies; the wings of the passing zephyrs fanned our "royal *cheek*," and the flaky cloudlets hung like a canopy of lace, woven by fairy fingers, over head, and we sat among the spirits of the air peering out from the rich folds of our throne and gazing down, down, down, upon the common world below. A green pasture in the vale beneath was dotted with a loving herd, and we heard them loo in their lowly vale—some black, some brindle, and others pale. They nipped the grass and wagged their tail, or scratched their sides against a rail. The lambs in the pasture skipped and jumped, the jaybird sang and the bittern pumped. **The** soft rays of an evening sun fell warmly upon the landscape, and tinged the blue lake with streaks of gold, and made darker the shadows of the distant hills. As we gazed out and down upon the beautiful world filled with its fretted throng, we felt like a king—a sunbeam for a scepter, and the crescent moon for a crown. This fancy did not last long, however, for just as our imagination had placed us as a kingly commander at the head of the human family, a "business" fairy rested on the south corner of our ear and whispered softly that it was time we "climbed down" from our elevation and proceeded home to saw some wood with which to cook the supper. This broke the beautiful chain of fancy, and we felt anew our common mortality; we pinched ourself to make sure, and cried "Ouch!" and then, lighting our cob pipe, we prepared to come down from among the guests of heaven's portico, to the common level of the wheelbarrow brigade. But, some day, we shall ascend the cliffs again, and wink love to Venus and flip pebbles into the clouds beneath us.

A Chicago communist predicts that the red flag of the commune "is destined in the near future to occupy a higher position than the 'Star-spangled Banner.'" That chap ought to be spoken to by a cannon, loaded with skunks.

If "charity covers a multitude of sins," about how many does an average church fair cover?

OUR AMBITIONS.

IN EARLY life the average American boy becomes infatuated with almost everything, but permanently attached to nothing. Of course, his opportunity for seeing the world has a good deal to do with his ambitions during boyhood; generally, the more things he sees, and the less he sees of them, the more ardent is his desire to adopt the life of every kind of man suggested by the sights he has witnessed—the strange and attractive glimpses he has been favored with. The country boy, for instance, is liable to have his ambition aroused to do something in the world, for the first time, when the old chap comes round to mend tinware—the *iti*nerant tinker. When he sees his mother getting out her leaky coffee-pot, her dipper that needs a new bottom, the biscuit-cutter that wants the handle soldered on, and sees the professional man locating himself in the corner, with all the assurance of a public benefactor, and the professional *nonchalance* of a man who has mastered his business in its various ramifications, from mending a pint cup to fastening the handle on to a tin pepper-box, the young American receives his first stroke of do-somethingness. He generally takes

up a position in front of the tinkerinktum professor, and
with his hands behind his back, his tongue out, and his
legs bowed back, he gazes with admiring wonder, giving evidence of the intensity of his thoughts by sort of
snoring and working the big toe of his left foot; and
the old tinsmith can rest assured that, for once, he is
looked upon as the greatest known mogul—the dia-
mond-pointed, and crowning glory of the human family,—the sunflower of creation. For the month following, he teases his mother to try and prevail upon his
father to have him educated for a tinker, and this is his
first ambition—the first visible development of the bud
that one day is to develop into the full-blown rose of
success. Of course, this disturbance of his soul is but
the beginning of the series, and only lasts till the clock-
fixer comes around, or the family cobbler makes his annual visit—when he revels in pictures of the future, composed of brass wheels, pendulums, and of pegs, half-
soles, awls, bristles and wax. All these and many other
grand vocations he resolves to adopt, in their turn, and
dreams of them at night, in undisturbed bliss until he,
unluckily for his peace of mind, attends the first circus
—then, his contentment and serenity of mind are literally torn in tatters. The wonderful beings he sees
there, and the still more wonderful things he sees them
doing, bewilder his senses for a year afterward. The
clown, the riders, and the tumblers who spring through
the air in their spangled tights almost upset his reason,
and he soon conceives the idea of aspiring to even so
great and dizzy a height in the catalogue of human
possibilities. Thus he goes on from one object to an-

other till he reaches his majority, and is next seen in the streets of the city, starting out for himself in the world. With his earthly treasures done up in a bandana handkerchief, and a card of gingerbread in his hand, he saunters along the crowded thoroughfare, with upturned face reading the world of signs along the street, in almost unconscious astonishment. Right here is one of the most important points in his life-journey. He is all adrift with no other object in view than the procuring of his first job. His natural abilities and his attainments are sufficient, if developed by the proper friction, to make a man of him; but not enough, probably, to raise him from the misfortune of a first wrong or unlucky step—a start into a channel that will lead him gradually lower instead of steadily higher. So, really, we seem to be children of fate, and after all, chance settles our lives, in a majority of cases; for, as we all have experienced similar ambitions during our earlier days, so have we drifted into the various positions we occupy in life—into the vocations we now follow—without scarcely choosing in advance, or knowing beforehand what was likely to transpire to fix our after course in the world. A "straw" can, and does, make or unmake a life.

LEARNING TO MILK.

URING a somewhat varied life, we have taken a hand at almost everything, from being boss of a stone-quarry down to running the culinary department of a flatboat. We had come to boast that there was scarcely anything we hadn't done, and there were mighty few things we couldn't do—in our own mind there were not any of the latter. It was only recently that we ran against something that we hadn't tried before, and which we have not accomplished, even at the present writing. Our folks got a cow; the question was raised as to who should do the milking; after a good deal of earnest caucusing, it was unanimously resolved that,—your "Uncle Dudley" should have the honor of attending to that little ceremony, morning and evening. Having been chosen to the position of milkmaid by an unanimous vote, we could not find it in our gizzard to decline. We never had milked, and were somewhat bashful in the presence of a cow, anyway,— and this one was a frisky sort of heifer, too. But, we had always heard that kindness would enable a person to become ever so familiar with a dumb animal of almost any sort; so, with a tin bucket suspended from our left arm and our hat over on our right ear, we started for the quarters occupied by her heifership out in the barn, whistling "Comin' thro' the Rye," by way of keeping our courage up, and letting her know that we were in a kindly frame of mind.

As we entered the barn we remarked, "So-o-o, Mariar! nice cow-y, so-o-o!" She responded, "Baw-aw-aw!" or words to that effect, as she surveyed us by a long, interested stare, and she stepped around somewhat nervously and observed, "Moo-oo-oo-e!" We said "So-o-o-a!" several times, and then slipped in along side of her, called her pet names, and kind of reached full arm length, to catch hold of the dairy division of her anatomy; she kicked up terribly on *that* flank, and we retired precipitately, though in tolerably good order, to the rear—the tin bucket catching the heft of the first pass made by her north-west heel. The bucket sort of caved in some on the side where she struck it; pretty soon it occurred to us that we might have advanced on the "wrong side"—that possibly she was used to being milked left-handed. After saying several endearing things that we imagined would come within the appreciation of an intelligent cow, we ventured in on the other side, and stroked her a little with the tips of our fingers. Then we got down on our knees and reached out and grasped hold of one of the protuberances underneath, that was a part of the lacteal tank, or udder. She immediately scratched our hand off with her hind foot, and a second pass knocked off our hat and skinned our left ear. Then we took a back seat again, and contemplated the situation and made a few

remarks, more or less pertinent to the condition of
things, as they then stood. Our Irish blood commenced
racking our Yankee frame, and we concluded if that
was her game, we'd see. Getting the wrecked bucket
well up on our arm, we advanced to the fray with a determined caution, that meant business—we had first
thought of throwing up earthworks and advancing under cover, but that last kick altered our plans. Watching a favorable opportunity we closed in with her, got
our left leg locked in with her hind ones, to keep her
from kicking the bucket or our ear again, and gobbled
on with both hands to the protuberances aforesaid;
about that time the "bawl" opened. She gave one
challenging snort, ran ahead into the manger, flew up
behind, and before we had time to get settled to our
work we were standing on our head and shoulders out
in the middle of the barn floor. Our pants were half
torn off, and several teeth had become loosened in some
way, and that bucket looked like a gaudy tinsel, and
was about the shape of a saddle-flap or a Chinese fan.
Then we took another rest—the exercise was almost too
vigorous to keep right at it all the time. After figuring
on the probability of our winning or dying by following
that sort of amusement up, it seemed to figure out that
many such onslaughts would wear us out, while the cow
would remain in good health. Besides, it was well to
find some one thing in life that we couldn't do, else our
vanity might ruin us—and to milk that heifer seemed
to be the one thing we couldn't do, successfully, in this
world. Some people can never get the "slight" of
milking a cow. We returned home and told the family

that our "slight" was bad, and that we should be re-
luctantly (in a horn) compelled to decline the honor
they had seen fit to confer—that we could do anything
else but milk.

COLLECTING.

COLLECTIONS are lively these days. We
traveled all day on Monday last, determined to
"raise the wind" or nearly perish in the attempt—for we had grown weary of gazing at the old
unpaid accounts that adorned the pages of our account-
book. After laboring all day with our delinquents, we
sat down about dusk on a lonesome corner of a back
street to take an account of what we had collected during the day, and found we had accomplished wonders
—when considering the fact that we are a very poor
collector, and that it is a close time for money. We
found that we had collected the following amounts of
money and chattels, all of which we were carrying
homeward in a monster tin pan—which was one among
the number of articles we had secured—to wit: First,
we pulled out a large iron spoon, and laid it down on
the grass; next came a tin pepper-box; then a ten-cent
scrip; a pound of starch, two bars of soap, a pound of
stearine candles, and then a twenty-five cent scrip;
next came a tin stew-pan, and a match-safe; some more
scrip, and a dollar bill, with its northeast corner torn off
and missing; next was fifty cents worth of coffee and

four ounces of tea; a sack of dairy salt, and a stone-china butter-dish; then a set of tea-spoons—crinkled tin—and another pepper box; this seemed to us an undue number of pepper boxes, but never mind—it was a second hand box, and was the only thing the poor man had, who owed us, and so we took it, that he might be entirely unencumbered with personal property. Then we yanked out a gridiron, and a dozen patent clothes-pins; three five-cent, and five three-cent nickels; then a bottle of pepper-sauce, a box of condition powders, and a large piece of earthen ware with a handle on one side. This was the result, and after all, we flattered ourself that there were many worse collectors in the world than ourself. As the entire bill of goods lay all about on the green grass, the sight was a rich one, and we fancied ourself an East Indian merchantman, recently returned from a successful voyage. After feasting our eyes for a time, we gave a stout boy the odd pepper box to help us repack our effects and bring them into camp. Those persons who still owe us, can rest assured that we are "well heeled" on everything except money; we could handle a good deal more of that than we possess, with considerable satisfaction.

AFFECTATION.

THIS age is full of it; and when we think of its universal existence it is with a feeling of *unaffected* disgust. Look into all grades of society; look out upon the street; look into the public halls; into the churches, even, where the supposition is that sinners gather only to kneel in supplication for mercy and forgiveness. Upon every hand, as a rule, and with only isolated exceptions, the false stands out so brazenly and so universally as to have well-nigh crushed out the last vestige of the honest simplicity and true-heartedness that characterized a century ago. The poison of self-show having gained the upper hand in all the public channels of life, is even storming the sacred battlements of the domestic circle, and of home—the only remaining asylum where candid humanity may expect to find a refuge from the blighted mould of the prevailing affectation of the time. Dignity has been exchanged for it; true comfort has been extinguished by it, and virtue itself is allured from its throne and totters into the foul gulf set for its destruction.

This is a strong picture, but one that will prove itself by reflection. Halt, for an instant, in the current of life, and gaze at the picture as presented, and then consider the underlying reality—the comparison of a thing you have thought but little about, perhaps, because of its universality, will at once amaze you, as you gaze upon the false character, false show, false pretenses, false words and false system of living that you now realize actually exist. And once you realize the conditions of life now prevailing, you must needs resolve to do battle against the mocking monster that strides through the land, instead of encouraging his ravenous destruction by " doing as others do."

It has actually come to such a state that it is unpopular, not to say unprofitable, to do right on all occasions. Persons are even made to blush, who seek to act in life as God intends they should, in the presence of what is *popular* and fashionable.

To pay as you go, and dress accordingly, has become absolutely ridiculous.

To live as becomes your means soon brings the finger of showy and empty pride to point you out as an unworthy associate.

To soil your hands with honest toil very quickly unfits you to mingle in " society; " for, affectation's laces are very sensitive to the brown of nature's callings, and starts like a guilty thing, that it is, from the honest **touch** of industry—reality.

The world, basking as it has for many decades of time, beneath an overload of blessings and earthly stores, is becoming a very Sodom, that needs a carnival of destruction to sweep and purify it, and bring its people back to simple reality, and an unassuming mode of life, in principles and appearance, and to a *real* and not an affected worship of the Author of all good.

Even many of the leaders and teachers of the time have become stained with the prevailing plague of affectation, and if the counselors of the young are to assume that fashion must take the place of simplicity, where are the generations yet to come, to look, for a guide to the true, the dignified and the real virtues of life? For we claim that to practice affectation in a single thing will lead to the unreal in all things. We are reminded forcibly that this affectation is invading many precincts which should lie out of reach of its contaminating influence, by what a writer in one of our leading magazines recently said, after examining certain school reports from the Western States. He says: "By the way, we do not like the speaking of the salaries of teachers as 'wages,' which is so common throughout these reports, as this in itself alone is sufficient to degrade the office in popular estimation to the level of the mechanic or the domestic servant." If this be true, "popular estimation" in the West is very badly informed, and who but the school teachers are responsible for the fact? "Wages" is used altogether as a word, and it means exactly the thing which it is used in the reports to signify. The use of "salary" as a more dignified and dignifying word is an absurd affectation which no sensible school teacher should encourage, and the thought implied in the writer's words, that the man or woman who receives wages for honest work, honestly done, is in some way degraded by the payment, is one which, if it exists in the popular mind, ought to be driven out as soon and as thoroughly as possible. It is for correcting precisely such notions as this that we pay our public school teachers their *wages*.

A PRINTER'S REVERY.

'T IS night, now, and here we stand at our printer's case, all alone, and in solitude—for it is very late, and the town, as well as this vast continent, is asleep, and unconscious of the events of the stilly night. We use no "copy" by which to be guided in our thoughts, but pick up the leaden types and form them into words and sentences as dictated by the force of a midnight revery of a laboring mortal away here on the borders of civilization. It is so still that the nibbling of a little mouse, off in one corner of the dingy room under the ink-board, sounds like the filing of a mill-saw on a frosty morning. We love deep, dark solitude sometimes. It seems to allow one to step between mortality and immortality, and look back over the troubled sea of the one, and ahead upon the enchanting landscape of the other, with the beacon of hope standing in relief, indicating the haven of final and eternal rest. The night-view from our window is one of almost supernatural splendor. All nature is hushed; the earth is draped in her first annual robe of purity, which glitters as if set with diamonds 'neath the rays of a full bright moon; the dark pine trees are laden and drooping with snow, and seem like pearly-draped willows standing sentinel o'er the sepulchres of the departed dead; the dancing Aurora in the icy north, casting a weird light upon the landscape, finishing a scene which, added to the still solitude of the hour, creates within one's soul an awe, becoming a child of Him who is the Author and perfecter of all these profound **wonders.** The candle burns low in the socket, the embers are fast dissolving into ashes, and we are reminded that this is but typical of life—first, feeble in our mortal weakness, then ablaze with life and fiery ambition, soon but a flickering flame, and quickly like the dying embers of the fire, fall into ashes and are forgotten of earth; we have run our race, fulfilled our mission, and passed away.

WHISKEY FOR A COLD.

HAVING an awfully grievous cold, we went down town to find a remedy. It had settled in the neighborhood of our bread-basket, and was so very bad that we began to fear consumption, and resolved to root it out at any cost, and no matter what the character of the remedy. Meeting a friend on the corner, we asked him did he know what would knock a bad cold, and says he, "I do, for a fact"—he had tried it, and knew it to be a dead-shot. He told us to go right off—if we could find any place where it was sold—and get a pint of whiskey, then four ounces

each of black and cayenne pepper, then go home, put
the pepper into the whiskey, warm the mixture, and
with our feet to the fire, spend the evening in its ab-
sorbtion, in the usual way. The idea was somewhat
revolting to a temperance man—particularly the pepper
part—but we went right off and got the things and returned home. We told our good wife to cease fretting
about our cough, ₁cause we had it now right by the appendix, and showed her the prescription. She advised
us to start in kind of gently on that kind of medicine,
till observations might be made of the effect, and a
guess arrived at as to the probable result. We felt awfully bad, and our newspaper would suffer if we got
sick, and so we absorbed about a gill at the first dose,
then drew a chair up to the hearth, and asked wife how
was her health. Pretty soon we commenced talking
rather cheerfully about "old times," and asked if she
remembered when we were married; and if so, if she
dreamed at that time that ourself was to be a great man,
and she to be our wife all the same; and if she thought
then that it would require at this date four trundle-beds
to hold the miscellaneous assortment of young tow-heads
who slammed doors about our domicile at the present
time. Then we felt so greatly improved in our general
health, that it was voted we should proceed immediately to get our vest around the outside of another gill of
the pepper, which we did. At about this stage in our
recovery, some old songs came into our mind, and we
sang, in a splendid wheel-barrow tone, everything in the
catalogue, from " Greenland's Icy Monntains " down to
"We Won't go Home till Morning." When we got

into some of the star pieces, a large proportion of our
posterity rolled out, and came tumbling into the room
to attend the concert and see what was the row with
their sire. We induced eight or ten of them to mount
our knees and shoulders, and had a family pyramid.
After a short season "among the Pyramids," we assured
the whole family that their immediate ancestor was entirely cured, or would be in a very short time; we felt
the cold that had penetrated our system, steadily cours-
ing its way out through the pores in a million little frosty
columns, and to keep up the mildness of our physical
temperature we drew on the commissary stores again.
We now happened to think of a little story, or incident
in our life, that would be almost sure to please the children. It was to the effect that when a boy, another
boy wagered his black-alder whistle against our barlow-
knife, that we couldn't stand on our head on one of the
joists above the cow-stable; and that we made the attempt, but turned clear over, and went down into the
stable, lighting astride of old brindle's back; how that
she waltzed about the stall, pawed the floor and bel-
lowed, finally throwing us off, and nearly kicked the
daylights out of us before we could scramble through
one of the little holes that usually appear in the rear end
of a cow stable. This recital pleased them to an exaggerated degree, and we prescribed again for our cold,
and cut a pigeon-wing about the room. Abraham
seemed delighted at the extraordinary antics of his usually staid, exacting sire, and asked what kind of medicine it was that was making us well so fast. He was
informed that it was a vegetable decoction called, by

the doctors, " Leonte-donte-terracticum," but common-
ly called " Opadildoc," or " Bug-juice," upon this occasion, done in red-pepper.   Jonathan, our second hope-
ful, said that Jo Smith could stand on his head on a
chair, and he wanted us to try it; of course we would
do anything to please the children, and up went our
heels, over went the chair, and down went the stovepipe.
About this time, wife advised that we go to bed, and
take a rest; and we did, for we felt a little tired, like.
Next morning we ascertained that our cold was slightly
worse, and our head immensely so—strange as it may
seem.

A MAN down in Indiana dropped dead at the polls
during the recent election.   We could not learn which
ticket he voted; therefore, we shall say nothing about
a special visitation of Divine wrath, until we learn the
man's politics.

WERE we to strive more, to practic *common* sense,
and less, to achieve *extraordinary* sense, we would be
considered far more sensible.

SECONDS chase the moment, the moment the hour,
the hour the day, the day the week, the week the
month, the month the year, the year the man, until he
is frightened over the brink of Time—a last leap, and
that, " a leap into the dark."

A GOVERNMENT MULE.

A GOOD deal has been said and written about the mule. We have often heard the expression, "Tougher'n a government mule," and many other similes at the expense of his long-earship. But not till a few days ago did we ever have a real good opportunity to get right down to solid and satisfying contemplation of this famous animal. There were 210 of them, and they were *en route* to the front to take a kick at the hostile Indians on the frontier. They had been packed—like sardines in a box—in the cars, for two mortal days, and then let out into a mule-pen, to rest and refresh themselves preparatory to being again packed in the cars to continue their journey to Fort Lincoln. We expected that after their enforced abstinence for so long a time from food and water that they would scarcely be able to walk when taken from the close, stifling cars to the pen; and we would not have been surprised had some of them been found to be dead. But no, that isn't the way with a mule, even under such painful circumstances. Though thin as wafers from the terrible squeeze through which they had gone, they came out rearing and tearing, making the cars fairly

rock with their scrambling **to get out,** literally clambering over one another to get into daylight. Each car
contained about eighteen, and the carnage that followed
their egress was nothing short of a terror. The **enclos-
ure was** small, and they were pretty **well crowded.
Each one of the** 210 seemed to vie with **the** other in
the matter of braying, and such an opera as set in would
put pandemonium clear in the shade. We took a posi-
tion astride the high board fence, and gazed intently
down into the forest of **ears and** heels for three mortal
hours, studying mule character. **As a** vocalist, we consider the mule ahead of **everything.** Comparing it with
a chorus by 200 **mules,** an earthquake—with Vesuvius
as head singer—sinks into insignificance. When **they**
had become hoarse by their vocal efforts, and had exhausted the programme of the opera under consideration, they opened the ball, and commenced the regular
business of a mule wherever he has room to elevate his
after-deck. Each of them kicked the other, **and** the
other kicked each, and they all kicked together. When
any one exhausted his particular batch of mules to kick
at, he would go for the fence, or any other object that
seemed worthy of his heel. After an hour or so **of such**
amusement they were again run into the cars through
a sort of " spout," and when a car would get so full that
another one could not **squeeze in,** the " mule whacker "
would frighten him until **he would run** his head in among
the others, when two or three men behind would drive
him in with clubs, much like driving in a wedge,—
when that particular car would be pronounced loaded,
the door closed, and another car moved up to the spout.

Verily, nothing can be "tougher than a government mule."

A CHAT WITH A BOY.

INTERVIEWS with prominent men are common—with boys, not so common. We sat, the other day, on a plow, at the depot of a western village, waiting for the train. It was rather a lonely depot, and, in fact, the village itself was a lonely spot. A boy straggled along, however, and we captured him for company. He took a seat on the other end of the plow, and he looked like the thing he was—an inhabitant of the extreme West; but we soon discovered that between that coon-skin cap and the earth—inside those frontier clothes, which presented almost a total wreck in the rear—was located a genius—or the making of one. We asked him how old he was, and he said he didn't know; we wanted to draw him out, and so asked his name, and if he lived far around there; he said Bill Jefferson, and that he did live close away from there. We told him that was an honored name, and asked him if he knew we had a president, once upon a time, by that name, only that it was Tom instead of Bill; he said he know'd him right good; Tom Jefferson was his cousin and lived right neighbor to him in Pennsylvania, and he (Bill) had "belted" him just the week before he came out to Minnesota. We told him that must have been another Thomas Jefferson, and asked him if he

didn't know it was wicked to fight. He asked:
"Didn't you never fight nobody?" We said: "No,
never." Said he: "Well, I'll fight any boy that calls
me ragged-kneed Bill, at the drop of the hat." We
told him Pennsylvania was our native state; that in the
old Keystone State was where we first saw the light,
grew from infancy to boyhood, from boyhood to manhood; among its craggy mountains and nestling valleys
was where our education was received; its rippling
brooks and crystal springs were yet very dear to our
heart, and that during our leisure hours our heart filled
with mingled joy and sadness when we reflected upon
the scenes of our younger days; and ended the sentence
by singing the first verse of "There's no Place like
Home." The boy had gotten straddle of one of the
plow handles by this time, and his mouth was in the
proper position for the reception of a huge potato, and
said he: "Look here, old man, do you git them spells
very of'en?" We begged his pardon, and assured him
that it was the remembrance of the old Keystone State
that had brought it on. He asked us what a keystone
was, and we told him it was a stone that was neither
oblong nor square, but that, as we had just used it, the
term was only a typical one, and had an allusion to
Pennsylvania—his and our native State. He said he
"hadn't never seen no stones there only the common
sorts and some grindstones." We said "Yes," and
asked him how he liked Minnesota. He said he liked
it right good, 'cause he could ketch jest slathers of rats
here—muskrats. He was going to work away till he
got enough rats to buy a railroad. We suggested that

he must mean some railroad bonds, and then "hold the bonds." But he replied, "Hold nothing," and knew just what he meant without any of our help. He said he wanted to be a brakeman, and if he could buy a railroad of his own, he'd be a brakeman all he wanted to. Just then the train whistled, and we bade him adieu, and told him to be a good boy, and then he would grow up a ditto man. As we stepped aboard the train we heard him remark, that he didn't care a durn about our ditto, nor our keystones, neither—it was rats and railroads he was after.

"I WILL drink vinegar; I will drink rancid milk, or foul water; I will drink what of the contents of the filthiest cess-pool it is possible to drink, and call it good. But, I will never again drink any intoxicating liquid, though it be the most delicate "elixir," sparkling with the most brilliant "beads," served in a diamond glass, and reflecting in its bowl the tiniest rainbows from the mellow light of the stained windows of a palace, to tempt my lips. This is what we heard a man say, a day or two since. He was "swearing off." The following day, however, he was just as drunk as though nothing had happened.

HOLDING A CIGAR.

OW harrowing it is to one's feelings to see a new smoker hold a cigar—or try to hold one. He will get it in the center of his mouth, poke out his lips, as though he were going to seed; first shut one eye to keep the smoke out, and then the other; and finally he has to take it out and lay it down on the sidewalk while he wipes the water from his eyes with the sleeve of his coat. Sight recovered, he picks up the cigar and, after getting it carefully balanced right end too, he sticks it into the east corner of his mouth and runs it out past his left ear, so as to get rid of the smoke. Of course, he has not gotten the "slight" yet of doing it that way, and when he steps off the end of the sidewalk the cigar jostles out of his mouth and falls into the mud—and is gone. He looks at it with smarting eyes, gives it a kick and passes along in disgust. Now, if boys, or young men, who are bent on "victory or death" in this matter, would practice on a clothes-pin for a few weeks, the art would be accomplished without a struggle, or a pain, or a watery eye. Just carry a clothes-pin in your pocket, and at every opportunity, when no one is looking, wear it in your mouth, and in

a remarkably **short time** you'll have the knack to a
dot.

～～～～～～～～～～～～～～～～～

A TEST OF PATIENCE.

THE snow **has been** "too thin," for real good
hauling **this week,** though **our** wood-haulers
have tried to make the most of it.   A green-oak
granger got stuck in the street Tuesday, and his patience
was put to the severest test; he was a very nervous
man, and he had a very bad tongue in his sled, and a
pair of mules that evidently considered that they had
just naturally pulled that cord of green oak around
as much as was necessary. The mules stopped on a
rather bare spot, and looked around at the driver; the
driver said " Git," but neither of them " got;" he tickled their after deck with his brad, but they simply
passed him up one which very nearly struck his shin;
then he stepped down and off, and tickled them a little,
at arm's length, with the brad, between decks; one
jumped forward and the other stood on his head in order to get his heels high-up as possible, and then the
tongue pulled out of the **roller;** thereupon **he said**
" **Whoa!**" and **made one or two other remarks that the**
occasion probably warranted, though they seemed somewhat foreign to the subject in hand. He got a rope
and secured the tongue to the roller; then he put his
brad where it was thought it would do the most good;
and the crowd, which gathered about, thought every-

thing would soon come right. The mules tightened up on the traces and the front end of the tongue came out of the neckyoke, and the other end of the tongue pulled out of the rope. Then the captain of the craft walked clear round the load, and examined the mules, to see if anything else had pulled out. The boys standing around offered a multitude of " suggestions," all of which conspired to make our granger friend more than ordinarily nervous; he took the tongue and put it up on the load, thinking probably it might make wood; then he walked around the mules and said "Whoa!" again, which seemed to correspond with their idea of the matter exactly; then he hitched the doubletree to the roller by means of the rope, and when everything was right he told them to whoa! which they continued to do. He geed them off sort of obliquely, so that the whole craft might not be thrown upon its beam-ends, when the draft commenced, and then he put in a few with his brad; the mules took a tack to the southwest, the rope came untied and one of the mules kicked up; the granger repeated a few stanzas, and induced the mules to stand up by the sidewalk and whoa, while he went and borrowed a team of horses that didn't know as much about that load of green oak as the mules appeared to, and the sled disappeared around the corner.

BEING A FAMILY MAN.

TO BE a family man of good repute, unexceptionable character and good square application, is an accomplishment rarely met with. Fast men, ladies' men, and men-out-o'-nights, are numerous; but a family man is about as seldom as a chicken's tooth. The labors and attentions expected from a genuine family man might be compared to the sands of the sea shore, or musquitoes of a warm night in July. He must be bright, apt, capable, loyal to nothing save the hearthstone of his ranch, and must, withal, be a keen observer and a good judge of human nature—particularly of the member of the human family with whom he keeps house. He should observe the nature and disposition of his wife most studiously for the first five years, by which time he will know just what's the matter every time he sees her coming for him—if he learns easily, he will also, by this time, be expert in the principal items that go to make up one of those enviable creatures, a family man. He can sling an early breakfast together with elegance and dispatch, iron a shirt, darn a stocking, twist the head off a chicken for dinner, milk the cow, take every young-one in the house across his knee and polish them off respectively, and do many other needful things about the house and get off to his work "an hour by sun," every morning; this is only ordinary; there are men who can also bake bread, scrub, make the beds, saw a cord of wood, tie up the dog, go to market and churn, before breakfast; but we never could get quite up to that stratum of excellence as a family man; having rather a delicate constitution our better half always restrained our laudable ambition for fear we might become prematurely racked. If a person hopes for rapid advancement in becoming a family man, he must imitate, to all appearances at least, the noble example ef Joseph, and he will find the atmosphere of the kitchen not nearly so sultry as it would otherwise be, and his promotion and general comfort will be augmented in a wonderful degree. An estimable family-man is never out late, unaccompanied by his family, but "goes to bed with the chickens," and gets up as much earlier than the chickens as possible, especially in cold weather, when things need thawing out. The study of how to make good hash should be given much attention, until the mysteries of this article of diet are fathomed; for good hash for breakfast is a wonderful "elixir" toward starting the home circle for the day.

GATHERING WILD CATS.

AST winter it was the wolves that annoyed our good people who lived in the suburbs of the city, and along the bluff and ravine ranges in rear of the town—up and down the valley. We made a raid upon the wolves, however, and abated the nuisance. This winter, a streak of wild-cats seemed to be on. A few days ago we felt it a duty we owed to posterity, to change the wild-cat condition of things; and so, we hired a cheap boy—a regular baked-mud specimen of street urchin, who had long since become a stranger to fear, and to soap,—and started for the hills. We always have use for just such a boy when we go out to gather wild-cats. We promised him that if he would go along and carry the cats, and do all that we required of him on the trip, and would skin the cats and dry the hides after we got home, he would be entitled to a one-third interest in the peltry.

We reached a rocky ridge early, and just about the time the vermin had gotten comfortably settled in their holes after their night's raid on the hen-roosts of the neighborhood. It was not long before we found a hole in the rocks accompanied by what we considered infal-

lible signs of the presence of cats, and we at once prepared to clear that hole of its occupant or occupants as
the number of cats therein might indicate, and told the
boy to button up his coat and prepare to go in on a little tour of inspection whilst we would remain outside
and just above the hole, and "polish them off" when
they came out, with our long-handled tomahawk.

That boy, although he was probably dead to fear,
seemed to retain a slight smattering of good judgment,
though his appearance didn't seem to indicate that he
possessed the slightest discrimination between a proper
and an improper proposition.

He looked into the hole, turned and looked at the
"signs," and then at us, and said: "See here, boss,
what do you take me fur, anyway?" We told him we
took him "fur" to go into holes to drive out the animals; that if we had taken him along just for an ornament, we wouldn't have agreed to pay him such an immense margin of profits; that a one-third interest in the
net proceeds of a wild-cat hunt, when we let ourself
loose, was not to be sneezed at. He looked down into
the hole again, and then asked about how much his
share would amount to; and we informed him that it
depended altogether upon how he panned out as a
"driver"—that if he drove enough cats under our
weapon, there wasn't any telling how many hundred
dollars it would figure up. Then he wanted to know
the best way to drive them out; and we told him to go
in feet foremost and allow the cats to "shut dcwn" on
his pant-legs, or on his coat-tail, and then to come out
with his game—let them drive *him* out; if they didn't

bite, then he was to drive *them* out. He said he would go into that one hole, just to show us he wasn't afraid of wild-cats, but if he didn't bring out a hundred dollars' worth of cats the first pass, he would quit and go home —'cause it was worth that much to go into a hole where " signs " wuz so fresh.

Pulling his old hat over his ears and drawing his head down inside his coat-collar, he backed down into the hole, and soon was out of sight, whilst we squared our-self just one side of the mouth, with tomahawk raised and muscle swollen up like a hickory-nut.

" How goes it, Si? " we yelled down the hole.

" I'm a gittin' 'im ! " he yelled back, " He's snappin' at me now, an'—an' oh, lordy—look out, I'm a comin' —he, whoop !—wah !—phew—ew—here we come, dod-rot us ! "

Just at that Si came rolling and tumbling up out of the hole, and, sticking tightly to the broadest part of his dilapidated breeches was the cat ; we went for him with our tomahawk at the first glimpse we caught of him, and then—oh, shades of the stately cedar ! The cat commenced to defend his position, after the true fashion of his race, and quickly did we receive his copious and unerring shafts. Great guns and little fishes ! Before we could reach a place of safety, or a place where we could lie down and roll in the mud and hate ourself to death, we had become a walking pest-house. Si had brought out the wrong kind of a cat. Si had rolled clear to the foot of the hill, whilst we turned a somer-sault over a precipice fifteen feet high, and struck in a friendly mud-hole—but even that beat a skunk-hole all to death. We put ourself to soak over night in a solution of weak lye and ammonia, and the next day made out to appear as usual, but every body wanted to know why we looked so "bleached out." Poor Si, we haven't seen him since; but we feel sure he is satisfied without calling on us for a further share of the dividends of our wild-cat hunt.

THE dog in the manger, that would neither eat the hay himself nor let the ox eat it, has been denounced for ages as the worst example of selfishness that ever came to light in the history of the world. The wisest men have given the subject much thought, and have all arrived at the same conclusion: That the dog had no reason under the sun for such conduct, only pure, downright meanness. It never occurred to them that, as a good bed is next to a good meal, the poor dog wanted the little bunch of hay for a bed, and had as good a right to it as the ox; hence, the ox was the meaner of the two in seeking to rob the dog of his bed. So old Æsop had better take in his sail, while we tally one for the dog.

A CANINE DISCUSSION.

A DAY or two ago there was some fun on Supe-rior street. Fun for everybody except the two dogs engaged in the "discussion." The mud was thin, and was about six inches deep, on the average. One dog was somewhat smaller than the other, but he was a thorough-bred "bull," which made up for his deficiency in size. He was mostly the "under-dog," but he got in his work all the same; he was a great dog to attend closely to business, and he seemed to glory in being industrious. He just shut down on the cheek of the big dog, and while the big dog was mopping up the mud with him, he held the fort regardless of the condition of things. After they had "fit" half an hour or so, and they both assumed the appearance of two great mud cakes, the friends of the respective contestants thought they would wade out and quell the disturbance. They each got hold of the after end of their several dog, and braced themselves for a pull. Their hold slipped, however, and they both sat down in the mud. This made them somewhat vexed, and they finally came to the surface and promised each other that they'd pull them dogs apart, if it took all winter. So, they advanced again toward the surging mud-pile, inside of which were the dogs, and each got hold of what they presumed to be the tale-end of their respective dog, and hove away with an energy that did them great credit. After slipping their hold several times, they found that they were pulling at the same dog—one had hold of a leg and the other the tail of the same quadruped.— When this was discovered, they both slipped up and sat down again in the mud. Then they excavated around until they were sure they had hold of each of their respective dog, respectively, when they sawed them around a hitching-post until it was about half sawed off. At about this juncture in the war, the dogs thought they would just let go until they could get a fresh hold ; this proved fatal, however, to the progress of the fight, as it did to the further comfort of the pullers; for, they both went headlong into the mud, each taking his dog with him. After rolling over a time or two, they assumed an upright position, and, dripping with thinness, they started off, each with his dog on his shoulder, and the half hour's entertainment was over, although the two men were interested the remainder of the afternoon in trying to find themselves. The smaller dog, however, is on deck again, and is peeking around all the corners usually frequented by the enemy. But, the owners declare in terms that cannot be misunderstood, that if they quarrel again, in the mud, they may everlastingly skin each other, before they will interefere.

GOING FOR THE "BULL'S EYE."

ARCHERY may be considered as fairly ripe in this city at present, and the harvest of bull's-eyes has begun. When a stripling, we spent a number of years among the frisky Sioux Indians on the Minnesota border, and used to sit by the month (or less) in the villages and watch the Indians shoot at five-cent pieces, at a distance of from twenty to a hundred yards. They would put a five-cent silver piece of their "hard-earned annuity money" into the end of a tiny split-stick, and an Indian who had attained the age of five years who would miss it more than once in three, was considered a very unpromising American. We never would unbend our dignity enough to engage, ourself, in such tom-foolery, but still we knew just how it was done, to a tetotal dingtum, in every pose and posture. Hence, for the past year we have been chuckling in our shirt-sleeve, thinking how we should stalk into the archery clubs, when they got well under way, and get away with any dozen of the best of them, all put together. In other words we should knock a five-cent center at any distance, even so far off that it would have to be illuminated in order to show its locality. When we first

saw the targets they were to use—about the size of a
large wash-tub, all circled off with stripes three inches
wide,—and to be shot at forty yards away, we just had
to go off to some secluded spot and laugh till well nigh
into the night—in fact we never did get through laughing about it—that is, *hardly* ever.

We resolved to watch our chance, and soon we found
what we were looking after. We discovered a lady or
two, etc., with whom we were on speaking terms, exer-
cising on a back lawn, and so we leaked through a crack
in the fence and went over to where the carnage was
abounding, and asked could we take a shot or two.
The ladies—bless them—were sincerely delighted, and
we picked out a bow of streaked snake-wood, or something, and threw our symetrical form into a position
which was a sort of compromise between William Tell
and a first class Indian. Of course the great target was
uncomfortably close, and we felt sure of our ability to
lay hands onto the tail of a two-year-old steer and throw
him by said narrative and hit such a bull's eye at that
distance. Still, being modest, we did nothing of the
kind, but thought we would toy with the mark a little,
and get them sort of used to our bow-ideal ere we had
the great thing moved half a mile away. The ladies
exclaimed, " My, *what* grace," and we let 'er went—
that is, let fly the unerring dart, which would have utterly demolished the aforesaid " eye " had it struck it,
but it didn't. It went about forty feet to the left, and
three rods above the section of daylight occupied by
the target. We apologized by assuring the ladies that
our foot had slipped just at the fatal instant when it

oughtn't to have done so; they said "yes," and so we planted ourself firmly, yanked our left shoulder well aft and got a magnificent poise to withstand the concussion, and without any further apologetic discussion—except an inward dis-cussing—let the thing go again straight for the center. This time, it went a little too far to the right—too far by about three rods,—went through the lower crack in the fence, through a dog, and then shied across into the street to the right and came nearly killing a cow. This time, we assured the ladies it had gone off at half-cock, and of course could not help being an imperfect shot. One more shot, however, succeeded in thoroughly alarming that whole neighborhood. The people all around that part of town, who had been observing our agility, began closing the blinds, calling in the children and shutting the doors; some of the more timid families went down cellar and remained till the shower was over. We never learned just where the third arrow did go; but feel, somehow, as though it went up among the little stars to sail around the moon, and it will doubtless appear in due time as a celebrated comet. We told the ladies we had a touch of the cholera-infantum that day, and weren't very well ourself; hence, it was not our day for archery, as might reasonably be inferred, and with a a magnificent awkwardness we excused ourself, slid through the same crack in the fence, and went to business fully resolved never to do anything again until we learned how it was done—never to laugh at other folks until we learned, somewhere near, what it was we were laughing at.

"WHAT ARE THE WILD WAVES SAYING SISTER?"

PRIMER LESSON.

THIS is little Dan and his small sister. His sis-ter's name is Jane. Dan and Jane are down on the lake-shore. There is a north-easter on, now, and the *sea* on the *lake* is ver-y rough. See the ship out on the lake. Dan is ask-ing Jane what she thinks the wild waves are say-ing. Jane gives it up, and so does Dan. Dan is a good boy. He is not proud, and does not say bad words, when Jane is near. He knows that Jane would tell his Ma, if he swore. Dan has on a wide hat. It is his Pa's hat, I think. The day is warm, so, he has left his coat at home. He should have worn his coat, (if it is a long coat,) as he might take cold. Jane has her bon-net on. It keeps the bright sun-light out of her face. Jane will not get freck-led when she wears her bon-net. Jane is a good lit-tle girl, and loves Dan. They will soon gath-er Dan's hat full of ag-ates, and then go home, when Dan will go down town and play " keeps " with the boys.

FIGHTING A GARDEN RAKE.

WHEN a boy, it used to be our delight to boast of being able to tramp out a little bigger yellow-jacket's nest than any other boy in the school-district. A bumble-bee's nest was only an ordinary affair, and was used simply as an initiatory step in working up to the *neplus ultra* of genuine pluck; and, when a boy could get right into a mother-colony of able bodied yellow-jackets, with his bare feet, and tramp the life out of the last jacket that belonged to the settlement, he became entitled to his diploma—which was a " pressed " hornet on an oak-leaf. But, we wander. What made us think of these feats of our boyhood, in our bare feet, was seeing a barefoot boy, not long since, trying to " tramp out " a garden-rake; or, rather, he was trying *not* to tramp it out. His paternal parent sent him out into the wood-house to get an armful of wood that he had neglected to bring in before dark. The boy— whom we shall call John, because his name was something else,—went for the wood; but, if it had been light enough to see the shape of his mouth and the general expression of his frontspiece, even the most casual observer would have noticed that John was somewhat up

on his ear at having to go into a dark woodhouse to get
something that he *ought* to have gathered in previous to
the deep twilight that then existed.   In fact he was
mad, and stepped rather recklessly as he stumbled along
in the direction of the woodshed.   Boys have been
known to do something like that before, both in ancient
and modern times.   Saul of Tarsus, for instance, when
a boy, kicked a chained lion in the mouth because his
mother asked him to run down to the meat-market and
get twenty-five cents' worth of smoked sausage for breakfast.   The lion came out first-best, however, and that is
the history of most such bad actions on the part of
boys, when they have to do something in response to
orders from headquarters, that they don't like to do very
well.   John went bumping along, just aching to kick
something, or to step on a toad and mash it, for very
spite.   He stamped his feet heavily upon the ground,
and when in the very height of his anger he found a
garden-rake that had been left in the path, lying on its
back, teeth uppermost.   He changed the bent of his
mind very suddenly, the instant he discovered that he
had found something to tramp on and mash.   All of a
sudden, he wasn't so mad at having to bring in a little
wood as he was previous to the time when he stepped
on the rake.   In fact, he felt just as though he would
rather carry in wood than not.   When he stepped on
the sharp teeth with one foot, he made a leap upward
and then came down with the other foot in the same
place.   This tipped the rake up and the handle pretty
nearly knocked his left ear off, and it fell back in its
original position.   Then John, in his agony, sat violent-

ly down in the same spot, which induced the rake-handle to again come for his head, taking him gently across the bridge of his nose; he sprang up with a yell of pain, when the rake detached itself from his seat of empire, and in some unaccountable manner raked him down the back of his neck and fastened itself into his yarn suspenders, and there held fast until John landed in the midst of the frightened family, in the sitting room, the worst chopped-up boy that could have been found in a day's walk. In about ten days afterward, John was able to sit on a soft chair, and tell the folks about how many rake-teeth he thought he could accommodate and still live.

RIDICULOUS SUICIDING.

SUICIDES are becoming of daily occurrence. Some days there are a dozen of them, and the fact is, the thing is getting monotonous. We don't object, particularly, to this, because we have a big stock of people on hand, in the world, and the suiciders don't interfere with the business, by shuffling themselves off, to any perceptible extent—the profits tail up at the end of the year just about the same. It is the way in which they go about it, respectively, that disgusts us. There isn't one in twenty who approaches a genteel, neat style of going to glory. One will slip out to the barn, take an old halter-strap, tie it to a beam, put his head through the place where the horse's nose

belongs, stand up on an inverted half-bushel measure,
kick it away when he gets ready, and is found afterward
looking about as picturesque as a last year's scare-crow
after a hard winter. Another will saw his head pretty
nearly off with a dull razor, and after living long enough
to wish he hadn't made such an unsightly mess of it,
climbs the golden stair. Some will jump into an old
well, and smother themselves with dirty water and liz-
zards, and after their friends spend a great deal of valuable time in hunting the country all over for ten miles
in every direction, discover their late lamented friend in
the old well, besmeared with mud, so that it takes half
a day's hard work to put him into presentable shape for
a respectable funeral. Another will put his mouth down
over the muzzle of a heavily charged gun in the parlor,
and utterly ruin a seventy-five dollar carpet and knock
a lot of plastering off the ceiling. Some jump into the
river, and become a great "what-is-it" to the catfish.
And so we might go on, enumerating the various styles
of doing it, all of which would be the most unromantic
ways imaginable. Of course, if *we* felt bent upon self-
destruction, ourself, we should much prefer to be pet-
ted to death, if we could afford to hire some proper person to do it. But still there are many other ways that
might be adopted, which would neutralize the prevailing monotony. Even if a person felt it his duty to go
out on the rope-walk, he owes it to himself and the public, to take a little more pains, and have a little more
style about him. He should dress up in his best clothes,
get a very nice new rope, decorate it with a blue ribbon,
wear a mashing button-hole boquet, and then pendul-

27

umize himself from the stair-bannister in the front hall.
There are various things that might be suggested, that
would greatly improve the present style and make the
custom more popular, no matter by which route the
suicide might want to travel; but **we** simply give the
above suggestions as a sample of how either of the many
ways might be bettered, and how they might after their
departure, instead of " **presenting** a ghastly sight," **leave**
themselves looking "just too nice for anything."

WE KNEW it would come out! We were always
told that the ancients believed that the world was flat,
like a cold pancake. That one could walk to the edge
and look down into nothing, and up, into the same article. That if a fellow wanted to commit suicide, all he
had to do was to walk out to the edge, grapple himself
by the slack of his ulster and pitch himself over the
crag, and die falling, keep on falling through all eternity. Also, that this pancake of a world was toted
around "from one town to another" on the back of a
turtle. It never was stated in any book we ever saw,
what the ancients thought the turtle stood on, but it is
supposed they concluded that that was the turtle's business. It now transpires, however, that the earliest races
of men of whom we have any authentic account, knew
mighty well that the world was round, and not flat;
they knew it better than the generations who followed
later—subsequent generations evidently forgot it; hence,
we later chaps have found it out by accident, thought
ourselves alfired smart, and imagined we had struck a

discovery. But, it turns out now, that we have only been working an old claim, that was abandoned by a generation of old rabbi several thousand years ago. We are mighty smart people now-a-days, but there's a whole spelling-book full of new things that we haven't caught on to yet.

TORN DIGNITY.

THERE is scarcely anything more harrowing to a sympathetic nature than to see an elderly gentleman, who is as chock-full of cold dignity as an oyster is of sea-weed, "taken down"—sort of knocked out of time, as it were. We have one fault that we have noticed, even ourself; and that is, we are almost foolishly sympathetic. While riding on the cars not long ago, we noticed a well-dressed old gentleman, with a very respectable sized rink on his head and a pair of gold-bound specs surmounting a most exacting nose, who sat nearly opposite the seat we occupied. His face alone would prove to the most ordinary judge of human nature that he could prove an alibi, if a smile were ever to be perpetrated in his region. He would freeze Charles Francis Adams to death in a harvest-field, and probably never committed a charitable act in his life. The dignity of his pose and motions could have been cut into chunks and sold for frescoing cathedral windows. After awhile the train arrived at the station where he, evidently, desired to leave the train. The brakeman opened the door and bawled out, in four different keys, the name of the station, when our frigid friend grabbed his "grip" and stood up, adjusting his vest and collar, and depositing his specs in his watch-pocket, as he moved out into the aisle and waited for the train to stop. For some reason, the engineer seemed to yank the throttle of his air-brakes wide open at that station, and the stopping of the train was almost a shock to even those who were sitting. Our dignified friend suddenly found himself cutting a multitude of vulgar monkey-shines, which were very aggravating to a gentleman of his fabric, and we could not help, (despite the fact that we love fun,) but feel deeply for him. He lost his balance entirely, and in trying to find it again he cut all sorts of pigeon-wings. He first struck out with his left foot, but instantly found that he *ought* to have *first* shoved out the right leg. His grip flew up and knocked off the side-lamp, and he sat down astride the arm of one of the seats. He made a lunge for liberty and a becoming posture, and went full length over to a seat occupied by a fashionably dressed lady and literally mashed a whole millinery store, while his high hat went galloping down the aisle in the direction of the last station passed. He fairly groaned with shame, and we fairly moaned with sympathy for the old chap. As soon as the lady yelled "git eout!" he caromed over into our seat, when we gobbled onto him till he could get his legs *under* instead of over him, and by that time the shock had subsided; we went and got him his hat, gathered up his grip-sack for him, and balanced him along to the door. The old gent, as he struck the depot-platform, tried to say, "thank you," but failed, and instantly struck his wonted gait as he marched off as stiff and upright as though he had eaten a dinner of telegraph poles. Even under the most trying emergency this fine old gentleman did not lose his dig., though we really felt sorry for him.

"LO!" DIET.

WE HAVE often thought it a wonder that humanity were not visited by condign punishment for the great and prevalent sin of gluttony—of making "a god of their belly," or, more modernly speaking, their stomachs. People in these days not only eat *too much*, by an immense majority, but are too particular *what* they eat. It is getting so that it takes nearly as many people to prepare a table, as are required to eat what is prepared—in some instances, even more. There are thousands of tables spread every day in this country, upon which there are so many kinds of victuals that the feasters do not pretend to get half way round, just for lack of capacity to hold even a tidbit of each article—grease their stomachs, or stand up, as they may. Yet, all these dishes must be regularly prepared, for appearance' sake, and the overtaxed stomach does its best to reach them, and failing in this, looks longingly after the rest, and wishes them well— wishes it could furnish storage for all before it. Enough is absolutely wasted each day to feed every hungry

creature in the land, with a lot of cannibals and Ute
Indians thrown in.   Speaking about Ute Indians, reminds us that *they* are free from the sin of *being particular* what they eat, even if they *do sometimes*, probably,
eat a little too much.   But for this latter failing we cannot be severe on them, because they labor altogether in
the open air, and the character of their work—scalping
folks, stealing horses, murdering women and children,
etc.,—is very arduous, and conducive of a hearty ap-
petite.   Any sins of commission in this respect, however, are more than counteracted by the simplicity of their
diet, and the utter disregard in which they hold fancy
nixnax, or their equally admirable carelessness of *how*
the simple articles they have, are prepared.   Whatever
mild faults the Ute may possess, fastidiousness is not
one of them.   The testimony of Miss Meeker—who
was a captive among them—again substantiates the as-
sertions of thousands of others who have had opportu-
nities to note the simplicity of the daily "chuck" consumed by the noble red man, as also his little concern
as to how it is prepared and dished up.   For instance,
Miss Meeker assures us that the Ute Indians live principally on bread and meat.   Now, this is simple as well
as healthful, and speaks volumes in praise of their character, as a frugal, contented people.   Then she says
that when they can't get bread, they eat meat; and
when there is no meat in plain sight anywhere, they eat
bread.   Note what a picture of contentment this is—it
is a subject that would make an artist's mouth water.
She neglects to state what they do when they can get
neither meat nor bread, but we presume they must eat

a small ration of dried apples, and "swell up." This is
another pretty subject for the brush. When they have
a large quantity of " grub " on hand, they just sit around
and eat until the last " tat " is consumed, before worry-
ing themselves about " where the next meal is coming
from," as we poor grasping, wicked pale-faces do.
They think not of the morrow—they let each day provide for itself. They sew not, neither do they spin, to
amount to anything. They never steal anything they
cannot reach, nor take a scalp unless one presents itself.
When they have only a limited amount of provisions on
hand, they do the same as when they have plenty—eat
it up in perfect contentment, and never talk back.
They are not proud, and are magnificently reckless as
to the condition of their person or clothing—in the
Greek tongue, they are dirty; which, translated into
Hebrew, means excessively filthy. Their meat is permitted to lie about on the ground, as they fritter away
none of their substance on cupboards, ice-boxes or cel-
lars. Each family is provided with a dog—all the way
from eight to fifteen of them. These dogs are kept to
" make night hideous," and to lick the gum-biles on the
Indians' heels; they help themselves to the meat, when
there is any, just the same as the Indians. After the
dogs have satisfied themselves, Miss Meeker tells us, the
Indians cut off from the same piece on which the dogs
feed. There is nothing small about this, and nothing
fastidious, that we can discover. They generally boil
their meat, and commence eating it as soon as it is
warm. They use the same water, over and over again,
in which to cook their dog-bait, until the same is thick

enough to stand alone—Miss M. says until it becomes
"a perfect slime of filth." Of course, right here we
deem the Utes a little off; we can see nothing that
would be inconsistent with simplicity, nor anything that
would be particularly wicked, if they would occasionally change the water, and even once in a while scour out
the kettle with soap and sand. Still, this is purely a
matter of taste, and would entail a few minutes' labor
every day—and the people whose religion will not permit them to "spin," cannot be expected to scour out a
kettle nor change the water on their dog-meat; they
eat out of the vessel, and then the dog licks out the
leavings. Miss Meeker says they are generally clothed
in the skins of animals. Now this is primitive and good.
She continues: "They take a skin and cut a hole in
it and throw it over their heads, cutting arm-holes and
fastening the garment at the waist with a wide belt,
while they close up the neck with a buckskin string.
When the garment wears out, they cut the string and
let it drop, but not before. Sometimes the Indians will
wear as many as five of these garments at a time, always
keeping the cleanest one on the outside." Now, these
are the main differences between the Indian and the
white race. Is it to be wondered at that the red man is
"the *noble* red man," and that the white man is frequently punished for his stomach's sake, by the demon
of dyspepsia or the gout? The one is the simple life
of a perfect contentment; the other is a wicked, waste-
ful life, where discontented, greedy man is constantly
struggling to bite off more than he can chew, and is
always found chewing at more than he can bite off.

PUTTING DOWN A CARPET.

T IS one of the neatest, not to say most interesting jobs that is contained in the spring catalogue. When the lady of the house intimates that a thirty-yard carpet must be taken up, pounded, and then put down again, all in the same day, the man of the house has been struck with one of the greatest calamities of his life. He doesn't realize it, however, provided he has never had a tilt with that kind of a job, and starts in as though it were the merest trifle. He just peels his spring ulster, and rips that carpet up around the edges, sending the tacks in a shower against the opposite walls, sings "Hold the Fort," and wishes somebody would give him some hard job. Then he yanks the thing out into the yard, and after a deal of "spraddling around" gets it on the line. Then he digs the sand out of his eyes, scoops the gravel and dust out of his ears, wipes the first flow of dampness off his forehead with his white sleeve—which isn't *white* any more —and he unconsciously switches his singer off from "Hold the Fort" to "Life is a Weary Way." He begins to suspect that a thirty-yard carpet is about as big a fort as one man can garrison. For the next hour or two, as he pounds the dust and gravel out of the goods, he can be seen but faintly, as he moves around in a cloud which fills that whole neighborhood. Being full of *sand*, he mauls the establishment until it is clear of dirt, and he is a walking mud-man ; the little rivers run down his face, making his whole countenance look like a miniature map of Sahara—supposing Sahara to be blest with rivers. His real grief hasn't begun yet, though. He gets somebody to shovel part of the dirt out from between his collar and his neck, behind, and then drags the carpet back into the room and gets it sort of squared down again. He has a dinner-plate full of tacks, grabs the hammer and, on all-fours, gets the thing secured along one side—his left thumb is pretty well *struck* by this time, and he sits down to breathe a little, with one hand on the small of his back and the other thumb in his mouth. He succeeds in securing another side of the fabric along the south side of the room, and now the stretching era has been reached. He knows it must be pulled till there isn't a kink to be seen. After putting himself into fifty different agonizing positions, so as not to be lying on the very width he is trying to tighten, he is so tired and "broken in two" that he determines to rest again and look the thing over a little. Accordingly, he reclines squarely in the plate of tacks. Of course, the hammer goes flying through the opposite window about this time and he stands up suddenly and remarks emphatically. His first impression is, that he must have sit down on a hornet's nest, or something, but it was only the tacks. After he travels around the room a few times, as though he was trying to walk a thousand quarters in a thousand minutes, he gets calmed down, stands up in the corner, tries to solve the problem, and admire the improvements. He gets down on hands and knees again, and attempts to stretch the goods with his grip, and springing up off his knees. But, when he bobs up from the floor, of course he loses his "push," and when he pushes, he loses his "bob-up." He tries this about twenty times—his hammer in hand and his mouth full of tacks,—when he feels completely broken to pieces— if his feelings indicate anything—'fore an' aft and cross-wise. Then, after looking around to see where the plate of tacks is located, he sits down, in some place where the plate isn't, and declares to himself that he has struck *one* job where words fail to do the subject justice. At last he strikes an idea· He calls in a strong, cheap boy; he lashes the broom-handle up and down his back, so as to sustain the suspension ; then, armed with the im-plements of his profession he has the boy grasp him by the two ankles as he would a wheelbarrow—and, lo and behold, here is a carpet-stretcher, tacker, and swearer, combind. This fixed, he grasps the edge of the carpet, the boy shoves him up to his work, the broom-handle prevents his saging down in the middle, and in course of time the carpet is stretched and nailed, his thumb has also been "nailed," and he is finally bathed, rubbed down and put to bed. In a week, if he is of a strong constitution he is able to be out again. No man who is not a natural born lunatic, ever puts down more than one carpet—very few live through a second job of that kind, anyway.

THE AUTUMN WOODLAND.

AS IS our wont, when the season permits, we go for a stroll in the woodlands—the primeval forests, which constitute the proud and waving plumes of our beautiful continent. A stroll through the woodland, to the contemplative mind, is as a banquet-season, and fills the soul with a stirring sensation that is a nectar to our existence. We enter the brambles of the "forest's shore," which close behind us, and lock their thorny portals as if to bar all comers, and allow us an uninterrupted ramble among the products of Nature's studio. Soon, the last sounds of a "busy world" die on the wings of the empty air, and we find ourself the one animate form among the towering giants of the woods; we halt in our zig-zag wanderings and look about us; standing on a carpet of moss that no loom of art can duplicate, we become almost smothered in thought, as we stand in the mottled halls of the forest, that are silent as the tomb, though fragrant as an Eden. We gaze about us; the chambers of the woods present one endless gallery of beauty; the earth is thickly carpeted, and all the trees have sprinkled in the colors, and the gentle zephyrs have formed the web and woof, in a matchless pattern of Nature's chosen tints. Here and there, as if jealous of the leaves and boughs, the earth has shot upward her "figures" of green and gold, and with the humble moss has inlaid "Beauty" with tints too delicate to be described by mortal pen. As we tread along in respectful awe, with sturdy sentinels on either hand, and reaching arms, forming a triumphal arch of beauty o'erhead, we cannot but believe that the forest is the ante-chamber beyond whose bounds must open the golden portals of a better world.

The clinging vine, which climbs the trunks of the great trees, form the garlands along our path, and with gentle patronage hand down a wreath to the passer-by more beautiful than a golden coronet, more precious than a crown.

Up through the boughs, as if to crown this earthly loveliness with a beauty ineffable, is the dome of the heavenly blue—in daytime too delicate to be copied, and in the silent night, set with sparkling gems too glorious to be described.

Among the arbours of the boughs the happy songsters chirrup their songs. The plaintive lay of the robin but adds to the solomn grandeur of the time, and while standing in deep contemplation of the beauty about us, and amid the sacred stillness of the wood, we involuntarily ask, "Is Nature, God, or is God, Nature?"

ON THE WAVE.

He ask'd the Captain why it seemed
   As though his head went 'round—
One eye kept squinting to'rd the sky
   The other to'rd the ground.

He said his stomach "pucker'd up"—
   "Water" was in his mouth,—
In turn he sweat like a butcher-man
   Then suffered from a drouth.

The boat kept rolling to and fro—
   He wish'd he'd "side-hill" legs—
He grew so sick and dizzy, like,
   He could hardly keep his "pegs."

At last the sky turned bottom-up,
   And held within its bowl,
A rolling world and a ship tipped up,
   And a "heaving" sea-sick soul.

Sometimes he fear'd he was going to die,
   And then he feared he wouldn't;
At times he could see a rod or two—
   At other times he couldn't.

He hove and retch'd and retch'd and hove,
   Till he could taste his leathern boots,

And was left a wreck on the tipping deck,
  To be gather'd up as "scoots."

He finally lived to tell the tale,—
  To wish, his soul to save,—
To find the miserable——who wrote
  "A life on the ocean wave."

GLOOM.

I sit alone in my oaken chair,—
  Peer out through the window pane,—
And watch the angry sea-waves roll,
  And heed the patt'ring rain.

The misty clouds, like a mourner's pall,
  Hang low upon the hill-tops' crest,
The muddy ground and thickning air,
  Shed gloom from east to west.

A silence reigns o'er all the scene,
  Increasing the weight of gloom,
No sound is heard, outside the waves—
  Their hoarse and solemn "boom."

All Nature's sad, and weary, too,
  The birds have sought their rest—
A day to dream of times now gone—
  Of friends now with the blest:

In hours of sunshine, hopes are high,
  And thoughtless manhood strives

To conquer *all* with puny hands—
   Grasp *all* within their lives.

When somber days come on, apace,
   And gloom the world o'erhangs,
'Tis then we halt, in the race of life,
   And feel life's sober pangs.

DOT'S VISIT TO FAIRY LAND.

Little Dot was a bright-eyed child, and happy, the live-
   long day,
And in a thousand ways, from morn' till night, she
   passed the hours away.
She gave no pain to any one, by naughty act, or word,
But chirruped, through the summer days, a happy little
   bird.
She loved to hear her mamma read about the fairy
   lands,
And all about the pranks and games of the little fairy
   bands.
She asked mamma one starry night—as she laid her
   toys away,
If she might see these little folk, and with them spend
   a day.
Her mamma told her, in the morning bright, that she
   could go and see
The fairy lands, and fairy bands, in the boughs of a
   forest tree.
So, in the morn, when Dot arose, all dressed in gossa-
   mer blue

She sprang upon a spider's web, and through the air
  she flew.
The little fairies laughed and sang, and played on their
  little harps,
As on they rode, on the spider's web—escorted by
  meadow-larks.
They were wafted on, by zephyrs soft, until their home
  was seen,
Among the boughs of a forest tree, and ruled by a fairy
  queen.
The royal guard of her **majesty,** when Dot's approach
  was known,
Brought honey in a butter-cup, and daisies freshly mown.
The silken web to a leaf was tied, and with music they
  entered in
To the palace of the fairy **queen,** whose favor Dot
  would win.
The queen sat on her crystal throne, with a tiny crown
  of gold,
And about her stood her courtiers, all fairies, young and
  old.
When Dot approached, the queen arose, and bade her
  welcome there,
And told her she had heard her fame, and of her name
  so fair.
She said the fairies always loved good little boys and
  girls
And always welcomed such as she, to their pretty home
  of pearls.
The pearls, she said, were of dew-drops made, and
  bound with sunbeams bright,

That fairies had but a single law, and that was this—
    " Do right."
Then, a feast was given to little Dot, and to the fairy
    band,
And the fairies all invited there, throughout all fairy
    land.
And so the hours rapid sped, such joy Dot never knew,
As with the fairy queen she danced, all dress'd in her
    goss'mere blue.
At sunset hour, by the queen's command, the fairies
    closed the day,
And Dot, upon her spider's web, sailed for home away.
She told her mamma all she'd seen, and how they called
    her good,
And how she loved the fairy queen, and her palace in
    the wood.

ONE of the most interesting things in the Holy
Land, says a writer, is the fact that one meets everywhere, in daily life, the things that illustrate the Word
of the Lord. The streets of Jerusalem are very narrow,
and no one is allowed to go out without a light. You
will hear the clatter of sandals as the late traveler rattles
along. You will see that he has a little lamp fastened
to his foot, to make his step a safe one. In an instant
the verse comes to your memory, written in that same
city three thousand years ago, "Thy word is a lamp to
my feet, and a light to my path."

IN THE TWENTY-FIFTH CENTURY.

E IMAGINE we live in the twenty-fifth century, and are a young man, seeking information of the past, from an old gentleman who was born in the nineteenth century, and has lived five hundred years. He loves to sit in the cool shade of the old elm, and talk of the centuries he has seen come and go; for even yet he retains a bright recollection of all important events since his young manhood. His long white hair lends a singular, and almost supernatural look to his keen, sharp eyes, and ashen complexion. He leans over the top of his short, stout staff, and looks at us sharply, and even severely, as he begins:

"Yes, young man, I was born before the middle of the nineteenth century, and here it is, almost the middle of the twenty-fifth. I have, with these old eyes,—pointing to one with his long bony finger—witnessed vastly more scenes and changes in this world's appearance and affairs than you glean from the best of your histories. Even now it seems but yesterday since I was a drummer-boy in the first civil war in this country—the war that abolished human slavery from this fair land; now, it is *very* **fair,** but it has cost a sea of blood and a mountain of treasure to make it so."

"You remember, I presume, when, by an agreement between nations, war was done away with?"

"That was not till late in the twentieth century. Yes I remember it well. The proposition of arbitration was advocated by a few of the more humane far-seeing people, as early as in 1856; but it was not until over a hundred years later that the ambition of men—with more of the savage brute in their natures than humanity and Godliness—could be curbed and cultured up to the idea that war was a disgrace to the world and a curse that always left its greatest calamity upon the humble poor who, until two hundred years ago, made up the mass of the human family. All through the war ages it was a fearful thing to live; and indeed, men did not live long at best; for, the excitements of the times soon wore out the human constitution, even if it escaped being the victim of crime, or of war; man soon gave way under the stress and vicissitudes of his day and by overwork in the great race for gain and earthly glory that so characterized the first two centuries in which I lived. Dissipation, too, of all kinds marked those ages, and sowed the seeds of moral and physical misery that has reached even to the portals of the present reign of peace and good-will on earth. Even the highest and most sacred positions in both State and Church, were debauched by the most ungodly excesses, until political life became a stench in the nostrils of all good folk, and the Church was forced to purge itself, and come out of the unclean paths into which it had been lured. And, speaking about the Church, reminds me that I have lived to see the Christian Church break up into a hundred fragments—each fragment claiming superiority and right over all others—and after a series of decades of disorder in the Christian religion, have witnessed them coming together again, until now, as you see, all Christians are training under one banner and worshipping the true and living God in essentially the same sanctuary."

"But how did all this happen?—history on that subject is rather indefinite."

"Well, young man, I don't wonder that it is. To have written a precise history of how the hundreds of branches of the christian church were cemented, at first slowly, and then rapidly, would have required an almost superhuman observer, who would have had to live through three hundred years, and made the subject a constant study and care. The Reformation which occurred centuries before I was born, was well for the world, and even the subsequent breaking into bitter sects was no doubt in accordance with the grand plan of our heavenly Father; now, I can see that it *was* all for the best; then, I used to almost renounce my faith, at sight of the awful confusion, jealousies, and evils that grew out of the cutting up of the simple Christian faith, until the pieces were so small that really they seemed not worthy of serious attention, or of admiration in any degree. But, after a time these sects ran their race, and gradually one after another receded to more reasonable grounds, cemented with one another, until at last all superfluities were dropped by the older, and the essentials were adopted by the newer branches, until by an almost imperceptible process all Christians grew into one common worshipping mass, with Christ as an example, and enlightened reason as their guide in the true path to human redemption."

" You lived, also, to witness the many and most important political changes in our country, and the final adjustment of political affairs to the present system ? "

" Indeed I have, young man.   During the first two centuries of my career I led an active political life, myself; after that I retired to private life on my humble but happy estate as you now see me.   Here I have followed a life of ' industrious ease ' amid the blessings of Nature, spending my hours of leisure in reading and contemplation.   In all the decades of my life in this beautiful hill-bound spot I have more and more become acquainted with my God, more abundantly, day by day, thanked Him for the grand provision he has made for his people, and even now I but begin to appreciate his blessings and perceive his mighty character, his love for fallen man, and learn the outcome of the great problem of the creation.

" Yes, the seathing furnace of national politics that lasted with this nation something over two hundred years, was an important agent used in the purification of men's minds, the advancement of the people in intelligence, in science, in general knowledge, and rationalism—by which they were enabled to break through the dark clouds of superstition, and establish certainties where before they were hemmed about on all sides by doubts and perplexities.

"Your histories, however, will give you a very clear idea of the progress made by this country in a political sense. Until nearly three hundred years ago, we had presidents, two houses of Congress, as they called them, and a score of national and state dignitaries and bodies that have long since been done away with. A thousand national questions perplexed the country, but as time advanced, daylight gradually dawned, entering into the body politic through the windows of intelligent reason and a purified and more Godly intellectual nature.

"Now, as you are aware, our country is governed by a council, composed of our wisest and best men—ex-Governors of our several States. You see, each State elects one of its best fitted citizens—mentally and morally—to the position of Governor, for a term of ten years—half the States electing at one time, only, and they being States geographically located in all parts of the country; these governors are elected by the direct vote of the people of the respective states, but no man can vote at any election who cannot read and write, repeat the Lord's prayer and the ten commandments. These ex-Governors, at the end of their terms, respectively, take seats in the national council for a term of ten years, after which they retire from official life. In the council they have one vote for every ten thousand votes they represent. They have power to make all the laws for the nation, provided their acts, before going into effect, have been pronounced constitutional by the nation's supreme court, which affixes its great seal thereto. This council also fills all appointive offices by a majority vote, and has power to amend the constitution by a two-thirds vote. It elects one of its members to preside each year, and the heads of departments are appointed every five years.

"Our state councils are formed in a similar manner, by one member from each county, elected for five years, meet annually, and each has one vote for every thousand voters he represents. They are vested with the power to make all the state appointments including the judges of all the courts, and amend the state constitution under the same rules that govern the national body, and all their acts are to be passed upon by the state supreme court. The governor, however, retaining the veto power, and the right to appoint his own private officers.

"This, in a general way, comprehends our present system of government, both state and national. Because our system of government is now almost perfect, and because mankind has grown to be, not only wise, but good—a God-fearing and God-loving people— official corruption is now an unheard of thing. Since it has been so, there has been no cause for complaint, and all dangerous rocks have easily been avoided, the nation is running in the interest of love and good fellowship, and all to the honor and glory of the God of worlds and of nations.

"One of the most trying dangers—after the war of the emancipation of human slavery—through which the nation passed, occurred in the opening years of the Twentieth century. It is known in history as the poor men's war. The country had become so effectually within the grasp of rich and greedy monopolies and capitalists, that the hundreds of thousands of miners, operatives, mechanics and laborers, whose sole dependence rested upon their whims and edicts, became sorely oppressed, and though our land was a land of plenty, the amount of suffering that existed among the masses of the manufacturing portions of the country incited all classes of "workers" to open revolt—first, only in sections, and they were crushed time after time, but finally in a gigantic and well organized uprising all over the union. It required the whole energy of the government, at that time, to subdue the revolt, and the cost was immense, both in treasure and thousands of precious lives, to say nothing of the billions of dollars in private property that was destroyed."

"How was the great evil finally remedied, and what was done to better the condition of the laboring classes?"

"Well, young man, if you would look up the history of that bloody and distressing period, you would see, that after the government had asserted its authority, the wise men and philanthropists—now fairly frightened into activity—held councils together, and with the representatives of the suffering masses. They knew that something was radically wrong, when thousands and tens of thousands of the most honorable and industrious people of the country were driven to assert their rights by force of arms, and to seek redress by passing through a sea of blood and fire. In brief, a special 'Congressional Council' after first providing for the immediate wants of the oppressed classes, a minimum rate of pay was fixed for the various grades of working men, and

an act passed that all those who could not be provided
with employment should be given—each single man or
head of a family—eighty acres of the government land,
given transportation thereto and *loaned*, on ten years'
time, with six per cent. interest, a sufficient amount to
purchase a team, implements to till the soil, and enough
supplies to live upon for eighteen months. The parties
receiving this aid had to, of course, make proof that
they were such as came within the scope of this pro-
visional act. By this means, the laboring classes were
not only relieved, in a measure permanently, but the
transportation lines were safely operated, the manufac-
tories were placed on a safe foundation in their conduct
and the mines were worked with perfect order and satisfaction to both the employers and the employed.
Further, by the provision of these small but self-sustain-
ing homes to the poor but industrious masses the resources of the country were greatly increased, and the
government rapidly pushed ahead toward a permanent
prosperity. Following these wise provisions—which
ought to have been made long ere the date that the
terrible shock came—a uniform system of internal improvements was adopted by the government, and
throughout many succeeding decades annual appropri-
ations were made for a vast number of internal improvements—just to an extent, from year to year, suited to
the capabilities of a prosperous nation like this, without
crippling herself—and now in this twenty-fifth century,
you can travel from one corner of the country to another and behold, everywhere, the wisdom of such a
policy, in the manifold advantages that have been de-

rived, aside from furnishing employment for the thousands of dependent workmen, that under any circumstances, are always found to exist. Here you see, the
mighty watercourses—the great transportation arteries
for heavy products—that sprangle like a tree-top
throughout this great continent, are almost 'walled rivers,' vieing, in the character of the work and many times
exceeding in extent, the similar improvements of China
in the palmiest days of that powerful country. By reasonable encouragement, also, railroads have been built,
so that every nook has almost equal advantages in a
market, and the productions, natural and artificial, find
easy and cheap transport to the domestic markets and
those of the outer world.

"By the settlement of the broad domain before re-
ferred to, and the construction of railways across the
continent, the Indian problem solved itself; and by the
whites settling among and around them, they were preserved instead of destroyed,—civilized instead of being
made more savage,—and for two centuries past, the
most remote fastnesses of the redmen have bloomed as
a rose, by the hand of a christianized and happy people—even the breasts of the great Rocky Mountains
are purple with the vineyards, whilst the valleys leading
out from either slope of the great continental chain are
waving with golden corn, and studded with glittering
and prosperous cities, towns, villages and happy country homes.

"To-day the man who would do a wilfully dishonest
or dishonorable act, is condemned of men; he who
would dare to become a beast of prey upon virtue, is

sent out into the world with a mark, that all passers may know his vileness, and his victim is sought out and comforted in proportion to the great wrong she has borne.

" Men, for more than three centuries, have been possessed of all the mental gifts given them by their Creator. They have not lost their responsibility, their honor and their constant recollection that they are responsible, God-made men, through drunkenness and by means of all the terrors that followed like scavenger-carts in the drunkard's train. The *cause* was completely, though in a gradual manner, removed, and the effect, the results, of its removal have been so innumerable, for the good, that no human soul has been capable of enumerating them or of computing their value. Look at the world, however as you now behold it, young man, and compare it with what it was at the close of the nineteenth century, and the glimpse may serve to impress you, but the extent of the blessing will be found beyond your grasp in its manifold and gigantic proportions. The bringing of this nation out from the gloom of intemperance, rescued it from nine-tenths of its sins, and crimes, its poverty and moral degradation at one fell stroke, and blessed, as if by magic, the country with a race of *men*, instead of a people where sinners were the rule and righteous men the exception.

JOHNNY CUTTING.

IN THE year 1856, long before a railroad was built from St. Paul to the head of Lake Superior, when the vast region lying between the two points named was a peculiarly hideous wilderness, the writer was one of a party of four who penetrated that country nearly up to the St. Louis river. Our object was recreation and adventure. At Cross Lake, where the early Catholic missionaries for a long time conducted an Indian mission, we halted for a month, with our headquarters not far from where the old mission buildings stood. The Indians in the neighborhood were friendly, and it was not long before our party was on such good terms with them that we could leave our camp for days together without finding anything disturbed on our return. From this point we made lengthy trips away into the wilderness, in various directions, taking with us a light camping outfit, of course including guns and compasses, and carrying enough provisions to answer for the trip in view. Sometimes, however, we were thrown wholly upon the resources of the country; though we were never sorely in want of provisions, as game was quite plentiful, and we killed many deer and three bears, besides considerable smaller game, during our month's explorations.

One of our longest trips was to the northwestward of Cross Lake, in making which we came one day, about the middle of the afternoon, to an immense windfall. A particularly fierce tornado had passed through the dense forest, uprooting the trees and piling them confusedly in a ridge that extended for miles, This windfall was the greatest and most difficult to cross of any the writer has ever seen, though he has observed many in the thick pine woods of the far northwest.

We had designed going some distance further in the direction we were traveling; and though the huge windfall we encountered was a barrier not easily surmounted by men with tired limbs and heavy packs, we resolved to cross it on account of the novelty, as well as for other reasons. The point where we struck the windfall was in a dense pine growth where the trees had stood to a great size and height. Their trunks, as they lay piled upon each other were as white as bones, and formed a very high ridge about twenty rods in width.

After a rest of half an hour, a little luncheon and a smoke, our party commenced the ascent. In our clamber we met with not a few mishaps, and indulged in hearty laughs as one or another of the party tumbled, pack and all, down among the great logs. At length we gained the summit, the writer having the good fortune to reach the topmost log of the ridge a trifle in advance of the others; and to his utter surprise he met, at the highest point, face to face with a human being, who was known at a glance to be certainly not an Indian. Both were equally astonished, apparently; for as we came up simultaneously to the same log, the stranger gave a sort of gutteral exclamation of surprise, and started backward, with a critical look and a decided air of distrust. He was not over five feet, five inches in height, and was rather slightly built; though he evidently possessed great wiriness and agility, with a capacity for extreme endurance. He had a small beard, yet his face was strikingly effeminate, with a finely-cut mouth and nose, and eyes that were wonderfully expressive—a pretty dark blue, and wearing a look of saddest cast. His hands and face were extremely small for a man, and his entire appearance, though weather-beaten and careworn, betokened refinement of person and character. His hair—the most striking feature about this singular being—though evidently little cared for, hung in long, brown ringlets about his head and shoulders. He was dressed entirely in buckskin, excepting his cap, which was of mink fur trimmed with beads and porcupine quills.

Our party, on reaching the place of meeting, took seats on the log, while the mysterious stranger seated himself on the heavy pack he had been carrying, a rod distant. For a moment we looked him over without speaking, and he gave each of us a searching glance, from head to foot. The writer first broke the silence by an inquiry as to who he was. He said he wasn't anybody, and returned the question. We briefly informed him who we were, and what we were there for—our mission in that region being nothing in particular. He asked us where we were going; and we told

him it was our wish to go in the direction we were traveling as far as the upper Kettle River. In response to
our questions regarding that region, and the exact direction to it, he informed us in a few words that we would
be quite the opposite from welcome in the Kettle river
country, as the Indians would consider us interlopers
upon their hunting territory, and might conclude to
make it extremely warm **for us**.

This man did not seem disposed to do much talking,
and his mode of speech was decidedly strange. There
was a peculiar cut-off to every sentence, and to almost
every word. We judged this to be owing to his long
association with the Indians, as in his speech there was
the gutteral tone common to most Indian languages.
In reply to our question as to the location of his headquarters, he told us that they were almost anywhere,
but that just then his camp was about three miles distant, where, as it was nearly night, we would be made
welcome, if we chose to accompany him. After a brief
consultation we determined to accept his invitation, be-
cause, aside from a desire to find a camp already made
for the night, we had a strong desire to learn more of
the peculiar being we had met in so singular a manner
in so outlandish a part of the country.

We all shouldered our packs, and were soon in Indian file, following our guide, through the mossy cran-
berry marshes and over pine ridges. He carried a pack
which consisted of furs, deer skins, dried meat and a
few blackened and battered utensils, the whole weighing nearly one hundred pounds. He packed in true
Indian style. The bundle was secured by rawhide

thongs, and around it a wide belt of the same, which he passed over his head, allowing the band to rest on his forehead. When he rose to his feet the pack rested at the small of his back, just above the hips. It was a perfect wonder to our party to see a person of so slight a build carry such a load, and that, too, with apparent ease. He traveled fast, and stopped but once in the **three miles, and then for** a moment only. Whilst the strongest man in our party, with but half the load, was well-nigh fagged out in keeping pace with our guide, *he* seemed but little jaded.

We found his camp in a romantic spot, on the shore of a small lake, the waters of which were clearer, if possible, than plate glass, whence flowed a beautiful little stream. Both lake and stream were inhabited by thousands of the most luscious trout. His camp consisted of a roomy birch-bark wigwam, in which there was evidence of neatness and good order. At one end was a low, wide bunk, and the bed was wholly made of skins and furs. First was a lot of dried grass, gathered from the neighboring meadows; on the top of this were spread sheets made of deer-skins, which had been tanned after the peculiar mode of the Indians, and were as soft as velvet. At the head was a large pillow filled with moss. Over all were two fur spreads or robes, which had also been tanned so as to leave them pliable as a woolen blanket. At the side of the wigwam was a rude table made of rawhide stretched over stakes which were driven into the ground. Above this were two or three ingeniously constructed shelves, containing various articles. Of the latter, some bore evidence of being the

productions of civilization, and others were ingenious
and pretty specimens of the handiwork of native women. In one corner were arranged, in an orderly way,
quite a number of steel traps of various sizes; and close
by them was a receptacle for hunting knife, ammuni-
tion, gun, tomahawk and other implements of the
chase. The floor, which was the ground, was covered
with coarse matting, braided from the marsh flag.
Two or three rude stools, in addition, composed the inside furnishing of this strange abode. In a hasty glance
at the articles on the shelves, we discovered a small,
cracked mirror, in a frame of bark, a dingy copy of
Scott's poems, and three or four other very smoky-look-
ing volumes, the titles of which we did not learn. His
fireplace was outside, and directly in front of the aperture which served as a door. It consisted of two forked
sticks driven into the ground, with a pole across, from
which latter a very ancient-looking iron kettle was suspended by a small iron chain, This kettle, with a
broken skillet, a dinted copper vessel and a birchen
bucket, constituted the culinary outfit.

Seeing we were tired, our entertainer asked us to enter his wigwam and rest, whilst he prepared some supper. We complied; but the writer, however, after
resting inside for a few minutes, volunteered to assist in
preparing the meal. After starting a fire by means of a
flint and steel and some dry spunk-wood, the host produced from behind the wigwam what he called his
"trout-persuader," and started for the lake beach. This
contrivance was simply a net, about three feet square,
finely and evenly woven from the fiber of a water-plant,

and stretched on two parallel sticks, held in position by two cross sticks, lashed at each end by thongs of raw-hide, the tension being such as to admit of the net bagging down slightly in the center. It was with no little curiosity that we followed him closely to the shore of the lake, to see how he could capture the wary trout with such a contrivance; and indeed, as we soon saw, no ordinary mortal could have succeeded with it. He motioned us to remain a little back, while he, taking the net by the two handles, glided softly along a small bay, driving a school of the speckled treasures quietly before him, till he came near a sharp nook, which, through a narrow passage, led to a minature bay within, a few feet across. When the school was about opposite the entrance to this, he made a quick upward and outward motion of the net, and simultaneously with this he leaped, with the quickness of a flash, and set his net nearly perpendicular in the mouth of this natural trap. Of course the fish, recovering from their first fright, would dart instantly for deep water again, but not until his net was snugly placed in their way. He had made it to fit the entrance to the little grotto exactly, and when the trout darted back for their freedom they ran into the bag of the net, and the next instant found themselves—a dozen or more—landed high and dry upon the beach by another motion of their captor equal in quickness to the one that had imprisoned them.

What with dried meat, chipped up and stewed in the iron pot, trout fried in deer's marrow, and the bread our party carried, seasoned by the keenest of appetites, our

supper and breakfast with this lone man of the wilderness were among the most enjoyable of all the meals we
ever ate.

After supper, as we all reclined about the camp-fire,
enjoying our pipes—all save our host, who said he never
used tobacco—we essayed to draw out the stranger,
and ascertain, if possible, something of his history.
This, however, we knew to be a delicate task, as his
manner, though courteous and hospitable, seemed distant and reticent, save on topics of the present. Nevertheless we resolved to try, though every inquiry was
put in the most casual way lest we should arouse in him
a feeling of resentment, or a suspicion that we intended
to be rude. In response to various questions we were
told by him that it had been several years since he saw
a white man; that he never went out to the trading-
posts, but that he did his trading through the Indians;
that he was thirty years of age, and had entered that
region alone when a very young man, and never intended to abandon the wild life he had led so long—a life
of constant adventure and hardship, with no companion
save his gun, and holding no intercourse with the human family save the Indians of that remote region, nor
often with them; that the Indians were friendly at all
times when he met them; that his name among the
whites was John Cutting. It was with some hesitation
that he told us his parents and relatives were among the
first families of central Illinois, and wealthy. His reason for abandoning a life of ease and luxury, at an age
when he was just entering upon the joys and plearures
of the world, he declined to state.

After breakfast in the morning we made preparations for returning to our camp at Cross Lake, and Johnny said he would accompany us a few miles, as soon as he could put his own camp in order and get a few things packed for a tramp; that he was going to the lower Grindstone river on a trapping expedition, to be gone **several days.**

Accordingly, an hour after the morning meal, we all started with him as our guide again. Just before noon we reached a trail, by taking which, Johnny said, we could save considerable distance, and pointing in the direction we must go, without saying a word he took each one of us warmly by the hand, turned sharply to the left of our course, and in an instant more " the lonely white man," as the Indians called him, had disappeared in the forest.

Nearly five years after our exploring party had returned from the remote region of the St. Louis river, the tocsin of civil war was sounded, and thousands of the young men of the country quickly responded, the writer among the rest. I went alone and on foot to the barracks, found the commandant and mustering officer promptly, and told him what regiment I desired to enter. He informed me that my chance was hardly good even in the last company of the regiment beyond the one I desired to join, and that the one I had named was full already. Reluctant to join any but the regiment of my choice, yet enthusiastic in the idea of serving my country, I was mustered in and directed to report for duty to Capt.——, whose quarters in a certain section of the fort were pointed out to me. Going thither, I was admitted to a large room containing nearly a hundred new recruits. All was bustle and confusion. The Captain gave me a suit of regimentals, knapsack and blanket, and the orderly seargeant assigned me to a bunk with another recruit, in the quartets, and I found him engaged in fixing up the cot. As I stepped forward he turned around, looking me squarely in the face, as if to see what sort of a chum had been given him. The recognition was mutual and almost instantaneous—my bunk-companion was none other than John Cutting, "the lonely white man." To say that each was astonished beyond measure at this second strange meeting, but feebly expresses it; and that night we talked long and freely concerning matters that mutually interested us.

Cutting seemed to consider himself very fortunate in having met some one whose face he had seen before; and during the years that followed, although he was ever courteous and obliging to all his companions in arms, he was never known to converse with those about him much more than the rules of war demanded, excepting the writer, whom he always sought to be near, and to whose mess he was always sure to belong.

No man in the Union army was a better soldier than Johnny Cutting. He always kept his clothing clean and orderly, his gun and equipments bright and ready for use at an instant's notice. He was orderly to an extreme; and his example in the company was more potent in enforcing good order and discipline than the scowls of an exacting officer. When the long roll was sounded, calling the regiment to arms, night or day, he was sure to be the first to report on the company's parade ground, in perfect readiness for battle, with not even a button out of place. I never saw a man who was as quick, and yet undemonstrative, in his motions as he, nor a soldier who so persistently sought to be at the front in every danger and hardship that presented, of which there was no lack. His favorite place was on the picket line, and his commander was not long in learning his value in the most responsible position of the soldier—that of a picket in front of the enemy.

Little by little, and in a disconnected way, I gradually learned the story of John Cutting's life; and it was, in its beginning, the old, old story, of love and disappointment.

He was the son of a wealthy Illinois farmer. From childhood he had grown up in company with Mary Allen, the sweet, blue-eyed daughter of a near neighbor. They had attended school together, from the days of their a b c's, until they had graduated with honor from the best institution of learning in that part of the State. They had spent their vacations mostly in each other's company, and their heart's tendrils had become so entwined, that to part them would be worse than death— at least to the warm, true, devoted nature of Johnny Cutting. The story of his love may be a short one, though no number of strong words could more than do justice to a man with such a heart and nature as his— true to every instinct of nobility and honor, with an unwavering fidelity to all convictions of right, and whose affection, once bestowed, was placed forever and irretrievably.

When Mary Allen weakened in her love for John Cutting, and in the daze of an hour gave way to the blandishments of a fashionably-dressed and jewel-bespangled sprig from the city, who spent his summer vacation in the neighborhood, she blasted the life of one she **knew to** be her equal, and whose love for her had so increased in the course of their many years of companionship as to attain a strength the tenderness of which the trials of a life-time could not tarnish.

Alone, in her father's grounds, beneath the twinkling stars, they met for the last time, and the rose-leaves **let** fall their dewy tears as she told him of her perfidious rejection of his hand for that of another. Without a **word of reproach, he passed down** the avenue into the road, his frame quivering like an aspen in a storm. As he closed the gate he turned around and halted but for an instant to catch one more glimpse of her who had been the idol of his life. With uncovered head he waved her a parting kiss, exclaiming in a husky voice, "God bless you, Mary, my darling! Farewell, forever!" And he was lost to Mary Allen's sight for all time.

He hastily bade adieu to his parents, telling them he contemplated a trip to the northwestern part of the country. Packing together a few things, and placing his savings in his purse, he embarked on a Mississippi river steamer, buying a ticket for the city of St. Paul, at which place he turned his back forever, as he intended, upon his own race.

Almost at the very outbreak of the war he chanced
to hear the story of the attack on Fort Sumter, and
became aware of the certainty of a gigantic civil war
He sat musing by his camp-fire the entire night upon
the stirring news he had heard, by the merest chance,
through a trader who was making a trip in that region,
and whom he had met at a gathering of Indians assembled for traffic. By morning his decision was
reached. He gave all his effects to an old Indian family, they having nearly always, through their attach-
ment for him, camped in his vicinity, moving their camp
whenever he moved his, from one section of that wilderness region to another. He started the day following
that on which he had received the news, and in three
days' travel he reached Fort Snelling, and was mustered
into the army but an hour or two in advance of the
writer. He had determined, during his night revery,
far away in the wilderness, to do the only thing left him
to do, of any value to himself or others in the world,
by placing himself at the disposal of his country in her
hour of need, and lay his life upon her altar.

His regiment passed through many battles, and suffered its full share of the hardships of the field, and
Johnny Cutting stood in the front rank of his command
without the loss of an hour from duty. He had been
in the thickest of many a bloody battle, and come out
with scarcely a scratch. He sought the hottest of the
fight, steadily and coolly loading and firing, while in the
use of the bayonet his quickness of movement and unwavering courage made him a terrible adversary.

At the desperate battle of Mission Ridge, the Union

32

army had to charge up the bold range of hills, in their endeavor to get a footing on the uplands, where the Confederate army was massed in great force. The Federals were repulsed again and again in their terrible and heroic efforts to capture the Confederate batteries posted along the brink of the ridge, which were dealing death in all directions among the blue-coats on the flats below.

The day wore on in its terrible work, and the hillsides and plain were thickly strewn with the dead and the dying; but the hights were taken, and about the Confederate batteries the final struggle ensued. The after-spectacle told plainly the tale of the carnage, and the stubbornness with which the enemy had defended their guns. The depleted ranks of the Federals needed no explanation of what the victory had cost them, as the storming regiments bivouacked on the field of blood.

Among the dead gathered for interment the next day, the hero of this sketch was found, with many other bodies, on the verge of a ledge which he and his companions had scaled. He lay calmly, as if sleeping, his blue eyes gazing upward in death, and his lips parted as with a smile. He was laid tenderly in a soldier's red-stained grave, where he rests in a hero's last slumber. He had given his love to a heartless one, and his heart was blighted. He gave his life to his country, and now wears a patriot's crown in the world of glory.

JONES AND THE HORNETS.

E HAVE laughed over it a great many times. Even in the dead of night we have awakened, when Jones and the hornets would run through our mind, and we would have to disturb the black stillness with a quiet giggle, because it was too funny for anything—funny as far as we were concerned; Jones can't see where the fun came in, even to this day, however. When we ask him if he ever saw a black hornet (as we do occasionally, when we wish to get even with him on anything), he gives us a look that assures us that his hash is settled, for the time being, at least.

Jones and the writer migrated from "Cold Minnesota" to "Sunny Tennessee," and located at Nashville, where we proposed to "grow up with the country," and tame the gentle bull-dozer as a sort of life-work— teach him to love the Yankees, and persuade him by our winning presence that his getting "cleaned out" in the late misunderstanding was a blessing in disguise. Three years of missionary labor, however, proved to our minds that such a hope was a snare and a delusion, and so we gave up our labor of love, and the magnolia shades

and peanut-fields knew us no longer.   But we wander
from the text.

During a portion of the Sabbaths, we used to take
short tours into the adjacent country, for recreation and
to study country life in the land of cotton—in the land
where the tobacco plant gallops friskily over the plain
with the sweet potato vine.   More than one adventure
overtook us upon these strolls, for even the dogs seemed
to scent "furren blood" when we came within range of
a plantation, whilst black looks from white men, and
white smiles from black men, thoroughly convinced us
that our "shape" was recognized, and that our brogue
grated harshly upon the ears of our new made friends (?)
—the pale-faces, we mean.

On one of these occasions, when we had journeyed
much farther from the city than usual, we determined
to save considerable distance on our return by cutting
across a kind of deserted section of the country—
through barren, old abandoned fields, etc.   We finally
came to an old "pasture" of considerable extent, with
a hollow running through it with smooth slopes on
either side.   Shortly after commencing the descent—
and walking some way apart on our way down the hill
—we happened to look over in the direction of Jones,
and—and—well, it was terrible.   We first thought our
comrade had gone stark mad; that a southern clime
had gone back on him some way—at any rate he was
climbing for all that was in sight, and we soon discovered that it was hornets which were in sight.   Brother
J. was dancing a jig, worse than an Indian corn-dance,
for contortions, and was reaching frantically with both

hands, for something in the air. Taking in the situation at a glance, we had a notion, first, to fly to the rescue; but, upon second thought, we knew how hopeless it would be to "help fight hornets," and the only thing we possibly could do to relieve our partner would be to simply divide hornets with him, or in other words, take half the hornets off his hands. But this idea was very repulsive to our inclinations, because we didn't want any hornets—we hadn't any kind of use for hornets. So, we relieved our conscience in the matter by yelling to him to run for his life, and at that we made a bolt down the hill, across the hollow, and half way up the other hill, before we dared look behind.

A Tennessee black hornet is about the size of a Minnesota robin; there isn't as much "death" wrapped up in any other living thing, in proportion to size; an interview with one of them is three times worse than a long run of sickness; they carry a stinger about the size of a two-edged razor-blade, and they would rather fight than eat; a genuine black hornet would fly ten miles at the dead hour of night if he thought he could find a row, and when Jones stepped into their home, they just came to the scratch with the greatest imaginable pleasure. We had rather fight a flock of billy-goats or a pasture full of jacks, than three of those hornets, any day.

After getting well up on the other slope we fell down from sheer exhaustion, and rolled over to see how Jones was coming on. We found that he was too much engaged to do any good running, but was making a very handsome retreating fight, and had gotten pretty nearly

down into the hollow, and was still reaching out nobly
for the enemy. By way of encouragement, we yelled
to him to " go for 'em." And told him we'd watch
that no more of them should come down from our hill
to reinforce those already engaged. By the time he
reached the hollow, his **case** had been turned over to
just one old boss hornet, while the others had returned
to reckon up the damage done by his stepping into
their nest. Even from that distance we could see that
Jones' head was enlarging terribly, and that one eye
was fast closing, and so we volunteered to direct the
battle by crying out what was best for him to do from
time to time. The hornet would rise high in the air,
get his poise and then come down like a bullet at Jones'
ill-fated head, whilst J. would watch his movements
with upturned face and his " wellest " eye. Most of
the time he would parry him over by a tremendous slap
with his hat; but, occasionally, he would miss the
"brute," when he would get into his hair, and then
there would be a minute or two of terrible misery, at
his end, and (we blush to confess it) a season of side-
splitting amusement at our end of the column. Such
clawing; such striking; such turning somersaults, and
standing on his head never was seen outside of a **first-
class** circus. That hornet would fairly howl with rage,
and Jones kept up a continual muttering of something,
but we never could believe it was anything suitable for
Sunday-school talk. At last, Jones literally gobbled the
creature, sat down on him, and mashed him to a jelly;
then, giving one agonized look in our direction he started up the hill, and fell exhausted where we had recently

been reclining; we had moved further up, when Jones commenced coming, because we didn't know how our part in the affair might have struck his ideas as to our duty in the premises. We preferred, anyway, to get his first opinion at a respectful distance; and, beside, his appearance as he started up toward us, was enough to have appalled a stronger heart than ours; his head looked like an inflated balloon with one eye in it, and only a small pimple for a nose, while his hair stood up like the down on the back of an ill-humored porcupine. We finally treated with him, however, and at a late hour we got him piloted home, through a dark alley, and it took about a week to make " Richard himself again."

"*AUNT ZEBBY*" *REPORTS.*

YOUR Uncle Dudley (the "Country Editor,") is in receipt of the two following letters from one of his esteemed correspondents living in the "timber:"

"MR. EDITOR—MY DEAR MISTER:—My son Jim an' me was settin' by the fire last night an' we got to talkin' over matters an' things about 'most everything, from the price of indigo down to marryin'. While I was expashaatin' on the miserable indigo we get now a-days and what I used to get when my mother used to dye her own yarn, I sort of noticed that Jim was kind of oneasy, and seemed like as though he wanted to tell something that he thought he know'd. At last says I, 'Jim, what the tarnal ails yer to-night—yer keep a skwirmin' around like a fish-worm on a pin. If any-thin' ails yer, tell yer mother; you know I'm good on colic, or biliousness, or 'most anythin', in fact—if it isn't any new-fangled disorder you've caught. What's the matter with yer, anyway? Jim kind o' got red in the face, an' if I hadn't noticed he was swettin' freely I'd a thought sure it was fever. He grabbed holt of the poker and give the fire a shakin', an' says he: 'Now,

mam, I want to tell yer somethin', but I know you'll git
mad an' kick around like a turtle that's upsot, if I do,
an' so, I guess I won't.' 'Now, Jim,' says I, 'I'll wa-
ger all the rag-carpet balls there is up stairs, that I *know*
yer complaint right now. Yer *lovesick*, an' that's just
what ails you to a nat's heel, Jim, now isn't it?' Jim
he kind of moaned a little, and kicked the cat clear
across the hearth, and says he: 'Now, mam, *I* ain't
'zactly lovesick myself, but I guess Deb is, 'r else she
wouldn't uv said 'yes' so quick when I axed 'er if she'd
like to be next best man to your son Jim!' 'There
now,' says I, 'what did I tell yer! I know'd it long
go, an' I've been afeard that yer poor old mother would
be outshined in yer effections one o' these days,' says I.
But I've felt as though the calamity had got to come
purty soon, fur a long time now gone, and so I kind uv
doctored my nerves up with a purty bracin' quality of
young hyson, so's to stand the shock. 'Well,' says I,
'Jim, yer all I have left of my various families, an' it's
mighty hard; but still I'm sort o' reconciled, because I
don't know of any better girl than Debbie Sand; she
wears good honest clothes, her hair an' teeth's her own,
she's fair lookin' and is a good cook. She'll make yer
a good wife, Jim; but, J—,Ji—Jim, yer won't fer—fer-
git yer ole moth—mother, will you, Jim?' I just broke
right down, like a mother 'most always does in such a
techin' case; my tea hadn't been very strong that evenin', fer supper anyway. Jim he broke in two, about as
bad as I did; and fer about two minutes my poor boy
he bellered like a spring-calf. Then he come across
an' put his arm aroun' my neck an' kissed me, and said

33

I was the best mother he ever had, an' beat all three of his fathers, put together—son Jim is my last boy by my first husband—peace to his ashes.

'Well, Mr. Editor, we've arranged to have the weddin' just as soon after I get my spring's soap made, as I can get things cooked—an' Debbie, my darter-in-law, as is expectin' to be, says she wants to help me with the cookery, an' things that's to celebrate the kli- max of the happy disastur. If you can't come in an- swer to the invitation we are all goin' to send you, I'll write you about it, and have you put the disertion in your paper. You must excuse me for not writin' this time about some other things I had in my mind; **but** you see this Jim marryin' business upset me altogether, about other things that needs tendin' to. It's just like I'm apt to do, though—I always find so much to talk about, before I git to sayin' anything. But, some of your pesky latter-day readers will hear *something* about themselves, more'n they ever dreamed of afore I quit 'em; fer I always make it a part uv my religion to speak to people that needs speakin' to. Good evenin'.

AUNT ZEBBY.

" MR. EDITOR—MY DEAR MISTER:—Jim is mar- ried; and so is Debbie Sand; they both married at my house last Saturday evening, and the not was tied by Squire M——. The weddin' transpired at the house of the bride's mother-in-law, because I have more room than Debbie's folks, and besides, I was bound to see son Jim yoked into Himan's kingdom right in the house of his poor old mother, and see that it was done right, and no part of the contract overlooked. I've been married three times, myself, and I *think* I know the difference betwixt a weddin' that'll hold fer life, and one that won't run more than six months until it lands in a divorce shop. There's a wonderful heap of difference in weddins in these miserable times. They *used* to hitch people together so's nothin' short of death by lightnin' could sunder them separate again; but now, la me! they get divorces for cold feet, or for an oniony breath, or for a measly temper'ment.

Well, Mr. Editor, we had a real sharp lot of fun, and we had just as good a supper as you ever sot tooth over; I reckon I'm not braggin' when I say that I can cook a leetle better than any of your cook-book housekeepers of these days; I *season* my stuff so as a custard pie don't taste like a pan of mashed turnips; and when you've eat a supper, you feel as though you'd been there. Jim he looked just too good fur any girl,—'cept Debbie, bless her memory,—and the bride looked just like I've seen picturs where a duchess and a dutchman was gettin' married in a king's house. She had on a muslin dress, with flowers of dandelion, and lile-thred gloves, and white kerchief around her neck fastened with a boka of merigolds, morocco shoes and a chinese fan, hung with a red and yaller cord that I hed when I was about her age. She was the purtiest bride that I think was ever sot eyes on, outside of the three occasions when myself was the principal attracshun—though I ain't sayin' this in any braggin' spirit. But, so the world goes; Jim and Deb have gone to housekeepin' already, and they live up stairs over my granery. May the good Lord have mercy on each and every one of them.

'I had calculated to say something about various matters in a domesticated way. Something of real good to the people of this hifalutin' age of the world; something that the young girls would find well worth alluding at, occasionally, if they ever expect to be an honor to their sex. There's more outlandishness in one day now than there was, when I was a girl, in a day and a half; and sometimes I think I might as well try and hold my peace, instead of tryin' to give 'em a piece of my mind—and then, again, I hardly know which to do. It is natural for me to feel like sayin' something, when there is so much room in the world for sensible talk. But, when I get to writin' I find it such a hurculius task, that I hardly know where to begin, until I have said so much that I have to leave off. But, I want your female girl readers, as well as some that claims the exsalted posishon of wives and mothers, to remember that I haven't forgot *them,* nor their needy condishun; but I'll tell them somethin' or another one of these days that they'll thank me for until long after their dyin' day, —I don't care *how* long they live. Good evenin'.

AUNT ZEBBY.

AN EARLY-DAY TRIP—NUMBER ONE.

EARLY in our fifteenth year we had succeeded in persuading our paternal parent to permit his prematurely ambitious son to "Go West." After obtaining his consent, we could not "wait a minute," but must be off at once—in the latter part of February. Accordingly, after packing into a capacious carpet-bag a very plain wardrobe, as well as several very "useful books"—including a Holy Bible, Pilgrim's Progress, etc.,—we gripped our very weighty sack, bade adieu to parents, and numerous brothers and sisters, climbed aboard the old stage coach, and waved a last farewell to the old farm, the brook, and the hills and valleys of western Pennsylvania, and started on what to us was a literal "leap in the dark." That was in 1855. Railroads were not then so numerous nor so well regulated as now, and even a railroad trip to the far **West** was a journey, the thought of which was calculated to cause a shudder of trepidation to run up the spinal column of full grown men, in the rural districts of old eastern communities. They never undertook the trip alone, and even when a venturesome trio started off, they were considered regular heroes by all their old neighbors and friends.

We started away fully resolved to reach the then new and little heard of country known as "Minnesota Territory;" and, with our twenty-six dollars—more dollars than we had ever before seen congregated together— we felt sure we could get to Minnesota Territory, and have money enough left to buy the Territory, beside ; but, as we afterward learned, this was a mistake.

We had never before been out of the county in which we were raised, had never seen a railroad, knew no more of the ways of the world than we did of the moon, and didn't know the difference between a city and a watermelon-patch, or between a hotel and a haystack, as it were.

In due time we reached the town, thirty miles away, where the railroad was to be taken, and having arrived a couple of hours in advance of the train, we carried our weighty sack around the streets, or sat upon it near the wonderful railroad and contemplated the astonishing character of the iron road, and speculated greatly as to how the cars could "stick onto" such a thing, how they looked, etc. At last, we heard the roar of the approaching train, and as it grew louder and louder, and approached nearer and nearer—but was hidden from view by a sharp curve near the depot—our knees began to knock together with fear and excitement, and the bag was so heavy that we could scarcely lift it. In a moment the locomotive came roaring and plunging around the curve into plain sight, and very near, and we felt exceedingly like an orphan without friends, as

we contemplated for the first time a train of cars; and
when the engine came up and blew a terrible blast on
the first steam whistle we ever heard, we felt pretty sure
the whole thing, including the train, the depot, the railroad, the people, ourself, and in all probability the whole
world, had been exploded, and were going into a million
pieces. After running clear around the depot, clinging
to our only treasure, however, we saw that the people
didn't seem to think there was anything particularly
wrong, and so we calmed down a little—though we really wished ourself at home, where things were run with
less clash and thunder.

After figuring out where the proper entrance to the
car was, we made a bold push, and soon were ensconsed
in a corner-seat, with our grip-sack carefully guarded
between our feet; our greatest fear was that some of
our books might be stolen, and particularly, that our
Bible or Pilgrim's Progress might in some mysterious
way, go astray on us; hence, we were either tightly
hanging onto our 'grip' or else sitting on it, all the
time.

Soon the cars started, and were shooting along at a
fearful rate of speed, and we felt sure we must be
dashed to pieces; the trees, fences and all objects flew
past as if shot out of a gun, and all we could do at
times was to shut our eyes, hold tightly to our treasure,
and mentally repeat, " Now I lay me down to sleep,"
etc.

A man soon came along and demanded our money,
and we gave it to him; he said it would be five dollars
to Mansfield, and that was as far as he could ticket us;

he said the train arrived at Mansfield about midnight, and that we could be ticketed from there to Toledo, but would have to stay over at Mansfield until the next evening.

At Mansfield the hackmen got hold of us, and it was a fight for life, among them, to keep from going crazy, and maintain possession of our carpet-bag; after ourself and our bag had been pulled and hauled around among about twenty shouting hotel villains, one burly fellow picked both ourself and our treasure up bodily and chucked us into his hack, locked the door, and drove off. We were now terribly frightened, and fully believed we had been kidnapped and were being driven off to some cave where we would be robbed of our books and clothing, as well as our money, and then murdered. We rehearsed with great rapidity, over and over again, all the prayers we knew, and would gladly have contributed liberally for the foreign missions if there had been any one to pass the hat; we even tried to sing a hymn, and did everything that seemed good, as we were jostled around the dark hack in which we were imprisoned.

After a time, to our great relief the conveyance stopped in front of a well-lighted 'tavern,' and the driver opened the door, and after telling us to give him twenty-five cents, told us that was his tavern and to go in and stay all night. We went in and hesitatingly took a seat in a shaded corner on our carpet bag after feeling it over to find out if any of our books had been stolen in the scrimmage, or our treasure had been otherwise damaged. We took a general survey of the place, and felt sure we must have been ushered into some king's palace, so grand did everything look. Pretty soon a young man, with a beautiful moustache, and gold shirt-buttons came to us and asked who and what we were. We very frankly told him our whole story, when he laughed heartily, as he remarked: 'I guess you have never traveled much, young man?' We told him we had traveled a good deal within the last twenty-four hours; that if we traveled many more days like we had the last day we should be worn out, or torn to pieces. He said it would cost us two dollars to stay at that hotel until the Toledo train went out the next evening, and that he would show us to our room where we could go to bed. We thought that was a tremendous amount of money for the privilege offered, but not knowing what else to do, we followed him to a room, and went to bed. We did not retire, however, until we had taken an account of stock in our grip-sack, to see that our books and other property were all right, and counted over our money, which we found had shrunken at a fearful rate; but, having no adequate conception of the great distance to be traveled, nor the thousand and one additional demands that would be made upon us, we did not fear but that we had even yet sufficient wealth to get us through to St. Paul.

Daylight found us out of bed, and after taking a careful invoice of stock again we went down stairs, and the landlord—noticing that we were a clear case of 'buckwheat'—kindly proposed that he would take care of our baggage until the train started, and relieve us from its constant care; he promised to put it under lock and

34

key for us, and so we took the chances, and after breakfast started out through the town to see the sights.

After wandering around for an hour or so, reading
the wonderful signs, and beholding, with mouth agape,
all the wonderful things in the store and shop windows,
we came to a place where a man had an immense
' whirligig,' from the long arms of which were suspended wooden horses, carriage-seats, etc., upon which one
could ride, so many times round, for ten cents, and
could ride astride of one of the horses or in a carriage
seat, as he chose. An immense crowd of idle men and
cheering street boys were present, and whenever the
owner got his horses and seats full, he would start his
machine and away would go the whole twenty cheering,
yelling riders, until a hundred rounds had been passed,
when the thing would pull up and a fresh load be taken
aboard, or the same riders would go again by repeating
the ten cent part of the programme.

Of course, this just beat anything we had ever heard
of, and it did not take long to convince us that ten cents
would be well invested in a hundred trips around ·this
sweeping swing, and one of the beautiful wooden horses
was our choice, by a large majority.

We climbed onto a dapple-grey horse, paid our dime,
and soon all the seats were full and the swing started ;
we had forgotten that even to ride in a common swing
made us deathly sick—much less one of these flying cir-
cular contrivances—and before we remembered this,
and discovered this to be a ten-fold more 'sickening'
thing than a common swing, it was going so fast that
to jump off would have been death or broken limbs,

and we soon discovered to our horror that we were in for what would probably prove a ride of ruin, so far as we were concerned. We tried to yell to the proprietor to stop and let us off, but the din and clatter drowned our voice; we swung our hat at him, and motioned with our legs, in the most desperate manner, but all to no purpose, and we resigned ourself to our fate, and devoted our fast failing health to the task of hanging on to our dapple-grey horse. Very soon the houses, and the whole world was whirling like a buz-wheel, and we could scarcely hold our seat; pretty soon we leaned forward and hung on with both hands locked about our horse's neck, whilst groans of agony were sent out, as our contribution to the general jubilee, and the whole crowd sent up a howl of delight at the sight of our grief. We have read of the agonies of seasickness, and how landlubbers fairly threw up their boots over the bulwarks, but we beg leave to assert that the worst case of seasickness recorded, either in history or out of it, was a season of perfect bliss compared with our ride on that whirligig; such retching and bodily contortions; such awful sensations, as we went round and round, wanting to die and yet clinging to our horse for fear we should fall off and be dashed in pieces. But everything has an ending, and that ten cent ride also ended after what seemed an age of agony, and we rolled off and lay limp as a rag on the ground—our hat gone, our jeans pants ripped, our hair all over our face which had grown, alternately, ashen and blue. We became unconscious, and after an hour we awoke and found ourself in a grocery, with a doctor administering mild stimulants with a teaspoon. After a time we were enabled to walk slowly, and the groceryman's boy showed us the way to the hotel, where we were glad to find that our carpet-bag was safe, and for three or four hours we lay on the bed, at the end of which time the world ceased whirling around, our nerves became settled, and a cup of tea and a piece of toast kindly sent us by the landlord, put our internal fixtures into a pacified and somewhat improved condition; so that at the hour of our departure we were enabled to take full command of our grip-sack once more. The landlord in his generosity, said he guessed we had had a rough enough experience in Mansfield, and did not charge us anything for our stay. From that day to this we cannot think of one of those machines without feeling sick at the stomach.

After stammering out our thanks to the kind host, we found the depot after a deal of inquiry along the streets, found the place to buy a ticket to Toledo, and got aboard the right car, after boarding two or three wrong ones, and coming near being run over by a switch-engine. After getting ourself and our baggage safely stowed away in a corner, we looked over our money, and found we had fourteen dollars and sixty cents of a balance on hand; but, thinking Toledo couldn't be *very* far from St. Paul, we consoled ourself, and during the night that followed we curled down on top of our 'grip,' and wore away the weary night by snoozing and dreaming of riding on that whirligig, and morning found us shrunken in frame, troubled in spirit and haggard in appearance.

We arrived in Toledo in a cold, drizzling rain, and

succeeded in escaping from the hackmen, with our property, after having been nearly pulled in two, and started up through the dreary muddy town, looking cautiously along for some one with a benevolent face of whom we could inquire when and where we could start for Chicago. Our load seemed very heavy, and it was with difficulty we could carry it. Finally an old pea-nut man showed us the steam-ferry upon which we would have to cross the harbor to the Chicago depot. By watching the big folks on the other side of the har-bor, and by a good deal of inquiry, we finally found ourself aboard the Chicago bound train, with but five dollars and thirty-five cents left. So intense had been our concern, that it was not until noon that we remem-bered not having had anything to eat, except the toast and tea, since the morning previous; and at Michigan City we went into a coffee-house near the depot and ate twenty cents worth of bread and coffee, and bought five cents' worth of pea-nuts.

Near midnight we landed in Chicago, amid a howl-ing mob of hotel-runners, rain, mud and snow, with no more idea where we were—aside from the name—than if dropped into another world. By an inquiry we had made on the cars, we learned the fare from Chicago to Galena was just five dollars—Galena was the most northerly point on the Mississippi River then attainable by railroad.

After asking many questions, and receiving many a heartless rebuff, and derisive reply, we finally, by almost superhuman exertion, in packing our load, found a ho-tel, nearly a mile from the depot, where we timidly entered, and seated ourself on our carpet-sack in the shade of one of the great pillars in the palatial office of the large, brilliant hotel—one of the first in the city. We were exceedingly weary, and by this time had fully concluded that our money must run out long ere we reached our destination, and the fact began to weigh heavily on our spirits; we were not only ashamed to beg, but were afraid to let our destitute condition be known; imagining that our plight was the first and only similar misfortune that had ever befallen any one, we shrank from the idea of making it known, but fully determined to go till the last penny was gone, and then trust to Providence for the rest.

It was not long after we entered the hotel before all the guests had retired, and we were discovered by the man on duty in the place, who approached us and in a gruff voice said:

'Here, you young rooster, what are you doing here —you'd better carry yourself out of this, in less'n a flyin' minute!'

We seized our satchel, and with a terrible sense of guilt, or something of a similar feeling, we made for the door as fast as possible; but, turning and giving the man a frightened look, he seemed to relent, and in a milder tone called out:

'I say, boy, hold on a minute.' We stopped on the threshold, when he continued: 'Come back here, and tell me what you are doing around here, anyway.'

We hesitatingly sank into a chair near where he was standing, and in answer to his questions told him who we were, and whither we were bound, etc., and apparently being convinced of our honesty he told us we might occupy a chair in the corner until morning, and he also told us when the Galena train started—at eight o'clock—and gave us a general idea of the direction to the depot, though he said it was nearly two miles away. We thanked him for his kindness, and then 'snuggled down' into the big chair, with our sack on our knee, and enjoyed an uneasy kind of sleep until daylight, when we shouldered our sack and started out to find the depot.

By dint of great labor, we found it barely in time, and our general appearance was much the same as when we got through with our ride at Mansfield. In our ramble in search of the Galena depot we had passed through the hands of a couple of burly newsboys, who seemed to feel it their religious duty to give us a complete walloping; our concern was not so great for ourself as for our glazed carpet-sack, which we had saved only by great bravery induced by desperation; the poor grip-sack was worse used up than ourself when we reached the depot, having one side kicked in, our precious books badly jammed, and one of the handles of the sack torn off. At the depot we paid all our money for a ticket to Galena excepting ten cents, and left Chicago with many a heart-sickening misgiving as to what would happen next, for our special edification, with a dozen sore spots contributed by the newsboys, and a very poor idea of Chicago hospitality. During the day we got our needle and thread and, so far as possible, made a-*mends* in our wardrobe and reconstructed our poor dilapidated baggage.

We had nearly all day to reflect upon how we were getting on in the world, and were finally convinced that during the past three days we had learned more than in all the rest of our life—in fact we *felt* that we had. We also learned by overhearing others talk, that the upper Mississippi river was yet closed by ice and would be for weeks to come; that Galena was a miserable town in which to remain until navigation opened, that Dubuque was a much finer city in which to sojourn, but that the only way, just at that season, to go from Galena to Dubuque was to walk across a wild region a distance of eighteen miles to Dunleith, and there cross the river to Dubuque, on the Iowa side, on the steam ferry, which would cost ten cents. We had just that amount of money left, but how were we ever to reach Dunleith? Already two days with scarcely anything to eat, and another day and night yet lying between, with our sacred property, weighing some twenty-five pounds and with which we would no sooner think of parting than we would with our right hand—especially with our 'good books.' And right here we propose to relate one of the most noteworthy cases of physical endurance we have ever since heard of.

We can scarcely, even to-day, explain what it was that kept us from at least *asking* for something to eat; but we felt impressed with the idea that all humanity was our enemy, we were retiring and modest at that age—since outgrown, however,—to the greatest possible extreme, and withal possessed of self-pride, and a self-respect that formed an insurmountable barrier to our begging, even had we not considered it positively

dangerous to ask for anything without paying all that
was required, and, of course, in our extreme innocence,
we should have died a dozen deaths ere we would have
taken even the most trifling thing without the knowledge
of its owner. **Thus,** amid the most terrible condition
of the roads and weather we landed at Galena some
time after dark of a black and terrible night, and, **by**
following in the wake of the crowd soon found ourself
and our precious bag in the office of the principal hotel.

Here we met with some decidedly new *features* in
our eventful journey. The hotel was crowded with
travelers and adventurers, and with the rest there were
about twenty Winnebago Indian chiefs, who had
reached there the day before 'from a trip to Washington on a treaty tour. We had never seen an Indian
before, and when we suddenly found ourself in the
midst of a great crowd **of** these stalwart, painted and
blanketed warriors, with knives, tomahawks and war-
clubs lashed to them, we certainly felt that life with us
was to be but a **brief** session. But, though we were in
continual fear of them all of that, to us dreadful night
—**for** we were well read in all the horrors of Indian
warfare and massacres—we finally concluded **that by**
keeping in a shady corner, and conducting ourself with
the greatest decorum, we might be spared, for we noticed that the white guests were very familiar with them,
and the Indians seemed to be in a pleasant mood.

Supper-time came, and the guests were summoned
by a fellow beating on a terrible gong; we had never
before heard one of these tumultuous carriage-dispens-

35

ers, and it just about frightened what little life we yet
possessed, clear out of us. Of course, we were only
too glad to be allowed to remain inside, without daring
to even look into the room where the steaming viands
sent out their luscious odors, to only aggravate our
starving sensations.

It was late when all the guests had retired, and the
savages spread their blankets about on the office floor,
all around us, and alternataly slept, talked in their singular tongue, or smoked their pipes until the room was
densely filled with smoke. And there we sat, finally, all
alone with these armed red skins, afraid to even move,
and watching their every movement through all that
weary and painful night.

Morning eventually arrived, after a seeming age, and
such a morning! It had snowed nearly a foot, on top
of the almost bottomless mud, and was dark and murky
overhead. Breakfast was announced, the guests all
gayly responded to the call of the gong, after having
their morning dram at the bar, and we almost, at once,
made up our mind to ask the clerk for something to
eat; but our heart failed us and we did not do it. We
could see that the town was a repulsive looking place,
and as we had heard a dozen or more of the men agree
to undertake the trip through to Dubuque on foot, despite the horrible condition of the roads, we resolved to
follow in their wake, though we had also heard them
describe the route as lying through a barren, wild and
desolate country.

After breakfast they fixed themselves completely for
the trip; long boots, unencumbered by luggage, to

speak of, they filled their flasks with stimulants, their
cases with cigars, and finally all started in high spirits
through the mud and snow, with the writer at a respectful distance in the rear, with his carpet-bag on a
short stick across his shoulder.

We had no more than entered the barrens in rear of
the town when we began to realize that our undertak-
ing was a most desperate one, with such a load, and in
our condition, but still something seemed to impel us
forward through the mud and snow nearly knee-deep.
We seemed to feel that if we could reach Dubuque, it
would be vastly better for us, because it would be so
much further on our journey, and could not but prove
an improvement over Galena as a place where we might
find employment.

For a distance of three or four miles we kept close to
the well-fed travelers, though none of them deigned to
notice us, save to occasionally turn around and, with a
laugh, yell out, ' Hurry up, Bub, or the wolves will
make a dinner out of you!' After a while we began to
fall to the rear, and finally, in spite of our exertions to
keep up, they passed out of sight entirely. We shall
not attempt to portray our experiences during the remainder of that day, for such experiences are beyond
the power of pen or pencil. With nothing to eat or
drink for nearly three days, save the little lunch two
days previous, we now found ourself in the midst of a
wilderness, alone, starving, and weighed down by a load
too great for even a strong man to carry over such
roads. After traveling until nearly noon, as we judged,
we fell exhausted in the snow, and lay almost uncon-

scious for a time, when we aroused again, and struggled on, with only a desperate resolution as our last support. We knew, every time we fell, which grew more frequent as the day wore on, that if we lay until our joints became stiffened and set—and they seemed, finally, to be growing solidly together—that we should perish through sheer helplessness, or speedily be devoured by the wolves which were abundant then in that wild region. So, with all the horrors of our situation pictured before our eyes, we would scarcely more than fall to the ground ere we would begin the struggle to get up again. Our feelings can neither be conceived or described; and our ghastly and crazed appearance must have corresponded well with our awful physical sensations.

We must have been a picture of insane distress when, just before dark, we reached the wharf at Dunleith, and staggered aboard the steam ferry, that was just pulling out for her last trip across the great river for the day. In a moment after starting, and as we stood leaning against the rail, the collector came around and we gave him our last dime, then we staggered along into the low cabin, dropped our sack on **the** floor, fell prone upon a long bench, and all consciousness was suddenly blotted out.

Up to this time our trip had certainly been an eventful one, and one in which human endurance was tested to the quick. But fourteen years of age, very slightly formed and small of our age; two days and a half and two nights without a morsel of food of any kind, and scarcely any sleep, and on the last day made a march with a load and through a country and over a road that would have been very trying to a strong man to accomplish. We have always considered that trip a thorough proportionate test of what a human being could endure, and yet remain on the earthly side of the dark valley.

When we first realized where we were, after passing into unconsciousness on the steamer, we found we had been carried to the city hotel, in Dubuque, by direction of some kind-hearted gentlemen who saw us fall. Lying on a lounge in a beautifully furnished and lighted apartment, with a waiter and a physician sitting beside us, apparently watching with deep interest the result of the trial, of which they yet knew nothing. The first thing we remembered to have spoken was an inquiry concerning our precious grip-sack, and the waiter assured us it was safe in the office of the hotel—oh, that precious property! It was near morning, and the doctor, after seeing us safely revived, left medicine to be given us, and said he would call again during the day. We could not move even a muscle, much less a limb, and it was nearly a week before we were enabled to walk about again—in the meantime having suffered greatly.

The landlord—whose name we have now forgotten—had inquired into our history, and assured us that we should be taken care of until the river opened, and then he would see that some way was provided for our reaching St. Paul; and when we were able, he said he had some light duties about the hotel which we could do for him. It is needless to say that as soon as possible, we were a most faithful servant to our kind and generous benefactor.

After two or three weeks we were again taken sick, and for some time the balance between life and death quivered dubiously; our wiry constitution, however, finally triumphed, and we again became convalescent. This was the spring when the cholera broke out all along the river with such terrible fatality, and every steamer that came from below was loaded with death in most horrible forms.

The landlord finally told us one morning that if we were bent on going through to St. Paul, the steamer Hamburg would be in during the day and her master old Captain Estes, being a warm friend of his he would introduce us to him and request him to set us down in St. Paul as safe and sound as circumstances would permit, which he knew he would do.

Accordingly, when the Hamburg arrived our noble friend consigned us and our grip-sack to the care of Captain Estes, and with real feeling requested him to look after our welfare, which the bluff, kind-hearted old skipper most heartily promised to do—the old Hamburg at this day 'sleeps' at the bottom of Lake Pepin.

Though other steamers which had come from below were freighted with death, the Hamburg could certainly claim the palm in that line, and our slow trip up the river was a journey of death indeed. At every landing, more or less dead were put ashore from among the four or five hundred passengers, and at every wood-pile corpses were hastily interred by the deck hands. At the then young town of La Crosse, we painfully remember, there were seven dead brothers and sisters laid side by side, on the wharf, with their dead mother, and when the boat pulled away we beheld, the last object we saw, the frantic father and husband wailing over his loved ones gone, through the horrors of cholera, to another land from the one they had started for with such hopes and promise for the future.

Captain Estes was indeed very, very kind; his solicitude for our safety and care was all that the fondest father could have bestowed, and although we drifted speedily into the first stages of the dreadful disease that was constantly spreading death and agony all over the boat, he, with his great experience, doctored us and watched our condition so closely, that he battled away the disease, so that when we reached St. Paul, though but a respectable skeleton, we had safely passed the point of danger, and afterward gradually regained our wonted health and vigor, by means of the grand and salubrious climate into which we found ourself introduced.

Many a mental prayer have we since uttered in behalf of the landlord and Captain Estes—two among the most noble of God's noble men.

FLY TIME.

PROBABLY one of the most "interesting" times in the year is that known as "fly-time." By this we do not mean a time to fly, but refer to the little creatures that get drowned in the butter, strangled in the molasses and boiled, by pairs, in your coffee just in time for you to drink them both before you can "stop it." Hot coffee "with a fly in it" is a very common morning beverage just now, and beats lemonade "with a stick in it" by a large majority—it's richer. We kept a "last surviving" fly all last winter, in our sanctum, just through compassion ; the little rascal was all bunged up with the rheumatism, and had spells of "lumbago in the back," when the weather was severe, but by careful nursing we brought him through the winter. He grew very independent toward spring, and would go limping around on our table just as though he owned the office. Probably one thing that made him so "stuck up" was, that we fed him all winter on nothing but paste. We regret now that we preserved that fly's life, because he went off about a month ago and told all the other flies in the United States that he had struck a place where they could live the year through, and a silly man who would feed them, blanket them, rub the creaks out of their backs, and wait on their pleasure generally. The result is—flies. We never saw so many flies before. They seem to come from every location known to man, and are of every variety imaginable: Large black fellows, blue-bottles, gray, brindle, brown, silver-winged, line-back, short-horns, suckers, biters, red-headed, six-legged, four-legged, and other varieties too numerous to mention. In fact we've got 'em bad.

Things finally grew so serious, that our love for flies became exhausted, and after much candid reflection we resolved to make war on them, and instead of preserving their lives, destroy them. We put fly-paper to soak all around in numerous plates, bought enough fly-brick to build a smoke-house, and as many of the latest improved fly-traps as our modest apartments could accommodate, and commenced business. At first they fought shy; but finally we got their confidence in the matter of the new dishes we were serving up to them, etc., and they went for it. It actually grieves us to think of what followed; if it is wrong to kill flies, then we are a clean goner. They seemed to believe that the poison was medicine, intended by their benefactor to keep off summer-complaint, cholera-infantum, etc., and to toughen them up for a winter's campaign, and it was sad to see them come; at times the air would grow almost dark with the delegations pouring in from Wisconsin, Iowa, Missouri, Texas, Maine, California, and everywhere. At the end of two days—well, dear reader, we know you would scarcely believe it if we should say

36

we had seven bedticks full of the fallen flies, and more live flies than we had in the first place.

This is an awful season for flies, in this section, and we are to blame for it all—for which we are extremely sorry. If ever we devote our charity again entirely to **the preservation** of flies through the **winter,** we desire that somebody may persuade us that it isn't the proper thing to do.

~~~~~~~~~~~~~~~~~

THE congress of nations which met in Naples for the purpose of considering the propriety of a general disarmament of the world, with no more "wah" to fol-**low,** bu'sted up in a general row. The representative of each nation present became fighting mad, and engaged in every kind of war save actually knocking one anothers' heads off. They adjourned and started for home to load up their bayonets and whet their cannons to a razor-edge. Instead of inaugurating universal peace, they came mighty near working up a large piece of war. This illustrates how "nearly we are *not* ready," as yet, to substitute arbitration for war.

THE NIGHT-PRAYER.

THERE is no time so sad and sweet as the dead hour of night. Silence and shadow reign in perfect harmony. The pale stars, in endless clusters, look and twinkle, and keep their glorious vigil o'er a slumbering world. The very trees, with their dark, thick foliage, stand in seeming awe of the surrounding solitude; Heaven and earth seem to commune together, while angels weep their tears of dew in their sympathy with poor, fallen humanity. The uneasy sleeper is startled from his restless pillow, by the phantoms of his life, and is stricken as by fear; he tosses restlessly, and close his eyes as he may, no refreshing sleep seals fast their lids; a glimmering star peers in at the shutter, and its brightness beckons him from his couch; he rises and steps out into the silent beauty, and stands amid the pearly jewels of the dew as they reflect from their tiny crystals the glory from on high. He bows his head in submission, and his very soul cries out, "O, thou Author of all this, make me pure like these! Wash my heart with these angel-tears, that I may dare look upward into those eyes of glory! Blot out, forever, the sins of the past from Thy remembrance, that

even the stars may not see nor the angels know them.
Let Thy grace fall upon me, as the dew upon the grass,
that mine utter weakness may be changed to strength,
and the darkness of my soul made to flee before the
heavenly brightness of a conscience made clear.
Then, will restful peace guard my pillow, and noble
deeds grace my day-walks, and all to Thy glory."
Amen.

APPENDIX.

—§—

HON. J. PROCTOR KNOTT'S SPEECH IN CONGRESS, ON DULUTH.

IN January, 1871, while the bill for the renewal of the St. Croix land grant was pending in Congress, a large lobby was in attendance, in favor of this measure, and probably an equally large one opposed to it. The latter was composed exclusively of the friends of Duluth. They wished the bill killed, in order to prevent the building up of Superior or Bayfield, as a rival to Duluth. The people of St. Paul, generally, with the exception of those especially interested in Duluth, favored the bill. Hon. Eugene Wilson, member of Congress from Minnesota at that time, was the *champion* of the bill. A vigorous fight had been made over the matter and finally the day came when the vote was to be taken. The result seemed trembling in the balance and was exceedingly doubtful.

Just at this juncture, Hon. J. Proctor Knott, of Ky., who was no friend of Duluth, and who like many other congressmen, had a rather confused idea of the geography of the northwest, as it seems, got the idea that the people of Duluth and those of the St. Croix valley had a common interest in the passage of the bill, and he thought he would give Duluth a back-set by turning

the bill into ridicule; and so, to the sorrow of the friends
of the bill and to the delight of the friends of Duluth,
he arose and doubtless made the most amusing speech
ever made in the American Congress; and that speech
had just the effect that he intended—that is, it killed
the bill as dead as a door nail, but he found when it was
too late, that he had done just what Duluth wanted!

. It is a rare feast for the lover of the humorous, and
will be read by many generations yet to come with keen
relish—provided, like the present generation, they appreciate a thoroughly "good thing."

THE SPEECH.

MR. SPEAKER : If I could be actuated by any conceivable
inducement to betray the sacred trust reposed in me by those
to whose generous confidence I am indepted for the honor of a
seat on this floor; if I could be influenced by any possible consideration to become instrumental in giving away, in violation
of their known wishes, any portion of their interest in the public domain for the mere promotion of any railroad enterprise
whatever, I should certainly feel a strong inclination to give
this measure my most earnest and hearty support; for I am
assured that its success would materially enhance the pecuni-
ary prosperity of some of the most valued friends I have on
earth ; friends for whose accomodation I would be willing to
make any sacrifice not involving my personal honor or my fidelity as the trustee of an express trust. And that fact of itself
would be sufficient to countervail almost any objection I might
entertain to the passage of this bill, not inspired by an impera-
tive and inexorable sense of public duty.

But, independent of the seductive influences of private
friendship, to which I admit I am perhaps, as susceptible as
any of the gentlemen I see around me, the intrinsic merits of
the measure itself are of such extraordinary character as to commend it most strongly to the favorable consideration of every

member of the House, myself not excepted; notwithstanding my constitutents, in whose behalf alone I am acting here, would not be benefited by its passage one particle more than they would be by a project to cultivate an orange grove on the bleak-est summit of Greenland's icy mountains. [Laughter.]

Now, sir, as to those great trunk lines of railway spanning the continent from ocean to ocean, I confess my mind has nev-er been fully made up. It is true they may afford some trifling advantages to locate traffic, and that they may even in time be-come the channels of a more extended commerce. Yet I have never been thoroughly satisfied either of the necessity or expe-diency of projects promoting such meager results to the great body of our people. But with regard to the transcendent mer-its of the gigantic enterprise contemplated in this bill I never entertained a shadow of doubt. [Laughter.]

Years ago when I first heard that there was somewhere in the vast terra incognitia, somewhere in the bleak regions of the great Northwest, a stream of water known to the nomadic in-habitants of the neighborhood as the river St. Croix, I became satisfied that the construction of a railroad from that raging torrent to some point in the civilized world was essential to the happiness and prosperity of the Americon people, if not absol-utely indispensible to the perpetuity of republican institutions on this continent. [Great Laughter.] I felt instinctively that the boundless resources of that prolific region of sand and shrubbery would never be fully developed without a railroad constructed and equipped at the expense of the government, and perhaps not then. [Laughter.] I had an abiding presentiment that, some day or other, the people of this whole country, irrespect-ive of party affiliations, regardless of sectional prejudices, and " without distinction of race, color, or previous condition of ser-vitude," would raise in their majesty and demand an outlet for the enormous agricultural products of those vast and fertile pine barrens, drained in the rainy season by the surging waters of the turbid St. Croix. [Great Laughter.]

These impressions, derived simply and solely from the " eter nal fitness of things," were not strengthened by the interesting and eloquent debate on this bill, to which I listened with so much pleasure the other day, but intensified, if possible, as I read over this morning, the lively colloquy which took place on that occasion.

The honorable gentleman from Minnesota [Mr. Wilson], who I believe is managing this bill, in speaking of the character of the country through which this railroad is to pass, says this :

"We want to have the timber brought to us as cheaply as possible. Now, if you tie up the lands in this way, so that no title can be obtained to them—for no settler will go on these lands, for he cannot make a living—you deprive us of the benefit of that timber."

Now, sir, I would not have it by any means inferred from this that the gentlemen from Minnesota would insinuate that the people out in this section desire this timber merely for the purpose of fencing up their farms so that their stock may not wander off and die of starvation among the bleak hills of St. Croix. [Laughter.] I read it for no such purpose, sir, and made no such comments upon it myself. In corroboration of this statement of the gentlemen from Minnesota, I find this testimony given by the honorable gentleman from Wisconsin [Mr. Washburn.] Speaking of these same lands, he said :

"They are generally sandy barren lands. My friend from the Green Bay district (Mr. Sawyer) is himself familiar with this question, and he will bear me out in what I say, that these pine timber lands are not adapted to settlement."

Now sir, who, after listening to this emphatic and unequivocal testimony of these intelligent, competent, and able bodied witnesses [Laughter], who that is not as incredulous as St. Thomas himself, will doubt but a moment, that the Goshen of America is to be found in the valleys and upon the pine clad hills of the St. Croix ?

Who will have the hardihood to rise in his seat on this floor and assert that, excepting the pine bushes, the entire region would not produce vegetation enough in ten years to fatten a grasshopper ? [Great Laughter.] Where is the patriot who

is willing that his country shall incur the peril of remaining another day without the amplest railroad connection with such an
inexhaustible mine of agricultural wealth ? Who will answer
for the consequences of abandoning a great and warlike people
in possession of a country like that, to brood over the indiffer-
ence and neglect of their Government ? How long would it be
before they would take to studying the Declaration of Independence and hatching out the damnable heresy of secession ? How
long before the grim demon of civil discord would rear again
his horrid head in our midst, " gnash loud his iron fangs and
shake his crest of bristling bayonets ?" [Laughter.]

Then sir, think of the long and painful process of recon-
struction that must follow with its concomitant ammendments
to the constitution : The seventeenth, eighteenth, and nineteenth articles. The sixteenth, it is of course understood, is to
be appropriated to those blushing damsels who are, day after
day, beseeching us to let them vote, hold office, drink cocktails,
ride astraddle, and do everything else that men do. [Roars of
Laughter.] But above all, sir, let me implore you to reflect a
moment on the deplorable condition of our country in case of
foreign war, with all our ports blockaded, all our cities in a state
of seige, the gaunt specter of famine brooding like a hungry
vulture over our starving land ; our commissary stores all exhausted, and our famishing armies withering away in the field,
a helpless prey to the insatitate demon of hunger; our navy
rotting in the dock for want of provisions for our gallant seamen
and we without any railroad communication whatever with the
prolific pine thickets of the St. Croix.

Ah, sir, I could very well understand why my amiable friends
from Pennsylvania [Mr. Myers, Mr. Kelly and Mr. O'Niel]
should be so earnest in their support of this bill the other day,
and if their honorable colleague, my friend Mr. Randall, will
pardon the remark, I will say I considered his criticism of their
action on that occasion as not only unjust but ungenerous. I
knew they were looking forward with the far reaching ken of
enlightened statesmanship to the pitiable condition in which
Philadelphia will be unless speedilly supplied with railroad

37

connection in some way or other with this garden spot of the universe. (Laughter.) And beside, sir, this discussion has relieved my mind of a mystery that has weighed upon it like an incubus for years. I could never understand why there was so much excitement during the last Congress over the acquisition of Alta Vela. I could never understand why it was that some of our ablest statemen and most disinterested patriots should entertain such dark forebodings of the untold calamities that were to befall our beloved country unless we should take immediate possesion of that desirable island. But I see now that they were laboring under the mistaken impression that the Government would need the guano to manure the public land on the St. Croix. (Laughter.)

Now, sir, I repeat, I have been satisfied for years that if there was any portion of the inhabited globe absolutely in a suffering condition for want of a railroad, it was the teeming pine barrens of the St. Croix. At what particular point on that noble stream such a road should be commenced, I knew was immaterial, and so it seems to have been considered by the draughtsman of this bill. It might be up at the spring or down at the foot-log, or the water-gate, or the fish-dam, or anywhere along the bank, no matter where. But in what direction it should run, or where it should terminate, were always to my mind questions of the most painful perplexity. I could conceive of no place on " God's green earth " in such straightened circumstances for railroad facilities as to be likely to desire or willing to accept such a connection. I knew that neither Bayfield nor Superior City would have it, for they both indignantly spurned the munificence of the Government when coupled with such ignominious conditions, and let this very same land grant die on their hands years and years ago, rather than submit to the degradation of direct communication by railroad with the piney woods of the St. Croix: and I knew that what the enterprising inhabitants of those giant young cities refuse to take would have few charms for others, what ever their necessity or cupidity might be.

Hence, as I have said, sir, I was utterly at a loss to deter-

mine where the terminus of this great and indispensible road
should be, until I accidently overheard some gentleman the other day mention the name of "Duluth." (Great Laughter.)
Duluth! The word fell upon my ear with peculiar and indescribable charm, like the gentle mumur of a low fountain stealing forth in the midst of roses, or the soft, sweet accents of an
angel's whisper in the bright, joyous dream of sleeping innocence.

DULUTH!

'Twas the name for which my soul had panted for years,
as heart panteth for the water-brook. But where was Duluth?
Never in all my limited reading, had my vision been gladdened
by seeing the celestial word in print. And I felt a profounder
humiliation in my ignorance that its dulect syllables had never
before ravished my delighted ear. (Roars of laughter.) I was
certain the draughtsman of this bill had never heard of it, or it
would have been designated as one of the terminii of this road.
I asked my friends about it, but they knew nothing of it. I
rushed to the library and examined all the maps I could find.
I discovered in one of them a delicate, hair-like line diverging
from the Mississippi near a place called Prescott, which I supposed was intended to represent the river St. Croix, but I could
nowhere find

DULUTH!

Nevertheless, I was confident that it existed somewhere, and
that its discovery would constitute the crowning glory of the
present century, if not of all modern times. I knew it was
bound to exist in the very nature of things; that the symetry
and perfection of our planetary system would be incomplete
without it; that the elements of material nature would long
since have resolved themselves back into original chaos if there
had been such a hiatus in creation as would have resulted from
leaving out Duluth! (Roars of Laughter.) In fact, sir, I was
overwhelmed with the conviction that Duluth not only existed
somewhere, but that wherever it was, it was a great and glorious place. I was convinced that the greatest calamity that
ever befell the benighted nations of the ancient world was in

their having passed away without a knowledge of the actual existence of Duluth ; that their fabled Atlantis, never seen save
by the hallowed vision of inspired poesy, was, in fact, but another name for Duluth ; That the golden orchard of the Hes-
perides was but a poetical synonym of the beer gardens in the
vicinity of Duluth.   I was certain that Herodotus had died a
miserable death, because in all his travels, and with all his
geographical research, he had never heard of Duluth.   I knew
that if the immortal spirit of Homer could look down from another heaven than that created by his own celestial genius, upon the long lines of pilgrims from every nation of the earth to
the gushing fountain of poesy opened by the touch of his magic
wand ; if he could be permitted to behold the vast assemblage
of grand and glorious productions of the lyric art called into being by his own inspired strains, he would weep tears of bitter
anguish that, instead of lavishing all the stores of his mighty
genius upon the fall of Illion, it had not been his more blessed
lot to crystalize in deathless song the rising glories of Duluth.
(Great and continued laughter.)   Yet, sir, had it not been for
this map, kindly furnished me by the Legislature of Minnesota,
I might have gone down to my obscure and humble grave in an
agony of despair because I could nowhere find Duluth.   Had
such been my melancholy fate, I have no doubt but that, with
the last feeble pulsation of my breaking heart, with the last
faint exhalation of my fleeting breath, I should have whispered
"where is Duluth ? "   (Roars of laughter.)   But thanks be to the
beneficence of that band of ministering angels who have their
bright abodes in the far-off capital of Minnesota, just as the agony of my anxiety was about to culminate in the frenzy of despair, this blessed map was placed in my hands, and as I unfold-
ed it a resplendent scene opened before me, such as I imagine
burst upon the enraptured vision of the wandering peri through
the opening gates of paradise.   There, there, for the first time,
my enchanted eye rested upon the ravishing word " Duluth."

   This map, sir, is intended, as it appears from its title, to
illustrate the position of Duluth in the United States; but if
gentlemen will examine it, I think they will concur with me in

the opinion that it is far too modest in its pretentions. It not only illustrates the position of Duluth in the United States, but exhibits its relations with all created things. It even goes further than this. It lifts the shadowy veil of futurity and affords us a view of the golden prospects of Duluth far along the dim vista of ages yet to come.

If gentlemen will examine it they will find Duluth not only the center of the map, but represented in the center of a series of concentric circles one hundred miles apart, and some of as much as four thousand miles in diameter, embracing alike in their tremendous sweep the fragrant savannas of the sunlit South and the eternal solitude of snow that mantles the ice-bound North. How these circles were produced is perhaps one of those primordial mysteries that the most skillful paleologists will never be able to explain. But the fact is sir, Duluth is pre-emminently a central place, for I have been told by gentlemen who have been so reckless of their personal safety as to venture away into the awful regions where Duluth is supposed to be, that it is so exactly in the center of the visible universe that the sky comes down at precisely the same distance all around it. (Roars of laughter.) I really cannot tell whether it is one of those ethereal creations of intellectual frost work, more intangible than the rose-tinted cloud of a summer sunset : one of those airy exhalations of the spectator's brain which I am told are ever flitting in the forms of towns and cities along the lines of railroads built with government subsidies, luring the unwary settler as the mirage of the desert lures the famishing traveler on, until it fades away in the darkening horizon, or whether it is a real, bona fide, substantial city, all "staked off," with the lots marked with their owners names like that proud commercial metropolis recently discovered on the desirable shores of San Domingo. But, however that may be, I am satisfied Duluth is there, or there about, for I see it stated here on this map that it is exactly thirty-nine hundred and ninety miles from Liverpool, though I have no doubt, for the sake of convenience, it will be moved back ten miles, so as to make the distance an even four thousand (Laughter.) Then, sir, there is the clim-

ate of Duluth, unquestionably the most salubrious and delightful to be found anywhere on the Lord's earth. Now, I have
always been under the impression, as I presume other gentlemen have, that in the region around Lake Superior, it was cold
enough for at least nine months in the year to freeze the smoke-
stack off a locomotive. (Great laughter.) But I see it represented on this map that Duluth is situated exactly half way between the latitudes of Paris and Venice, so that gentlemen who
have inhaled the exhilerating airs of the one or basked in the
golden sunlight of the other, may see at a glance that Duluth
must be a place of untold delights ; a terrestrial paradise fanned
by the balmy zephyrs of an eternal spring, clothed in the gorgeous sheen of ever-blooming flowers, and vocal with the melody of Nature's choicest songsters. In fact, sir, since I have
seen this map I have no doubt that Byron was vainly endeavoring to convey some faint conception of the delicious charms of
Duluth when his poetic soul gushed forth in the rippling strains
of that beautiful raphsody—

> Know ye the land of the cedar and pine,
> Where the flowers ever blossom, the beams ever shine,
> Where the light wings of Zephyr, oppressed with perfume,
> Wax faint o'er the gardens of Gul in her bloom ;
> Where the citrons and olives are fairest of fruit,
> And the voice of the nightingale never is mute ;
> Where the tints of the earth and the hues of the sky,
> In color, though varied, in beauty may vie ?

[Laughter.]

As to the commercial resources of Duluth sir, they are simply illimitable, and inexhaustible, as is shown by this map. I
see it stated here that a vast scope of territory, embracing an
area of 3,000,000 square miles, rich in every element of material wealth and commercial prosperity all tributary to Duluth.
Look at it sir, (pointing to the map). Here are inexhaustible
mines of gold, immeasurable mines of silver, impenetrable
depths of boundless forests, vast coal measures, wide extended
plains of richest pasturage, all, all embraced in this vast territory, which must, in the very nature of things, empty the untold treasures of its commerce into the lap of Duluth. Look at

it, sir (pointing **to the map); do** you see, from these broad,
brown lines drawn around this immense territory, that the enterprising inhabitants of Duluth intend some day to enclose it
all in one vast corral, so that its commerce will be bound to go
there, whether it would or not. [Great Laughter.] And here,
sir, (still pointing to the map), I find within a convenient distance the Piegan Indians, which of all the accessories to the
glory of Duluth, I consider by far the most estimable. For, sir,
I have been told that when the small-pox breaks out among the
women and children of that famous tribe, as it sometimes does,
they afford the finest subject in the world for the strategetical
experiments, and any enterprising military hero who desires to
improve himself in the noble art of war, especially for any lieu-
tenant general whose

> "Trenchant blade, Toledo trusty,
> For want of fighting has grown rusty;
> And eats into itself for lack
> Of something to hew and hack."

[Great Laughter.]

Sir, the great conflict now raging in the Old World has
presented a phenomenon in military operations unprecedented
in the annals of mankind, a phenomenon that has reversed all
traditions of the past as it has disappointed all the expectations
of the present. A great and warlike people, renowned alike for
their skill and valor, have been swept away before the triumph-
ant advance of an inferior foe, like autumn stubble before a
hurricane of fire. For aught I know, the next flash of electric
fire that simmers along the ocean cable may tell us that Paris,
with every fibre quivering with the agony of impotent despair,
writhes beneath the conquering heels of her cursed invader.
Ere another moon shall wax and wane the brightest star in the
galaxy of nations may fall from the zenith of her glory, never to
rise again. Ere the modest violets of early spring shall ope
their beauteous eyes, the genius of civilization may chant the
wailing requiem of the proudest nationality the world has ever
seen, as she scatters her withered and tear-moistened lillies o'er
the bloody tomb of butchered France. But, sir, I wish to ask

if you honestly and candidly believe that the Dutch would have overrun the French in that kind of style if Gen. Sheridan had not gone over there and told King William and Von Moltke how he had managed to whip the Piegan Indians. [Great Laughter.]

[Here the hammer fell.]

[Many cries, "Go on!" "Go on!"]

The Speaker—Is there any objection to the gentleman from Kentucky continuing his remarks? The chair hears none. The gentleman will proceed.

Mr. Knott : I was remarking, sir, upon these vast "wheat fields," represented on this map in the immediate neighborhood of the buffaloes and the Piegans, and was about to say that the idea of there being these immense wheat fields in the very heart of the wilderness hundreds of miles beyond the verge of civilization, may appear to some gentlemen rather incongruous—as rather too great a strain on the "blanket" of veracity. But, to my mind, there is no difficulty whatever. The phenomenon is very easily accounted for. It is evident, sir, that the Piegans sowed that wheat there and plowed it with buffalo bulls. [Great Laughter.] Now, sir, this fortunate combination of buffaloes and Piegans, considering their relative positititions to each other and to Duluth, as they are arranged on this map, satisfies me that Duluth, is destined to be the beef market of the world.

Here, you will observe, (pointing to the map), are the buffaloes, directly between the Piegans and Duluth, and here, right on the road to Duluth, are the Creeks. Now, sir, when the buffaloes are sufficiently fat from grazing upon these immense wheat fields, you see it will be the easiest thing in the world for the Piegans to drive them on down, stay all night with their friends, the Creeks, and go into Duluth in the morning. [Great Laughter.] I think I see them now, sir, a vast herd of buffaloes, with their heads down, their eyes glaring, their nostrils dilated, their tongues out, and their tails curled over their backs, tearing along towards Duluth, with about a thousand Piegans on their grass-bellied ponies yelling at their heels!

[Great Laughter.]   On they come !   **And as** they sweep past the Creeks they join in the chase and away they all go, yelling, bellowing, ripping and tearing along amid clouds of dust, until the last buffalo is safely penned in the stock yards of Duluth. [Shouts of laughter.]

Sir, I might stand here for hours and hours, and expatiate with rapture upon the gorgeous prospects of Duluth as depicted upon this map.   But human life is too short, and the time of this House is far too valuable to allow me to linger any longer upon the delightful theme.   [Laughter.]   I think every gentleman on this floor is as well satisfied as I am that Duluth is destined to become the commercial metropolis of the universe, and that this road should be built at once.   I am fully persuaded that no patriotic representative of the American people, who has a proper appreciation of the associated glories of Duluth and the St. Croix, will hesitate a moment to say that every ablebodied female in the land between the ages of eighteen and forty-five who is in favor of " women's rights" should be drafted and set to work upon this great work without delay.   [Roars of Laughter.]   Nevertheless, sir, it grieves my very soul to be compelled to say that I cannot vote for the grant of lands provided for in this bill.

Ah ! sir, you can have no conception of the poignancy of my anguish that I am deprived of the blessed privilege ! [Laughter.]   There are two insuperable obstacles in the way. In the first place my constituents, for whom I am acting here, have no more interest in this road than they have in the great question of culinary taste now, perhaps agitating the public mind of Dominica, as to whether the illustrious commissioners who recently left this capital for that free and enlightened republic would be better fricasseed, boiled or roasted ; [great laughter] and in the second place, these lands, which I am asked to give away, alas, are not mine to bestow !   My relation to them is simply that of trustee to an express trust.   And shall I ever betray that trust ? Never, sir !   Rather perish Duluth ! [Shouts of Laughter.]   Perish the paragon of cities !   Rather let the freezing cyclones of the bleak northwest bury it forever beneath the eddying sands of the St. Croix! [Great Laughter.]

Affectionately yours,

"Uncle Dudley."

THE END.

www.ingramcontent.com/pod-product-compliance
Lightning Source LLC
Chambersburg PA
CBHW060600030726

47498CB00005B/1479